Julia W

SECRET CITY

Bella
BOOKS

2013

Bella Books, Inc.
P.O. Box 10543
Tallahassee, FL 32302

First Bella Books Edition 2013

Editor: Katherine V. Forrest
Cover Designed by: Kiaro Creative

ISBN: 978-1-59493-390-5

Some of the locations in this book are actual places, but the characters and story are fiction.

About the Author

Julia Watts is the author of numerous novels for adults, young adults, and middle-grade readers, including the Lambda Literary Award-winning *Finding H.F.* A graduate of Spalding University's M.F.A. program, she teaches at South College and in Murray State University's low-residency M.F.A. program. She lives in Knoxville, Tennessee, with her family and many pets.

Dedication

For my mom and dad, in celebration of their fiftieth wedding anniversary.

OCTOBER 5, 1944

"Monkeys!"

That's the first thing Baby Pearl said once the guard who checked our papers let us through the gate.

I looked around, expecting to see real, live monkeys. They wouldn't have been any stranger than what I was seeing: a black and white sign reading *Military Area: Stop No Firearms No Liquor No Cameras*, green-uniformed soldiers as identical as gingerbread men, barbed wire twisting over a tall fence, a guard tower that put me in mind of a prison movie. And the mud. There was no grass underfoot, just mud so deep my Sears and Roebuck saddle shoes squished in it all the way to my bobby socks.

Baby Pearl squeezed my hand. When I looked down at her moon-round little face, she used her free hand to point. "See?" she said. "Monkeys. Like at Granny's house."

I followed the line of her chubby pointing finger, and I finally did see. Hanging on the side of the guardhouse was a poster of three little monkeys, one with its hands clapped over its eyes, the next plugging its ears, and the last covering its mouth. Back home, Granny had a figurine of these same little monkeys with a caption in the base that said, *See no evil, hear no evil, speak no evil.* But the monkeys on the poster came with a different caption:

What you see here
What you do here
What you hear here
When you leave here,
Let It Stay Here.

The words made me wonder if soon somebody was going to tell us what was going on—was going to tell us why the government had built a whole city where a year ago there had been only farmland. If somebody had told me, I would've kept my mouth shut. I was—and am—as anxious for us to win this war as anybody.

But we've been here about a month now—Mother, Daddy, my sisters and me—and I don't know any more than I did when Baby Pearl first showed me those monkeys. All I know is the government is working on something here, and whatever it is, it's big enough to make people come from all over for jobs.

Compared to a lot of people, we didn't come far—just from Kentucky, the next state over. Daddy had been having bad luck for a while. He'd worked in the sawmill when I was a baby, but it closed down when the Depression hit. He was out of work like everybody else for a long time, until he got a job at the grocery store, stocking shelves, sweeping up, sometimes carrying out groceries. He stuck with it because he had a growing family and needed the money, but he hated it. "Seems like the only kind of work I care about is building things," he used to say.

Daddy is good at building things. He built our old house all by himself out of odds and ends he brought home from the sawmill. It's just a two-roomer that sits on the back of my grandparents' little patch of land, but it's probably the best house ever to be built out of scrap lumber.

One day when a fellow came into the grocery store and mentioned that the government was giving out jobs near

Knoxville, Tennessee, that there was a lot of construction work to be done there, Daddy took off his stock apron for good and told us we were moving. Those government jobs, the man had told him, paid top dollar.

We didn't have much stuff to pack, which was a good thing since we didn't have anything to pack it in. We didn't own a suitcase because we'd never been anywhere, so Mama just rolled up our clothes in one quilt and our kitchen things in another. She cried to leave our little house and her parents and the patch of land she'd lived on all her life, but Daddy promised we'd come back home just as soon as the war was over and with enough money in our pockets to build another two rooms onto the house.

My sisters cried, too. Opal, who's thirteen, cried about leaving the boy she was sweet on even though, as far as I know, she'd never actually gotten up enough nerve to talk to him. Garnet's ten and didn't want to leave Granny and Papaw. And Baby Pearl—who we really ought to stop calling Baby because she's five years old now—cried about leaving the mama cat and kittens that lived in Granny's barn.

I didn't cry. I was glad for the change. Maybe it was because I just turned sixteen, or maybe it was because there's always been a restlessness about me. I love my sisters, but we don't have much in common except that our mama named us all after jewels we're too poor to afford. I don't reckon I have much in common with Mama either, except for her mousy brown hair. I got my blue eyes from Daddy. His blue eyes and his restlessness.

So for me, coming to Oak Ridge has been an adventure, or the closest thing to an adventure I've ever had. Mama and Opal and Garnet would've been happier staying back home, but Mama said, "Well, war changes things," and she seemed to accept the move as her duty the same way a young man accepts being drafted. But I wouldn't have had to be drafted to live this life. I would've volunteered.

Back home, living like sharecroppers on Granny and Papaw's land, I was lonesome...lonesome and bored. We were too far away from town to walk there, and I had read every single book in the school library at least twice. Nobody else in my family reads except for the newspaper and the Bible on occasion, so I don't reckon they feel my need, a need that is as real and deep as the need for food and water, to fall into another world, to escape into words. Or, if they do, listening to the squawking voices on the radio is enough to satisfy them.

Here, everybody's right in town, and the public library over in the Ridge Recreation Hall is the best thing that ever happened to me. I go there after school at least twice a week, and every time I open the door the smell of books hits me, and I breathe in and smile.

Another thing that's good about here is the high school. The teachers like it that I read. Back home if I talked too much about books, the teachers would tell me I was getting above my raising, that soon enough I'd be quitting school and getting married and dropping such foolishness. Here, though, Miss Connor—she's my English teacher who came straight down here from New York University, if you can imagine that—smiles when she sees me with my nose in a book.

One day when she saw me reading *Now, Voyager* by Olive Higgins Prouty (for the third time, but I guess she had no way of knowing that), she said, "If you're going to fill your head with romantic notions, they might as well be beautifully written ones." She grabbed a book off the shelf behind her desk and handed it to me. *Jane Eyre*. And for a full week, my head was full of Jane and that crazy woman Mr. Rochester kept locked up in the attic, and the wind whooshing through the moors—not that I'd ever seen a moor, or knew what one was before I read the book.

It's funny what Miss Connor said about romantic notions, though, because except when it's in a book, I don't think about romance at all. I've never met a boy my age who had anything in common with Mr. Rochester, and I don't tend to go out and socialize with other kids much.

I pretty much keep to myself and love my books and my time in the library and my classes in school, especially English literature. It was that class that gave me the idea to write things down like this. We were reading some of the diary of this fellow Samuel Pepys—I thought his name would be pronounced like "peppy," but you say it like the sound baby chicks make. Mr. Pepys lived a long time ago in London, and he wrote about the things that happened to him every day: what he saw, who he talked to, what he was thinking about.

And I thought, maybe I can write something like that, too. Between studying for school and reading my books and helping Mama with the house and my sisters, I won't have time to write every day. But I want to write as much as I can about life in this strange, new place which is strange and new not just to me, but to everybody who lives here. And maybe one day, some girl will be reading my diary in her high school literature class. But probably not. You can see why Mama says I'm a dreamer and don't have a lick of common sense.

OCTOBER 9, 1944

This afternoon I was outside with Mama hanging out some wash, and this fancy-looking woman passed by the house. She had on a hat and gloves, and her high-heeled shoes were so mired up in the mud she had to do some high stepping just to walk. She looked at Mama and me for a minute without saying anything, so finally Mama said, "Hidy."

The woman wrinkled her nose and looked at the clothes on the line, then looked at Mama like she was on display at a carnival. "I do so admire," the woman said, in a nasal accent as flat as a prairie, "how you maintain your dignity despite living under such harsh conditions."

"Harsh conditions?" Mama laughed. "Shoot, lady, you shoulda seen where we was living before."

Whoever that lady was, she probably lives in one of the big houses on the hill where all the scientists and generals live— Snob Hill, people call it. We live in one of the many "prefabs" the government plopped down in the mud to house workers. It's a funny little house. Called a flat-top because there's no pitch to the roof, it looks like a white box sitting on top of stilts. It's not cute like the little house Daddy built back home, but once you're inside it's right comfortable and roomy. Because we're a pretty big family, we qualified for two bedrooms, so we have a living room/kitchen area with a big stove in the middle of it, a bedroom for Mama and Daddy, and a bedroom for us girls. At our old house, we all had to sleep in the same room—Mama and Daddy in the iron-frame bed and all of us girls on pallets on the floor. Daddy used to say it was like a game, trying not to accidentally stomp on little girls when he got up to go to the outhouse in the middle of the night.

This evening when we were sitting around the table eating some soup beans that would've profited from a hunk of fatback (with war rationing, meat is scarce), Mama told Daddy about the lady who watched us hang out our wash.

"Harsh conditions, my foot," Daddy said. "She oughta see the barracks where the single fellers is squeezed together like sardines. Or the hutments where they make the coloreds live. The roofs on them shacks don't even look like they'd keep out the rain." Daddy pushed back his sopped-clean plate. "Nah, me and my girls is doing all right, ain't we?"

My sisters and I all said "Yes, Daddy," but Mama didn't say anything. Her eyes looked far away and sad like they did when she was missing home, like they did most of the time. Daddy must've noticed, too, because he reached over and patted her on the hand and said, "And my best girl—is she doing all right?"

Mama smiled a little and let her gaze rest on Daddy instead of the faraway place she'd been staring at. "Well, it ain't heaven, and it ain't home, but I reckon I'm a little more all right with every paycheck you bring in."

"Daddeeee," Baby Pearl whined, "you just called Mama your best girl. I'm s'posed to be your best girl."

Daddy scooped up Baby Pearl from her seat and swung her around, then tickled her. "Mama's my best grownup girl, and you're my best little girl." He circled round the table and patted

Garnet on the head. "And Garnet's my best bigger girl"—then he patted Opal—"And Opal's my best next-to-the-biggest girl." His hand was on my head. "And Ruby's my best biggest girl."

By that time, we all were laughing, even Mama.

Daddy set down Baby Pearl and kissed her head, then looked at me. "And speaking of you being my biggest girl, there's something I want to talk to you about."

He sounded serious all of a sudden, and I couldn't figure out if I should be nervous or not. "I'm not in trouble, am I?"

Daddy grinned, his blue eyes crinkling at the corners. "And when was the last time you was in trouble?"

It was so far back I couldn't remember. Opal and Garnet and Baby Pearl got whippings from time to time, but I never did. Goody Two-Shoes was what Opal called me when she was mad at me.

Daddy sat back down at the table, took out his tobacco and papers, and started rolling a cigarette. "I just wanted to tell you about somebody I talked to today. I was over at the cafeteria, bellying up to the trough for some slop. Well, the girl who was dishing mine up wasn't no bigger than a minute. She had this curly blonde hair, so I said, 'Say, Curly, are you old enough to be working in this place? I've got girls at home that don't look no younger than you.' She told me she was sixteen. She said there's lots of girls her age, working jobs here and making good money. And I said, huh, I got a girl at home that just turnt sixteen."

"You want me to get a job?" I was starting to think that maybe I had been right to be nervous.

"Oh, I ain't telling you what to do. It's just something to think about is all."

"But..." I watched Daddy's work-hard hands roll the cigarette. "If I got a full-time job, I'd have to drop out of school."

"Shoot," Opal said, "I'd drop out of school to make me some money."

"Me, too," said Garnet.

"Me, too," said Baby Pearl, who'd say she wanted a sock in the eye if her sisters said they wanted one.

"Baby Pearl," Garnet said, "you've got to start school before they let you drop out of it."

Everybody laughed but me.

"I was just thinking," Daddy said, "with you and me both working, this family'd have more money than we ever seen. Course, you could keep some of what you made—buy yourself some pretty things, go to the picture show any time you wanted to. And since you'd be working for the government, you'd be making good money and helping the country win the war, too."

"I reckon I would be," I said. "But I was kind of thinking I'd stay in school till I graduated." Even as I said it, I felt guilty. I didn't want to disappoint my daddy or my country, either one.

"Hmm." Daddy's mouth was set in a straight line. "I just thought as grown up and independent as you are, you'd like going out and being a wage earner like your daddy. For two or three years anyway, till you get married."

"I don't want to get married," I said.

Mama, who was clearing the table, looked at Daddy, and they both laughed. "That's what girls always say until the right feller comes along." She put her hand on Daddy's shoulder as she leaned forward to clear his plate. "And your daddy come along when I wasn't much older than you are now."

It's funny. People live their lives a certain way, and they can't imagine that somebody else would want something different than they do. Because I've got my nose in a book every chance I get, Mama and Daddy should know I want to stay in school. Because I've never given a boy so much as the time of day, they should know I won't be getting married any time soon. But they judge me by what they've done instead of by what I do. Sometimes the people who ought to know you best are the ones who know you the least.

Since it was my night to do the dishes, I said, "I reckon I'd better head down to the wash house before it gets too dark."

"Listen at her changing the subject," Opal said. "You'd think she wanted to be an old maid."

I ignored everybody's laughter, grabbed the bucket, and went outside. I was trying not to cry.

I love my family, but there are things about me they'll never understand. Like how having a high school diploma in two years means more than making some pocket money right now. I don't know what I want to do once I get that diploma, but I know I'll have a lot more choices with it than I would without it. Then I think of my daddy's eyes—the same blue as mine—and how they shone full of hope when he said if I took a job, I'd be helping out my family and my country. Am I letting my family and country down out of pure selfishness?

OCTOBER 13, 1944

This morning everybody was joking about the bad luck they were going to have because it's Friday the 13th. "Don't you walk under no ladders today," Mama told Daddy when he got up from the breakfast table.

"Walking under a ladder on Friday the thirteenth—that'd do me in for sure, wouldn't it?" Daddy said, laughing as he put on his hat and jacket. "Don't you girls break no mirrors nor let no black cats cross your path now."

I may not believe in that kind of bad luck, but I sure believe in bad moods because I've been in one ever since Monday night when Daddy suggested I might want to get a job. I kept stewing and turning it over in my mind, but it's hard when you know the one thing that would make everybody else happy is the very thing that would make you miserable. What I needed was somebody to talk to, but it would do no good to talk to anybody in my family because I knew what they'd say. Mama would say having another wage in the family would be a big help, and Opal and Garnet would just go on and on about all the candy and trinkets an hourly wage could buy. I needed to talk to somebody who didn't stand to gain or lose anything from my decision.

It came to me in English literature class. Miss Connor was reading us this poem about how no man is an island, and I started thinking about how sensible she is. She even looked sensible, with her thick glasses and her brown hair pulled back in a neat knot and her flat shoes that wouldn't hurt her feet as she stood up at the blackboard. And she had to know school is important, or else she wouldn't be a teacher.

When class was over, I went up to her desk.

"Yes, Ruby?" Miss Connor said, smiling. She had a gap between her two front teeth. When she taught us *The Canterbury Tales* and got to the part about the Wife of Bath's gap teeth meaning she was amorous, she had blushed.

"Miss Connor, I was wondering...after school, could I maybe come by and talk to you for just a minute?"

* * *

When I went back to see Miss Connor, she was already putting on her sweater and packing up her things. "If you need to go, I can always come back another time," I said.

"No, Ruby, I'm happy to talk with you," she said. "It's just that I'm dying for some fresh air. I thought we could walk down to the drugstore for a soda. If it won't embarrass you to be seen at the drugstore with your old English teacher."

"You're not old"—I had stopped myself in time from saying "you ain't old," remembering who I was talking to—"you can't be more than twenty."

"Twenty-three," she said, with her gap-toothed grin.

I wasn't at all embarrassed to be seen out with Miss Connor. If anything, I was flattered that such a smart, educated lady was willing to be seen out with me. What I was embarrassed about, though, was that I didn't have any money. Would they even let me sit at the counter at the drugstore if I didn't buy anything? I'd just have to see what happened when it happened, I decided.

We walked through Townsite, the main shopping area. The A and P must've gotten something new in because housewives were lined up way outside the front door. With food and household goods in short supply, when the store got in a new shipment, the word spread like hot gossip. "Bacon," one wife would tell another, and off they'd race to the store, telling other wives along the way.

"Wonder what they got in today," I said.

"I don't know." Miss Connor eyed the women in line. "It must be something good, though. Those canned hams last week nearly caused a riot." A woman in a head scarf carrying a full grocery sack passed us then, and Miss Connor said, "What's new at the store today?"

The woman looked around like she didn't want to say anything, her cheeks flushing pink. Finally, she reached into the sack and held up a roll of toilet paper. "This," she said.

Miss Connor laughed. "Well, I know where I'm going when we're finished at the drugstore."

In front of the drugstore, Miss Connor stopped to study a new poster which showed a pretty young brunette woman wearing red lipstick and a housewife's dress and apron. Underneath the picture it said, *People died because she talked.*

"Well," Miss Connor said, "I hope this poster doesn't scare you out of talking to me about whatever it was you wanted to discuss. I assume it wasn't a matter of national security?"

"No, ma'am."

The drugstore was filled with kids around my age, talking and laughing, Kleen Teens in store-bought sweaters and new saddle shoes already caked with Oak Ridge mud.

"Any of these kids in your crowd?" Miss Connor asked.

"I don't have a crowd," I said.

"All the better." Miss Connor patted my shoulder. "This country was founded on rugged individuality. So…shall we have a soda?"

The moment of truth. "You go on. I…uh…didn't bring any money with me today."

"Well, in that case, it's my treat. Is a cherry Coke all right?"

I looked down at the black and white checked floor. "My daddy always says not to take handouts."

"It's not a handout," Miss Connor said. "You're my guest, and I insist that you have a soda with me. Now why don't you go find us a place to sit?"

When Miss Connor brought our Cokes to the table, she said, "I'm fairly sure it's not a breach of my professional ethics to buy a student a Coke. Besides, teachers here get paid so well I could buy everyone in the store a Coke if I liked."

"Jobs here pay good," I said, enjoying the Coke's sweet fizz. "That's why Daddy came here—for the money and to help with the war."

"That's why everyone came here," Miss Connor said. "What else could possibly bring someone to such a remote little place—a fondness for mud and wooden sidewalks?"

Until her words, I'd never thought of Oak Ridge as remote or little. "I love it here," I said, not able to help myself. "I was living in the country before, and it seems like here there's always something to do. There's the library and the movie theaters and the stores. Plus, all the people buzzing around and working on whatever it is they're working on. It's...it's..." I'd run out of words all of a sudden.

"Exciting?" Miss Connor asked.

"Yes, ma'am."

Miss Connor sipped her Coke. "Yes, I feel that excitement, too, but in a different way. For you, it's exciting because you're a country girl living in a town for the first time. For me, it feels more like I'm a city girl who's accepted a position teaching in a one-room schoolhouse on the frontier. I feel like a pioneer." She looked at me hard through her thick glasses. "But we came here to talk about what you wanted to talk about, Ruby."

"Well..." I stared at the melting ice cubes in my glass, not knowing where to start. "I guess it goes back to what we were saying about how good the pay is in Oak Ridge. My daddy talked to a girl my age who works in the cafeteria—says she makes enough to live on and some to save and spend, besides. So Daddy took the notion that I ought to quit school and get a job."

Miss Connor leaned in toward me. "Ruby, am I correct in assuming that if you wanted to obey your father's wishes, you wouldn't be talking to me?"

"Yes, ma'am."

"Because you know I'm going to tell you to stay in school. But I'll tell you something else: I'm not just telling you to stay in school because it's what I'd say to any student. I'm telling you because you, Ruby Pickett, despite your backwardness, despite the ungrammatical mess that sometimes comes out your mouth, have a fine mind. Except for the grammar errors, the first theme you wrote for me in English literature was more insightful and promising than anything written by the scientists' children who are your classmates."

Nobody had ever come right out and called me smart before, and I got so choked up I could barely say thank you.

"There's no need to thank me, Ruby. I'm just stating the facts. And for a girl with your backwoods background and your fine mind to end up in Oak Ridge, the new home of some of the greatest minds in the United States, is nothing short of miraculous. There is opportunity for you here, Ruby. Opportunity much greater than a job slinging hash in a cafeteria. Here, you can get the education that will help you rise above your circumstances."

It was such a stirring speech I felt like I should applaud or something. But before I could say or do anything, Miss Connor whispered, "By disobeying your father's wishes, are you in any... danger?"

It took me a few seconds to figure out what she meant, then I said, "Oh, gosh, no. Daddy wouldn't whup me or throw me out or nothing. He's the best feller in the world. That's why I hate to disappoint him."

"Ruby, has anyone every told you the story about the crabs in the barrel?"

"No, ma'am."

"When crabs are in a barrel, if one crab tries to get out, tries to rise above its circumstances, the other crabs reach up with their claws and drag it back down. Don't let your family drag you down, Ruby."

"Yes, ma'am." But even as I agreed with her, I thought, what if the crabs don't grab the runaway crab because they don't want it to succeed? What if they're trying to hang on to the climbing crab because they love it so much they can't stand to see it go? But then I wondered, do crabs really love each other? Do they even have brains?

"Ruby, would it help if I wrote a letter to your father explaining why I think you should stay in school?"

"Thank you, ma'am, but no. I don't think Daddy would take much stock in what you say because he thinks you're a dried-up old maid."

Miss Connor laughed so hard some of the kids at the counter turned around to look at her. She wiped her eyes with a napkin, then said, "You stay in school, Ruby Pickett. And you tell that father of yours that I'm happily engaged. My fiancé just happens to be a little busy fighting a war right now."

"Yes, ma'am," I said.

And I left her to go home to my barrel of crabs.

OCTOBER 15, 1944

A day like yesterday could never have happened back home, where I spent my Saturdays doing chores and wishing I had somewhere to go or something to read. But yesterday, in this strange, new, magical place, both of these wishes came true.

After I helped with the breakfast dishes I walked down to the library to return *Wuthering Heights*. I'd checked it out because Miss Connor said if I was going to read swoony stuff, it was best to stick to the Brontes. *Wuthering Heights* was good, but I have to say I liked *Jane Eyre* better. Jane was a good girl with good sense—somebody I'd like to have for a friend—but that Cathy, sometimes I wanted to slap her cross-eyed.

I turned in the book at the librarian's desk, then went to browse in the fiction section. If books were food, I'd be too fat to fit through a door. As soon as I finish one, I'm ready for another.

I was scanning over the books' spines to see if any of the titles sounded especially interesting when all of a sudden I heard a loud "Waah! Waah!" I looked up to see a young woman—pretty, with honey blonde hair—holding a bald, chubby-cheeked baby who was howling for all she was worth. The woman bounced the baby in her arms, made shushing noises, then whispered to me, "Please excuse little Sharon. Nobody's ever told her you have to be quiet in a library. And even if someone did tell her, she wouldn't listen."

"That's why it's great to be a baby," I whispered back. "No rules, just do whatever you feel like doing." I reached out and offered the baby my pointer finger, which she grabbed in her fat fist. Her expression unclouded, and she looked at me with curious blue eyes.

"She likes you," the woman said, sounding surprised. Her eyes were the same blue as the baby's, but they had the dark circles under them peculiar to under-rested mothers.

"Nah," I said. "She just knows a sucker for babies when she sees one."

I am crazy about babies—their jowly little faces, their soft skin. When Garnet was a baby, I played with her all the time and washed her and dressed her like she was my own baby doll. I was the same way with Baby Pearl. Even though I've never been able to see myself as a bride, I can imagine being a mother. Now there's a sentence that would make Mama's hair turn white! What I really mean is, I wish there was a way for a grownup lady to get a baby without being married. A respectable way, that is.

"So, Baby Sharon," I crooned. "Read any good books lately? Any recommendations?"

The woman laughed. "Oh, she's no help. She has appalling taste in literature. But maybe I can make some suggestions. What's the last book you read?"

"*Wuthering Heights*," I said. "*Jane Eyre* before that." I was surprised how easily I was talking to this stranger—a stranger with a Northern accent and a string of probably-real pearls around her neck. But this lady wasn't like the snooty one who had watched Mama and me hang out clothes. She was young, and she had a nice face...open and kind. Plus, she had a run in her stocking, and her red lipstick was smeared, which put me at ease somehow.

"Oh, then I know exactly what you ought to read, if you haven't read it already," she said. She stepped over to look at a certain section of the fiction shelves, and I had to step along with her because the baby still had ahold of my finger.

"Ah, here it is!' she said, pulling a book from the shelves. "It's not an old book, but it's got that same dark, romantic feeling as the Brontes'."

She handed it to me. *Rebecca* by Daphne du Maurier. "*Du Morey-ay*—is that how you say her last name?" I just started taking French at school, so I'd been learning that things that ended in *er* weren't necessarily pronounced *ur*.

"Yes."

"Daphne du Maurier—I believe that's the prettiest name I've ever heard. It sounds like music, don't it?"

"It's a lot more musical than Iris Stevens, that's for sure."

"Is that your name?"

She nodded.

"I'm Ruby Pickett."

"Ruby Pickett," she said, smiling. "I don't know...that's kind of a musical name, too."

"Hillbilly music, maybe," I said, feeling embarrassed at my country name and homemade clothes all of a sudden. Iris was wearing a simple skirt and sweater, but they were nice and obviously store-bought. "Well, Baby Sharon," I said, "I reckon I'm gonna be needing my finger back now." She was holding on so tight her little knuckles were white.

"Oh, sorry," Iris said, trying to peel her daughter's fingers off mine. "My heavens, what a grip! It's a wonder she hasn't cut off your circulation."

As soon as her hand was disconnected from mine, Sharon began to howl again, as if my finger had been the only source of happiness she'd known in her short life. "I'd better get out of here before they throw us out," Iris said. "It was nice to meet you, and Sharon thanks you for the use of your finger."

"Nice to meet you'uns, too," I said. "And thanks for the book."

* * *

That evening, as soon as we'd eaten our last bite of supper, Daddy clapped his hands and said, "Who wants to go to the show?"

"I do! I do!" Opal and Garnet and Baby Pearl yelled. Being older, I didn't yell, "I do! I do!" But I still thought it. We never went to the show before we moved here because we were too far out in the country and too poor besides.

"I don't know," Mama said, "I've got all these here dishes to get washed."

"Leave 'em till in the morning," Daddy said. "Won't nobody be here to see your dirty dishes if we're all out at the show."

Mama grinned, said, "Oh, all right," and went to change into her good dress.

At the show, Daddy told us girls we could each pick out a little box of candy. It took Opal and Garnet and Baby Pearl forever to decide what they wanted, but I knew I'd have chocolate-covered peanuts because I love them, and I have a special way of eating them to make them last. I pop a peanut in my mouth and let the chocolate melt slowly. Sometimes I suck on it a little, but I never chew until the last of the chocolate taste has disappeared from my mouth. Eating them this way, I can make the box of peanuts last all the way through the newsreel, cartoon, serial, and feature.

It's always exciting after you get settled down in your seat, and the lights go out so you know the show is about to start. The newsreels upset me sometimes, though, because they're the only times I really see the war. I hear about it on the radio and read about it in the newspaper, but there's something about seeing the faces of those soldiers up there on the big screen—a lot of them just two or three years older than me—that makes it almost too real to stand. And I know these boys are brave and strong, but I also know they're kids with mamas and daddies, and looking at them makes me wish even harder that the war could be won and over so they could home safe.

And then that made me think I wished I could do something more to help, and I thought again about quitting school and working. But would slinging hash in a cafeteria really help us win the war? Or could I do more for my country by getting educated and contributing to society in some way? I knew what Miss Connor thought, and I knew that in my heart, I agreed with her. But I also knew that sometime before long, Daddy was going to ask me if I had made my decision, and I knew telling him I had decided against his wishes was going to be the hardest thing I'd ever had to do.

But then the cartoon came on, and I knew Bugs Bunny wouldn't want me to sit there worrying. Bugs wanted me to forget my troubles for a while, enjoy the show, eat my candy, and laugh. So I did.

OCTOBER 19, 1944

When we sat down to supper tonight, Daddy said, "A right queer thing happened at work today."

My ears pricked up. I wondered if Daddy was going to say something that might give me a clue about what all the workers in town were so busy doing.

"There's this feller, Floyd Adkins, that started working on the crew about the same time I did. A quiet feller and a real good worker—never missed a day. But today he didn't show up." Daddy was slicing an onion over his pinto beans with a pocket knife while he talked. "Well, I was kindly worried about him. I was afraid he might be bad off sick or something, so I asked the foreman about him. All the foreman said is, 'He's gone.' That didn't seem like much of an answer, so I said, 'Did he quit?' The foreman said, 'All you need to know is he's gone. They'll be somebody to replace him tomorrow.'"

"Did any of the other fellers know what happened to him?" Mama asked.

"No," Daddy said, "but one of them said what happened to Floyd wasn't that quare after all. He said after you've been working here a while, you see that—somebody'll be here one day, then gone the next. Fired and shipped out of town, most likely for something they said or did. Can't keep anybody around who's a threat to security, he said."

"You reckon Floyd Adkins told somebody government secrets?" Opal said.

"I don't think he'd know any secrets to tell," Daddy said. "Nobody tells construction fellers nothing. All we get told is where to slap up another building."

"Maybe Floyd Adkins was a Jap spy," Garnet said, her eyes skinny with suspicion.

"I'd be right surprised if he was," Daddy said. "Old Floyd never seemed like the sharpest tool in the shed, if you know what I mean."

"Maybe he was just acting stupid so you wouldn't suspect him."

Garnet has a wild imagination, but unlike me, she doesn't read for fun, so the imaginary world and the real world get all mixed up in her head.

"Well, if he was, then he was a mighty good actor. I'd say he could give Gary Cooper a run for his money."

"Miss Rose at school says that *anybody* could be a Jap spy," Opal said. "You can't tell by the way somebody looks or acts. That's why you can't talk to nobody."

"My teacher says that, too," Garnet said. "She says loose lips sink ships."

This rhyme must've struck Baby Pearl as funny because she giggled and repeated it, but it must've been hard for her little mouth to wrap around because it came out, "Looth lipth think thipth."

"Say it again, Baby Pearl!" Daddy said, laughing.

Baby Pearl said it again and again, and every time it got funnier and funnier till we were laughing so hard we couldn't catch our breath.

OCTOBER 24, 1944

Last night I dreamed I went to Manderley again.

That's the first sentence in *Rebecca* by Daphne du Maurier. Miss Connor is always telling us how bad it is to plagiarize, so I wanted to give credit where credit is due. But Miss du Maurier's sentence is so beautiful I couldn't resist writing it down myself.

I wasn't worth a plugged nickel the whole time I was reading *Rebecca*. I couldn't put it down. I swept the floor reading. I folded clothes reading. Sometimes Mama had to tell me two or three times to do something before I'd hear her because in my mind I was wandering the dark halls of Manderley.

"That must be some book," Mama said.

And it is, but I don't want to say too much about the story here because part of it's a surprise and I don't want to spoil it for anybody. That Mrs. Danvers is a right biddy, though. I had nightmares about her.

I thought about Iris a lot while I was reading since she had recommended the book to me, and then when I walked into the library today to return it, Iris was the person I ran smack dab into. She was holding Baby Sharon, who looked like she was trying to decide whether or not to have a crying fit.

"Hey," I said, feeling friendlier than I usually do, maybe because the book gave Iris and me something in common to talk about. "It's funny you're right here when I'm bringing back *Rebecca*."

"It's not that funny," Iris said, joggling Iris on her hip. "I come here almost every afternoon. When you're home with a baby all day, you've got to have some access to intellectual stimulation, or your brain turns to tapioca pudding. Did you like the book?"

"I loved it." Iris's face was pleasant and friendly. A little bit of lipstick was smeared on her front tooth, and I noticed a place on her sweater where the baby had spit up and she'd tried to wipe it away. Something about these little flaws made me like her more. "You know, I just now realized something, looking at you. The whole time I was reading that book, I kept imagining the main character—the second Mrs. DeWinter—as looking like you. I guess since you told me about the book, you and it are all tangled together in my brain."

Iris laughed. "Well, as long as you didn't imagine me as Mrs. Danvers. You really should've imagined the main character as Joan Fontaine since that's who played her in the movie."

"They made a movie out of *Rebecca*?"

"Yes, a good one. About three or four years ago."

"Shoot, I would've loved to see it." I added another item to the long list of things I'd missed out on by growing up poor in the country.

"I'm checking out this Pearl S. Buck book," Iris said, lifting the book with the hand that wasn't holding Baby Sharon. "I love her, but she always makes me cry. I just returned *A Tree Grows in Brooklyn*. I think I was the last person in America who hadn't read it."

"The second to the last," I said. "I've not read it."

"Well, you should. It made me cry, too, but in a good way. I'll tell you what—come up to the librarian's desk with me, and we'll see if she'll check it out to you instead of reshelving it."

At the librarian's desk, Iris said, "I need to check this out, please, and I was wondering if you might let my friend Ruby check out the copy of *A Tree Grows in Brooklyn* that I just turned in."

I liked hearing her call me her friend.

"Of course, ma'am," the librarian said. "I'll just need to see your cards."

I pulled my library card out of my skirt pocket, but Iris was struggling with getting her purse open while still holding on to Baby Sharon. "They ought to issue an extra pair of arms to every new mother," she said.

"I can hold her for a minute." I looked at Sharon and reached out for her.

"She'll scream," Iris said. "She won't let anybody but me hold her, not even her daddy."

"Let me try," I said.

"Well, it won't be the first time she's disturbed the silence of this library," Iris said, handing her over.

But Sharon didn't cry.

"Her's a little Sharon Bear," I said in the baby-talk voice I'd used with my sisters, and Sharon broke out in a one-toothed gummy grin.

"That's amazing," Iris said, handing her card to the librarian. "She really likes you."

"Ah-boo!" I said and tickled Sharon's little belly. "That's because she knows I'm willing to make a danged fool of myself to make her happy."

"Hm," Iris said, as we walked toward the door with our books. "I'm not sure what the proper etiquette is in asking you this question…"

"You're not a spy about to ask me to spill secrets, are you? 'Cause I don't know any."

Iris laughed. "No. I was actually going to ask if you've ever done any babysitting."

"Well, I've been helping keep my sisters since I was practically a baby myself." Looking after Opal, Garnet, and Baby Pearl had always just been something I did because Mama told me to.

"Warren and I never go out at night anymore," Iris said, pulling Sharon's hat around her ears as we hit the crisp fall air. "It's not like this town is hopping with nightlife, but still, it might be nice to see a movie once in a while. And I could use some help during the day, too—somebody to mind Sharon while I go get my hair done or pick up something at the store or just catch my breath. I've not talked to Warren yet, of course—the idea didn't even dawn on me until I saw you holding Sharon—but I think he'd be fine with it if we let him decide on the amount of money."

I finally caught on that Iris was offering me a paying job. "I wouldn't have to quit school, would I?"

She laughed. "Gracious, no. I was thinking you could come over after school a couple of days a week…and maybe stay until it's time to go home for dinner."

Her saying *dinner* would've confused me a couple of months ago, but since we moved here, I'd gotten used to Northerners who said "lunch" for dinner and "dinner" for supper. "I could do that."

"And then maybe a weekend evening every now and then, if I can convince my husband to take me out, now that I've turned into the matronly, motherly type."

"You don't look old enough to be anybody's mother," I said. There was something about Iris that made her look like a girl in woman's clothing. "I'm sure he'll be proud to take you out."

"No wonder Sharon likes you," Iris said, reaching out to squeeze my hand. "You know just the right thing to tell a girl."

I looked down at my muddy shoes, embarrassed. I wasn't used to compliments, and between Miss Connor and Iris, I had been hearing quite a few of them lately.

"We couldn't pay you much, and as I said, I'll let Warren set the price. Men like it when you make them feel like they're in charge of things. I know he wouldn't offer you any less than a quarter an hour, though, and you'd be working somewhere from six to ten hours a week, so that would probably give you enough spending money to make it worth your while."

"Iris," I said, and I felt the tremble in my voice that meant I wasn't far away from crying, "that money would mean a lot to my family and me."

I had it all figured out. I'd hand every penny I made over to Daddy to use for the family as he saw fit. I wouldn't be earning near as much as I would if I was working full time, but I'd still be increasing the family income. And I wouldn't mind not keeping the money as long as I got to stay in school

"Well, that's good." Iris looked embarrassed.

I probably shouldn't have sounded so grateful, but I'm the kind of person who has a hard time hiding my feelings.

Sharon was getting squirmy and rubbing her eyes with her dimpled fists. Iris said, "I'd better get her home for her nap. I'll tell you what—why don't you come over for lunch on Sunday around one? We'll let Warren get a look at you and see how much money we can extort from him." Her smile was contagious.

"Okay, I'll see you Sunday, then. Should I bring anything?" I hoped she'd say no, but I'd been taught to ask that question if somebody wanted you to eat at their house.

"Just that extra pair of arms I need to hold Sharon," she said.

Walking back home, I felt warm even though my sweater was thin and the wind was chilly. I woke up this morning without a friend or a job or a way of staying in school, and now I was pretty sure I had all three.

OCTOBER 29, 1944

The way Mama and my sisters acted when I told them I wouldn't be joining them for Sunday dinner, you would've thought it was news that needed to be a front-page headline in the Knoxville *News-Sentinel*: *Ruby Pickett Misses Sunday Dinner, Reasons Undisclosed*. Of course, I can see why it would make Mama curious. I've never been one to miss out on her chicken and biscuits, particularly since Sunday's the one day of the week we count on having meat.

"Where you gonna be at?" Mama asked. She was at the counter, cutting up the chicken.

"I'll just be out for a while. It's nothing bad, Mama, I promise. If it works out, you'll be proud of me. I'll tell you about it when I get back." I didn't want to say anything specific about the babysitting job. I didn't want to get anybody's hopes up in case Iris's husband hated me on sight or was too tight with his money to pay a babysitter.

"Ooh, I bet I know what it is!" Opal said from the kitchen table where she was peeling potatoes. "Ruby's got a feller."

To make it worse, Garnet grabbed Baby Pearl by the hands and started dancing her around, singing, "Ruby's got a feller! Ruby's got a feller!"

"You'uns hush," Mama said, then she turned to me, the chicken knife in her hand. "If you do have a feller, Ruby, I hope you're meeting him someplace out in the open. Some of these town boys is fast movers."

"I am not meeting a boy," I said. "And don't ask me no more questions 'cause I won't answer them."

"Ruby"—Baby Pearl looked up at me with the extra-wide eyes she always got when she wanted something—"If you ain't gonna be at dinner, can I have your piece of chicken?"

"That was the last question I'm gonna answer," I said. "And the answer is yes."

* * *

Iris and Warren lived on Snob Hill in one of the cemesto houses the government builds for the people with fancy jobs. Their house was one of the smallest ones on the hill—still lots bigger than ours—and it sat on grass with some trees around it instead of just the mud that passed for our yard. Standing on their porch about to knock on their door, I was overwhelmed how much Iris had that I don't. I could see every scuff on my shoe and every place my skirt had been let out so I wouldn't grow out of it too soon. I wondered if I should just run on home and take my piece of chicken back from Baby Pearl.

But then I'd be a chicken myself, I thought, and I got tickled enough that I found the courage to knock on the door.

When Iris opened the door and flashed her easygoing smile at me, I felt better. After all, she'd already seen how raggedy my clothes are. If that had bothered her, she wouldn't have invited me to her house in the first place. "Ruby!" she said, like I was the Queen of England dropping by for a visit. "I'm glad you could come."

"Me, too."

She opened the door wider and patted me on the back as she let me in. Over her clothes, she was wearing a pink apron made out of some kind of filmy material with red roses on it. The house, I saw, was also heated by a stove, but unlike our house, it was broken up into more rooms. I was standing in a real living room, with a couch, and armchair, and a bookcase spilling over with books I was dying to get a look at. The coffee table was piled with newspapers and magazines. Half-empty coffee cups had been abandoned here and there, and the ashtray on the end table was full. The room was like Iris, pretty, interesting, and not quite neatly put together.

"Sharon's asleep," Iris said, "which is a blessing since it actually allowed me to cook lunch. I was afraid she'd be so fussy I wouldn't have time to put anything together but peanut butter sandwiches."

"Peanut butter sandwiches would've been fine," I said.

"Well, they might have been better than my meatloaf, which is what you're getting." Iris motioned me to follow her into the kitchen. "What with rationing, I'm afraid there's more 'loaf' in it than meat." She dipped mashed potatoes from a pot on the stove into a fancy china serving bowl, then did the same with some green beans. She opened the door of the oven and pulled out a ketchupy-looking meatloaf. I couldn't imagine having a kitchen so nice to cook in.

"Well, I guess we're ready," Iris said. "Warren's back at his desk in the bedroom, puzzling over something or another. Let me go see if I can lure him out with food."

When Iris came back, it was with a man who looked quite a bit older than my daddy. His hair wasn't all the way gray, but it was streaked with silver, which just made his face look tanner and more handsome. He was wearing a crisp white shirt, open at the collar. I thought of a word I had read in a book not long ago: *distinguished*.

"Ruby, this is Warren. Warren, Ruby," Iris said.

"Delighted," Warren said, but he didn't sound delighted. He didn't seem happy or unhappy to see me; he just seemed like his mind was somewhere else.

When he shook my hand, I noticed how soft his hand was, not rough and knotty like my daddy's. "Pleased to meet you, sir," I said.

To my surprise, he smiled a little. "Southern charm aside, Ruby, you don't have to call me sir. I bet you don't call my wife ma'am."

"She'd better not," Iris said, laughing. "It would make me feel ninety years old. Ruby, what would you like to drink? The only choices besides water are coffee or milk, I'm afraid."

I didn't want to ask for milk since it's a kid's drink, but I can't stand the taste of coffee by itself. "Coffee with milk, please."

We sat at the table and passed around the meatloaf, potatoes, and beans. We ate quietly for a minute, and then Warren said what I was thinking but would never have dreamed of saying out loud: "The meatloaf. It's crunchy."

Iris crinkled her nose and smiled. "Cornflakes," she said. "To make the meat stretch. I guess I should've soaked them in milk first."

"Oh, everything's real good," I said. "You shouldn't have gone to so much trouble."

"It's okay, Ruby," Iris said. "I know I'm not much of a cook. I'd never cooked a meal until I was married, and Warren's been really patient with me and my burnt casseroles and unleavened dinner rolls."

"And grease fires," Warren added. "But I'm fortunate in that my mother is a truly terrible cook, so I have very low expectations."

"Which I someday hope to exceed," Iris said, laughing.

A loud "waah" came from a couple of rooms away, and Iris jumped up. "I'll be right back," she said.

She probably wasn't gone for more than a minute, but it felt longer because I had no idea what to say to Warren. I couldn't ask him about his work because he wasn't allowed to tell me about it, and I didn't know what hobbies or interests he might have. I thought he might ask me something, just to keep some noise going, but he just went on eating. He was one of those people who ate only one food at a time. He had quickly finished his meatloaf and then his potatoes and had started in on his green beans.

"Look who's here," Iris said, carrying a sleepy-eyed Sharon.

"Hey, Baby Sharon," I said.

"Watch this, Warren," Iris said. She handed Sharon to me, and she settled into my lap without a peep.

"See, what did I tell you?" Iris said.

Warren shook his head. "I can't believe it. She never lets me hold her like that."

Baby Sharon reached onto my plate and helped herself to a fistful of mashed potatoes.

"Such ladylike behavior," Iris said, and we laughed.

"If you *ladies* will excuse me…" Warren rose from the table. "I always practice my violin after lunch."

"Warren?" Iris said.

He looked at her and nodded.

After he was out of the room, Iris leaned over and whispered, "You got the job."

"Really?" I squealed and leaned down to kiss the top of Baby Sharon's head.

"Really. How about you come on Tuesdays and Thursdays after school and the occasional weekend evening if I can strong-arm Warren into taking me out?"

"Sure."

"And is fifty cents an hour okay? Warren said anything less would be insulting."

"Well, I probably wouldn't be insulted, but I'll take fifty cents an hour if you want to give it to me."

"This is wonderful," Iris said. "I get some free time; you get some money. Can you think of anything better?"

I couldn't. I smiled that kind of foolish smile you get when something really good just falls into your lap, like Baby Sharon had fallen into mine. I hugged Sharon and breathed in her powdery baby smell, and the sound of Warren's violin filled the house like the music in a movie about love.

NOVEMBER 1, 1944

Yesterday was my first day working for Iris. When I hit the front door, I could hear Baby Sharon squalling her head off. I had to knock several times to be heard.

When Iris opened the door, she was smiling, but her jaw looked tight, like she was forcing it. "She's in a mood today," she said. "I'm tempted just to hand her to you and run."

"Go ahead," I said, "as long as you come back sometime." I stepped in the house and reached out and took Baby Sharon, who stopped crying instantly.

"Magic," Iris said. "You're some kind of baby bewitcher."

"Babies like me," I said. "Babies and animals. My papaw had a billy goat that used to follow me around like a puppy dog. If anybody else tried to get close to me, he'd butt 'em with his horns."

Iris laughed. "I bet your dad liked that goat. It probably kept your boyfriends from getting too friendly."

"I think the goat thought he was my boyfriend," I said. "And he never had no competition."

"Really?" Iris said. "I thought you country girls started dating early."

"Not this country girl. What I want is an education."

"Good for you, Ruby." Iris yawned. "You know what I really want?"

"What?"

"A nap." She laughed, and so did I. "You know, I don't think I've had one honest-to-goodness nap since I brought Sharon home from the hospital. I know a lot of mothers nap with their babies, but I'm afraid to. I'm such a sound sleeper I don't know that I'd wake up if she needed me."

"Well, take you a nap, then. We'll be fine."

"Thank you." She grinned. "It's kind of sad that my life is at a point where I can get so excited about a nap. If I'm not up by five, wake me. I need to start Warren's dinner. I actually managed to acquire a tin of corned beef at the store this morning, after mowing down a few other housewives. I think I'll make some corned beef and cabbage. Maybe the Irish blood in my veins will help me cook it without creating too much of a disaster." She kissed Baby Sharon's jowl. "Well...nighty-night."

I set Sharon in her playpen and used some blocks to prop up a hand mirror so she could see herself in it—an old trick I'd used with Baby Pearl. She looked at herself and laughed and gurgled.

With Sharon happy, I decided to explore a little. Not to snoop, mind you—I wasn't going to open any drawers or cabinets. I was just going to get a closer look at what was out in the open. And of course, the first place I went was the bookcase. It was big and long, made of nice, dark wood, and crammed full of books.

Except for my library books and my sisters' and my schoolbooks, the only book in our house was the family Bible, which was used to record birth and death dates and to hold newspaper clippings and pressed flowers, but wasn't read much. This, though, was a full case of books like at the library. There were lots of scientific books which must have been Warren's, and even though I made good grades in science, their titles might as well have been in Chinese for all I could make out about them. Then there was one shelf full of beautiful, leather-bound books with gold lettering spelling out the classic titles: *Don Quixote, Great Expectations, Ivanhoe, Silas Marner.* There were other novels, too, by Daphne DuMaurier and John Steinbeck and Ernest Hemingway. The bottom shelves were taken up by a full set of the Encyclopedia Britanica. An idea popped into my head. What if I read some of the Encyclopedia Britannica every time I came over to babysit? How far could I get in it before Iris didn't need me to watch Sharon anymore? I pulled out the first volume and read about aardvarks. I glanced at the playpen and saw that Baby Sharon had jabbered at her reflection until she talked herself to sleep. I sat down on the couch and got settled in with my aardvarks. I couldn't believe I was getting paid to sit in a comfy living room and read a book. I felt like a criminal—like I had broken into the Stevens' house and was stealing money from them.

When the clock on the mantel said five, I went to wake Iris. The bedroom door was open just a crack. I softly called her name through the opening, but she didn't answer. Swinging open the bedroom door made me feel even more like a burglar. The parts of the bedroom floor that weren't stacked with books were piled with laundry. Iris lay in the middle of the bed, snuggled under the covers, her face resting on her hands. Her long eyelashes were fanned out over her cheeks, and her lips were parted. Like all pretty people, she was even prettier while she was sleeping. She looked sweet and peaceful, like a child instead of a mother, and I couldn't bring myself to wake her.

I decided I would start supper myself. The head of cabbage, the can of corned beef, and three potatoes were sitting on the kitchen counter. I poked around till I found the knife drawer and peeled the potatoes and chopped the cabbage into bite-sized pieces. I poked around some more until I found a couple of pans. I set the pans on the eyes of the stove but then realized I had absolutely no idea how the stove worked. The only stoves I'd used got hot because you lit a fire in their bellies, but this one had complicated knobs and dials. I got down on my knees to look at them better. If I turned the wrong knob, I wondered, would I blow up the house?

"Ruby, what are you doing?" Iris was standing in the doorway. Her hair and clothes were a little mussed from sleeping, and she was barefoot. Her toenails were painted red.

"I was gonna start supper for you, but I can't figure out how this new-fangled stove works."

She laughed. "You don't have to do the cooking. But I will show you how to use the stove. You might need it to heat up Sharon's formula one day. Plus, you'll need to know how this new-fangled kitchen stuff works for when you get married."

"Which'll happen about the time pigs fly," I said.

Iris patted my arm. "It'll happen sooner than you think. Why, it doesn't seem any time at all since I was your age." She turned one dial, then another, and a ring of blue flames burned around the pan on the stove. "And now here I am with a house and a husband and a baby." She shook her head. "But it's not bad. You'll see. Marriage has its moments."

Baby Sharon wailed in her playpen. "She's probably hungry," Iris said. She looked at the pans on the stove that needed tending, then in the direction of the playpen.

"I can feed her while you cook," I said.

"Oh, could you? I can mix up some cereal for her if you can get her in her high chair."

Once Baby Sharon figured out she was going to eat, she calmed down considerably. I tied a bib around her neck and started spooning oatmeal into her wide open mouth.

"I told you I needed an extra pair of arms," Iris said, stirring the cabbage. "Oh, I meant to ask you...have you started *A Tree Grows in Brooklyn* yet?"

I used the spoon to scrape a plop of oatmeal from Baby Sharon's chin. "I'm about halfway through it, and Iris, I hate to admit it, but I judged that book by its cover, just like they say you ain't supposed to do."

"What do you mean?"

"Well, I just thought it wasn't gonna be interesting. A book about a tree growing don't sound interesting, you know? It sounds like watching the grass grow or something. And then there was the writer's name. Lady writers usually have these beautiful, fancy names like Charlotte Bronte or Daphne du Maurier."

Iris laughed. "And she's just plain old Betty Smith."

"Exactly. Betty Smith sounds like your old aunt, not like somebody who'd write a book. But you know, once I gave that book a chance…well, it may just be the best thing I've ever read."

"It's a good book."

"It is. And what makes it good is that it's honest. It might be a made-up story, but it feels real. It felt a lot like my life, really. I mean, my family ain't Irish Catholics in Brooklyn, and we ain't as bad off as the family in the book because my daddy ain't a drunk. But the way they have to work so hard and the way Francie loves to read but has to work to help her family…"

"She's a lot like you, isn't she?" Iris said.

"She is." I didn't tell her that like Francie, I had started writing about my life, too. "And I didn't know anybody would write a book about somebody like me. And even if somebody did write it, I wouldn't have thought anybody would want to read it."

"Well, *A Tree Grows in Brooklyn* isn't showing any signs of falling off the *New York Times* best seller list," Iris said. "So clearly some people want to read stories that aren't about mansions and moors and tortured love. If there are any books you want to borrow from our shelves, by the way, feel free to grab them before you go. You can think of our home as a second lending library."

The word "go" made me realize it was getting to be time for my own supper. I didn't want to leave, though. "Thank you," I said. "I might borrow something once I finish with Francie." I used Sharon's bib to wipe the oatmeal off her face. "I reckon I'd better go eat my own supper," I said. "Hopefully I'll do a neater job of it than Sharon here."

Iris reached into the cookie jar which, I had learned, was for cash instead of cookies. "Well, Ruby, you've let me have a nap and an actual adult conversation. You've definitely earned your money today."

* * *

On the way down Snob Hill, I kept passing little kids. One was covered in a sheet. One had his face blacked with cork to look like a beard and was wearing a beat-up hat and carrying a kerchief on a stick. Another had on a mask like the Lone Ranger. I was confused for a minute, then I remembered what day it was and that trick-or-treating was something town kids did. We had always lived too far out in the country for trick-or-treating.

Mama was getting supper on the table when I got home. "Sorry I'm late," I said, then I took the money out of my skirt pocket and gave it to Daddy, who was sitting at the head of the table.

"Well, look at that," he said, grinning. "You're a wage earner now—that's something to be right proud of. This money'll be a big help to your mama and me."

After we'd mopped up our plates, I said, "Mama, Daddy, there's a bunch of kids out trick-or-treating tonight. You reckon I can take the girls?"

Garnet and Baby Pearl started saying, "Can we? Can we?" right away. Opal didn't say anything, probably because she's old enough to know that saying "Can we? Can we?" over and over again doesn't do anything but get on your parents' nerves.

"We don't go door to door begging for food in this family," Mama said.

"It ain't begging," Daddy said. "It's more like a game."

"Well, it's a no-count game," Mama said. "This family made it through the Depression without begging. We ain't gonna start now."

"Aw, please..." Baby Pearl started to whine.

"I'll tell you'uns what," Daddy said, clapping his hands. "Ruby and Opal, you go fetch us some water."

"What for?" Opal said.

"Cause I said so, that's what for," Daddy said. "Take both buckets, and be quick."

Opal complained all the way to the wash house and back. "We never get to go nowhere or do nothing," she said.

"That ain't true. You just got to go to the wash house," I said. But the look on her face said she didn't think I was funny.

When we got to the house with the water, Daddy pointed to our big metal washtub and said, "Pour it in there." We did, and then Daddy pulled a big paper sack form behind his back and turned it upside down into the tub. Shiny red apples tumbled out and splashed into the water.

We bobbed for apples and laughed like idiots. Afterward, while we crunched our apples by the stove, Daddy told the story of Ol' Rawhide and Bloody Bones that used to scare the living daylights out of me when I was little. I guess I wasn't the only kid that story scared, though, because when it was time to sleep, Garnet and Baby Pearl ended up in bed with me. I guess they figured if I'd survived sixteen years without getting eaten by Ol' Rawhide and Bloody Bones, then they liked my chances of being able to keep them safe.

NOVEMBER 3, 1944

Today in biology class, Mr. Harris made us number off and pair up with partners. My partner was a scrawny red-headed girl whose face was as full of freckles as the sky is full of stars.

"Hey," she said, with a mountain accent even thicker than mine, "you live out at Happy Valley, don't you?"

"Yeah," I said. "My name's Ruby."

She shot out a long, freckled hand for me to shake. "I'm Virgie West from West Virginia."

I couldn't help laughing. "You're kidding, right?"

"Wish I was." Her grin showed a neat row of teeth so tiny they could've been baby teeth. "My daddy told 'em what to write on my birth certificate before Mama came out of the ether. She like to killed him when she woke up."

On the counter in front of us Mr. Harris set a glass mason jar with a fat green bullfrog in it. Next to the jar he set down a strip of white cloth soaked in something that stank to high heaven. "Do not open the jar yet," he said. "Await further instruction." Then he moved on and said the same thing to the next pair of kids and the next. Mr. Harris always talks fancy like that; he went to Harvard or Yale or one of those places. But smart as he is, the poor man still looks like a polecat.

"Now," Mr. Harris said, once all the jars were passed out. "Open the lid of the jar, being very careful not to let the frog escape. Drop the cloth in the jar, and then tightly screw back the lid."

But of course, one of the frogs did escape. It jumped right out of this blonde girl's jar, and she screamed like it was going to kill us all. It jumped off the counter and clear across the room. "I didn't know we was in Calaveras County," I said, thinking about a story I read one time.

"Huh?" Virgie said.

"Nothing." That's one reason I keep to myself. I tend to say things that make sense only to me.

I watched an overgrown boy in overalls catch the frog and stuff it back in the jar. The blonde girl—who, judging from her store-bought clothes, probably lived on Snob Hill—looked at the boy with about as much disgust as she'd looked at the frog.

"How 'bout I open the jar lid and you drop the cloth in right fast?" Virgie said.

She opened the jar lid just enough for me to slip in the cloth. She screwed the lid back on and set the jar on the counter. Nothing happened at first, but then as the fumes filled up the jar, the frog began to twitch and jerk. After a while he stopped twitching. I felt sick.

I must've looked sick, too, because Virgie said, "You all right?"

"Yeah." I couldn't get over how still the frog was. "I just feel sorry for the little feller is all."

"Shoot," Virgie said, "that was nothin. You ever been frog gigging? Now that's gotta hurt. This little feller never knew what hit him."

"You may open the jars and dissect the frogs according to the instructions in your manual," Mr. Harris said.

A lot of the girls didn't want to touch the frogs, but Virgie grabbed ours and splayed him out on the tray Mr. Harris had provided. "You wanna cut him open, or you want me to do it?"

"You go on," I said.

She picked up the blade and sliced down the frog's chest and belly, then across on each side, making flaps of skin that opened like a saloon's double doors in a Western. I still felt sick, but once I saw the frog's insides, I was interested, too: the tiny heart, the little lungs, how everything nestled together in that small space to make what had been seconds earlier, a living, breathing creature.

When the bell rang, Virgie said, "Well, that wasn't so bad. It beat sitting around with our noses in a book for an hour."

I would've rather had my nose in a book, but I didn't say anything.

As we passed Mr. Harris's desk, Virgie said, "You ort to take some of them frog legs home with you, teacher. Them's some good eating."

Mr. Harris massaged the bridge of his nose and muttered, "Sometimes I have to remind myself why I came to Tennessee."

"Say," Virgie said, once we were out in the hall. "You want to sit with me on the bus today?"

"All right," I said, surprised that she'd asked me.

After the final bell rang, I found Virgie outside the building with a lanky red-headed boy wearing faded dungarees that were too short for his long legs. "Ruby, this is my brother Aaron," Virgie said. "Mama learned her lesson when she had him and come out of the ether to name him herself."

"Hey," Aaron said without really looking at me.

I said hey back, but after that Virgie seemed happy to do the talking for all of us. After we took our seats on the bus, she said, "You like to go to the show?"

"Yeah," I said, "when there's something good on."

"Shoot, it's all good to me. As along as the pictures move, I'm happy. You wanna go to the show sometime?"

"Sure," I said.

"What else do you like to do?" she asked.

"I like to go to the library," I said.

"The libary?" Like a lot of country folks, she didn't pronounce the first "r" in the word. "What for?"

"I like to read."

"Shoot, no point in getting eyestrain looking at those little-bitty words when you can look at them nice big pictures up on the movie screen. Say…I roll bandages over at the Red Cross on Wednesdays after school. You wanna come with me?"

"Sure." I decided I'd be friends with Virgie even though we probably didn't have much in common. She was so easygoing and happy it was impossible not to like her, even if you could hardly get a word in edgewise.

I'm glad I met Virgie so I won't be alone all the time at school, but as I write this, I'm too restless to feel all the way happy. Mother and Daddy and my sisters are sleeping, and I'm sitting in front of the stove, wrapped in a blanket, writing by the light of a candle just like Samuel Pepys probably did. It's late, and I should write the same thing Mr. Pepys did at the end of his diary entries: "And so to bed." But I've already been to bed, and I couldn't get to sleep. Every time I closed my eyes, I saw the little frog I murdered, lifeless in its jar like Snow White in her glass coffin.

NOVEMBER 7, 1944

When I knocked on Iris's door today, she hollered for me to come on in. She was sitting in the living room chair with Baby Sharon on her lap. Two other ladies were sitting on the couch with cups of coffee. Like Iris, they were wearing good dresses with high heels and hats. Visiting clothes, I reckon. A little blond-headed girl who looked to be about two was sitting on the floor, scribbling in a coloring book with a picture of a pumpkin in it.

"Ruby, come have a cup of coffee with us," Iris said. "Milk, right?"

"Yes, please." I watched as Iris poured a cup about a third full of coffee and two-thirds full of milk, the way I like it.

"Ruby," Iris said. "These are my neighbors, Mrs. Hannah McGill and Mrs. Eva Lynch."

Mrs. McGill looked like she might be around Iris's age; she had a round face and mouse-brown hair and stopped just short of being chubby. Mrs. Lynch, though, was so rail-thin she made me think of how Daddy described skinny women: "a hank of hair and a bone." Unlike Iris, who always had lipstick on her teeth or a spot on her blouse, Mrs. Lynch looked perfect. Her chic little hat—that's how they always described them in ladies' magazines—was perched perfectly on her perfectly arranged hair and also managed to perfectly match her peacock blue dress. "Nice to meet you'uns," I said. The way they were looking, I felt like I should curtsy. But I didn't.

"What was that she said?" Mrs. McGill turned to Mrs. Lynch. "You-uns?"

"You'uns." Mrs. Lynch pronounced it slowly. "It's a plural form of 'you.' Nonstandard English, of course. Local dialect."

"Ruby's from Kentucky," Iris said. When neither Mrs. McGill nor Mrs. Lynch said anything, she added, "Ruby, after we finish our coffee, we're going downtown to vote. We shouldn't be gone long, if you wouldn't mind looking after Sharon."

"Of course she wouldn't mind," Mrs. Lynch said. "That's what you pay her for, isn't it?" She laughed.

"Doesn't it feel strange," Mrs. McGill said, "to be voting in the national election but not for any local government?"

"Well, in Oak Ridge, the national government *is* the local government," Mrs. Lynch said.

"True," Iris said. "For better or for worse."

"Which makes it sound like a marriage," Mrs. McGill said, laughing.

"It is a marriage," Mrs. Lynch said, but her voice was serious. "Scientists, soldiers, laborers, wives—we're all married to this town." Then she looked at me. "Ruby"—I was startled since everybody had been talking like I wasn't even in the room— "since we'll be gone so briefly I think I may leave little Helen with you, too." She nodded in the direction of the little blonde girl, who was engrossed in coloring a picture of a Thanksgiving turkey.

I said "all right" even though I was pretty sure I would've ended up with Helen even if I'd said a firm no.

When the ladies trooped out to do their patriotic duty, Iris was the last in line. She looked at me, smiled, and mouthed the word "sorry."

The reason for Iris's apology became clear soon enough. Once her mother was out of sight, little Helen started screaming—screaming the way you would if somebody was cutting one of your legs off with a rusty hacksaw. Her pretty face transformed into a red, twisted mask, and Baby Sharon—who probably figured that if a bigger kid was throwing a fit like that, then there must be something really bad going on—started crying, too. For sheer loudness, though, Baby Sharon couldn't hold a candle to Helen. Nobody better tell Helen any of Oak Ridge's secrets, I thought, or she'd scream them out so they could be heard clear to Japan.

"Helen," I said, making my voice as sweet as syrup, "why don't you show Baby Sharon and me how you color in your pretty coloring book?"

She snatched up a fist full of crayons and slung them across the room. "Mama!" she screamed. "Maaaaamaaaaaaa!"

"Your mama'll be back in a few minutes," I said. "I tell you what let's do, Baby Sharon. Let's see if Helen wants to dance with us."

I put a record on the record player and bounced Baby Sharon up and down in time with the music. She cheered up right away. Helen, though, kept right on screaming. No matter how big Glen Miller's band was, Helen's screams were bigger.

Finally, I took the girls into the kitchen and gave them each a cookie, figuring that Helen couldn't scream with her mouth full. But as soon as Helen started chewing, Iris came back with Mrs. Lynch, who took one look at Helen and said, "Oh, no, you've spoiled her dinner!"

"I wouldn't worry, ma'am," I said. "I think she worked up quite an appetite."

"Is she sarcastic with you, too, Iris?" Mrs. Lynch said.

"Oh, that's just Ruby's sense of humor," Iris said. "I like it."

Mrs. Lynch didn't like it, I guess, and she plunked down a nickel on the table in front of me, scooped up Helen, and left.

"That was a hard-earned nickel," I said, when Iris came back from walking Mrs. Lynch to the door.

"I know it was," Iris said. "Eva left Helen with Warren and me one Sunday afternoon. After an hour of her screaming, Warren said he found the first syllable of her name quite appropriate." She laughed. "Would you mind feeding Sharon a jar of sweet potatoes while I get dinner started?"

"Of course I wouldn't mind. That's what you pay me for."

Iris winced. "Ooh, she did say that, didn't she? Well, you've got to understand Eva's one of those rich girls who was raised with a whole household staff trained to do her bidding. Roughing it in Oak Ridge has been quite an adjustment for her." She opened and drained a can of tuna. "But she means well. At least that's what I keep telling myself."

I didn't feel like I ought to say anything else on the subject of Mrs. Lynch, so I spooned sweet potatoes into Sharon's waiting mouth and asked, "You reckon Dewey'll win the election like the newspapers want him to?"

"I don't know." Iris opened a soup can and dumped the gray, gloppy contents into a bowl with the tuna. "He didn't get my vote."

"Mother and Daddy like FDR, too," I said. "Daddy don't care for Mrs. Roosevelt much, though. He says a woman ain't got no business doing some of the things she does, like going down in the coal mines. He also says she looks like a mule."

Iris poured a little milk into the bowl of goo and gave it a stir. "And what do you think of Eleanor?"

"I like her. I think she's smart. And she can't help it that she looks like a mule."

Iris laughed. "I like her, too. And I think that a lot of FDR's good ideas are really her ideas."

"I think so, too. I hope nobody told my daddy that, though, or he would've voted for Dewey."

Iris smiled. "I like that there are women like Eleanor and like the ones working over at the plant—women who take an interest in what's going on outside their houses." She poured the tuna-soup glop into a baking dish and smeared it around. "I don't want to sound like I'm criticizing Hannah and Eva because they were really nice helping me get settled here, and we all take turns having each other over for coffee..." She crumbled up some saltine crackers and started sprinkling them over the tuna glop. It looked awful, and I was glad I wasn't staying for supper. "But when I'm visiting them they don't talk about anything but what their kids are saying and doing and what new recipes they've tried…sometimes I want to talk about something bigger than everyday life, you know?"

"Yeah. Sometimes I get to thinking about how my mama spends all her time looking after whatever little-bitty place we happen to be living in. My sisters say they're gonna marry rich men and be housewives in mansions. But no matter whether my house was a shack or a mansion, I think I'd get bored staying in it all day."

"You would." Iris slid the baking dish into the oven. "Sometimes I think that when Sharon's old enough for school— and who knows where we'll be by then?—I might get a job. My degree's in journalism, and some days I just picture myself sitting behind the desk in a newspaper office, checking the facts on some big story."

I grinned. "Like Brenda Starr."

"It wouldn't have to be that glamorous to satisfy me. I'd even like writing up run-of-the-mill stuff like wedding announcements and obituaries. I worked three out of my four college years on the school newspaper, and those are some of my happiest memories—staying up late to make deadline, the camaraderie with the rest of the staff. I'd like to have something like that in my life again once Sharon's older. I haven't talked to Warren about it, though. I guess I'm afraid he'll say no, and then I won't have my little daydream to entertain me anymore."

I wiped Baby Sharon's sweet potatoey face. "He shouldn't mind, if you wait till Sharon's bigger. Maybe you could find a part-time job and just work the hours she's in school. You should talk to him about it."

Iris took off her apron and sighed. "There's a lot Warren and I haven't talked about since we moved here. With him working six twelve-hour shifts per week, there's not much time for conversation. And then when he is home, I can't very well ask him 'what did you do at work today?' because he's not allowed to tell me. So I make pleasant conversation about the baby and the house and anything interesting or comical that I can think of, and I don't bother him with my worries or problems because I know he's working a lot harder than I am. Then he compliments me on the dinner I've prepared—most of the time I don't deserve it—and makes chit-chat about the new Oak Ridge Symphony he's been asked to join or an upcoming dinner party or social event. Warren and I don't get to spend enough time together, and the time that we do have, we've fallen into this pattern of being extraordinarily polite to one another." She lifted Baby Sharon from her high chair. "But apparently my politeness doesn't extend to you. I've spent far too much time talking to you about myself. It's just…there's something about you I trust. That's why I chose you to look after Sharon."

"That means a lot to me. Thank you."

"But just because I trust you doesn't mean I should unburden myself to you at every possible opportunity. I really am interested in what's going on in your life. What are you reading right now?"

"*A Tree Grows in Brooklyn*. Again. I finished it and then turned right back to the first page and started it again. I had to renew it at the library. For some reason I can't let it go yet."

"I can only imagine how much I would have loved that book if it had been around when I was your age."

I grinned. "'When I was your age'…that makes you sound old enough to be my granny."

"It does, doesn't it?" Iris laughed. "But Ruby, I did want to say, I appreciate your listening to me, and if you ever want me to listen to you…if you ever have anything you want to talk about—maybe some girl things it's too awkward to talk to your mother about—well, you know where to find me."

I felt my face heat up at the sound of "girl things." I didn't know what kind of things she meant, exactly, but I did know that whatever they were, they embarrassed me. I was even more embarrassed when I looked into Iris's clear blue eyes and saw and felt the trust she had mentioned. It was like being handed a nice present. I felt grateful and lucky but also awkward and unworthy. I did manage to say thank you, though. And then I slipped home to supper, also grateful that I didn't have to eat Iris's tuna casserole.

NOVEMBER 10, 1944

Well, whether you're reading this in 1944 or 1984, you already know that FDR beat Dewey, so I reckon we should be glad that in this country what the people want matters more than what the papers want.

"Unprecedented," Miss Connor said in literature class on Wednesday when she held up the newspaper announcing Roosevelt's victory. "It is unprecedented for a U.S. president to win a fourth term of office. I don't know what you students are learning in history, but as citizens of the United States right now—and as citizens of Oak Ridge, Tennessee—you are living history, and don't you forget it. You boys and girls will have no shortage of stories to tell your grandchildren."

That afternoon I went with Virgie to the Red Cross to roll bandages. Aaron went with us as far as the door but then wandered off without a word. "He'll be back in an hour," Virgie said. "Rolling bandages is women's work. I guess men's work is getting shot up so they need bandages."

We sat at a big table, rolling up strips of white gauze. "You know," Virgie said, "sometimes I think I might leave a note in one of these bandages and maybe the soldier who uses it will come back and find me after the war. He'll be real handsome, of course, and he'll have been dreaming of me the whole time he was getting shot at. And he'll take me out dancing, and we'll have a whirlwind romance and elope to Niagara Falls." She crinkled her freckled nose and grinned. "Is that the foolishest thing you ever heard?"

"It's one of them," I said. "You probably go to the show too much."

"Well, you read too much," Virgie said. "It makes you stand-offish."

"Am I stand-offish because I read too much, or do I read too much because I'm stand-offish?"

Virgie laughed. "Shoot, I don't know, Ruby. You're the smart one. You tell me."

When we'd finished rolling our bandages, Aaron was waiting for us at the front door. Some babysitting money was jingling in my skirt pocket, and I had an idea. "You'uns wanna stop at the drugstore for a Coke?"

"Ain't got no money," Virgie said, like somebody who was used to having no money and wasn't ashamed of it.

"I'll buy," I said.

Aaron ran a hand through his orange cowlick. "Girls don't buy boys no Cokes." It was maybe the second thing I ever heard him say.

"Sure they do," I said, "if they're friends, and one friend just happens to have some babysitting money in her pocket."

Aaron squinted up his eyes, like he was thinking hard. "Well, I reckon it'd be all right just this once."

The soda fountain was full of kids our age, playing Perry Como on the jukebox and talking and laughing. I thought of the day I'd come in with Miss Connor, with no money and no friends. But now I had fifteen cents for Cokes and two kids my age to sit at a table and drink them with me. Nothing like this would've ever happened back home. I sipped my Coke and patted my foot in time with the jukebox. "Did you'uns have a soda fountain back where you came from?" I asked.

"Shoot, no." Virgie laughed. "We lived in a coal camp. There was a school and the company store and a rec hall, and that was about it. They showed movies in the rec hall every once in a while, but they was always old ones. Here I get to see a new picture every week. I'm getting plumb spoiled."

"So you like it better here than you like it back home?" I said. "I sure do."

"I like some things better, mostly the movies," Virgie said, draining the last of her Coke. "But I miss home, and Aaron misses home real bad, don't you, Aaron?"

He nodded, but he looked a little embarrassed.

"In a lot of ways it's real different here than it was in the coal camp," Virgie said. "But some ways it's just the same. Everybody's here on accounta the same job, so it's a company town."

"It is," I said, "but the government's the company." I was beginning to notice that Virgie was a lot smarter than she thought she was. She's not book-smart like me. She does just enough in school to get by. But she can see things about the real world that I miss sometimes.

A fast song came on the jukebox, and that blonde girl from biology class dragged a boy to the floor and started dancing. I couldn't imagine dancing out in the open like that with everybody watching me, but then again, I didn't know any of the dances these rich city kids knew. The girl's shiny saddle shoes didn't miss a step. She'd probably had dancing lessons from the time she learned how to walk. Back home, lots of people thought dancing was a sin, and the ones that did dance clogged to fiddle music instead of jitterbugging to a jukebox. I liked this new music and the new dancing, though, even if I didn't know how to do it. I tapped my feet and sipped my soda. Virgie's and Aaron's glasses were already empty, but I wanted to make mine last.

Once the song was over, the blonde and her boyfriend walked toward the door hand in hand. When they passed our table, I said, "You'uns dance real good."

The blonde girl looked at us like we were the mud she scraped off her saddle shoe. She looked over at her boyfriend, spat "hillbillies," and they both laughed. I don't think she recognized Virgie and me from her biology class. I don't think she could even see people like Virgie and me.

Virgie was up on her feet. I'd never seen her mad before, and her light blue eyes were as cold as ice. "Danged right we're hillbillies," she said, loud enough that people turned their heads to look. "But you're here in the hills now, too, so that means you ain't no better than us."

The blonde girl raised a perfectly plucked eyebrow. "Excuse me, do I know you?"

"You ought to know me," Virgie said. "You've been in third-period biology class with me since the start of school. You don't know my name, but I know your name's Susie Thompson. And you know what else I know? I know my friend Ruby here paid you a compliment, and you insulted her."

Susie looked over at her clean-cut, square-jawed boyfriend. "You're not going to let her talk to me like that, are you, Rob?"

"This is stupid," I said. "Let's just forget about it."

But Rob had already shucked off his yellow cardigan and handed it to Susie. He slung back his shoulders, puffed out his chest, and pointed his finger at Aaron. "Hey, Li'l Abner, I don't know if she"—he nodded in Virgie's direction—"is your sister or your girlfriend or both, but whoever she is, you need to tell her to keep her mouth shut."

Aaron didn't say a word. He didn't even blink. He just stood slowly, showing himself to be a good six inches taller than Rob.

"Come on, Susie, let's get out of here." Rob grabbed Susie's hand and dragged her as he ran for the door. They bumped into a pair of soldiers in the doorway, one of whom said, "Hey, watch it, kids!" Aaron didn't sit back down until they were out of sight.

Virgie was laughing so hard she couldn't catch her breath. "They ran like scalded dogs!" she said when she finally had enough wind to speak. "They ain't got no right to be calling you Li'l Abner, Aaron. They're the ones that belongs in the funny papers. Blondie and Dagwood!" she said, then doubled over laughing again.

Aaron just wore a half smile.

I reached out and touched Virgie's arm. "You didn't have to do that. Stick up for me like that, I mean."

"Sure I had to," Virgie said. "You're my friend."

Being friends with Virgie was different than being friends with Iris. With Iris, I was always trying to be the best me I can. She brings out the part of me that wants to do more, know more, be more. Spending time with Iris is exciting, but it makes me a little nervous, too, afraid I'll say the wrong thing and show myself to be even more ignorant than she already knows I am. With Virgie, though, I'm just regular Ruby, not worried about what kind of impression I'll make. With her brains and education, Iris shows me what's possible—what I could grow up to be. But Virgie, with her common sense and mountain ways, meets me where I am.

NOVEMBER 14, 1944

When I walked past her desk after English literature today, Miss Connor said, "Ruby, could I keep you a moment before you go to your next class?"

"Yes, ma'am." I racked my brain trying to figure out what I'd said or done to get in trouble.

After everybody else had filtered out of the classroom, Miss Connor flashed me her shy little gap-toothed smile. "I kept you because I have good news, Ruby, so you can stop looking so worried."

"Yes, ma'am." I smiled back at her.

Miss Connor opened up a desk drawer and pulled out a typed sheet of paper. "The Society of American Clubwomen is sponsoring an essay contest," she said, glancing down at the paper. "I was asked to select a girl from each of my classes to enter the contest—the student I considered to be the best writer with the freshest perspective. And in English literature, that would be you."

"Me?" I felt like somebody was blowing up a balloon in my chest. "There's plenty of scientists' kids to pick—kids who can use big words and whose parents went to college."

"That's true," Miss Connor said. "But I didn't think they would have as many interesting things to say on the subject"— she glanced down at the paper again—"What America Means to Me."

"Shoot, you think anybody'll care what I have to say?"

"I already care. And I think others might care, too, especially if you clean up your grammar. The deadline for submissions to the district contest is January fifth, so you'll have time to work on your essay over Christmas vacation. And of course, the winner of the district contest goes on to compete at the state level." She held out the paper. "These are the rules. Do you think you might like to give it a try?"

"Yes, ma'am." It was all I could do not to snatch the paper out of her hands, but I made myself take it gently. "And Miss Connor, I just want to say that it means a lot that you picked me. It…it makes me feel like I've already won something."

Miss Connor smiled, but then she blinked hard. "Ruby, you really are very dear, do you know that? Now run along. I will not be responsible for making you late to your next class."

When I got to Iris's, I showed her the rule sheet and told her about Miss Connor picking me.

"That's wonderful!" she said and clapped her hands. Baby Sharon—who just learned to clap and seems right proud of it— clapped, too. "See, even Sharon is proud of you. We should do something to celebrate. How about a slice of pumpkin pie? Eva made it, not me, so it's edible."

"Sure, thanks."

Once we'd settled on the couch with pie and coffee, Iris said, "So what are you going to write about? What does America mean to Ruby Pickett?"

"I have no idea, to be honest." The pie was good, sweet and creamy and spicy. It was obvious that Iris didn't make it. "I've always felt about being an American the same way I feel about being a girl. I'm glad I am one and wouldn't want to be different, but I've never really thought about what being one means. Reckon I'd better start, huh?"

"Oh, I'm sure you'll come up with something outstanding. And can you imagine if your essay were to win the district contest, then the state contest? You'd get to compete on the national level."

"Ain't that kindly counting your chickens before they're hatched? Or counting your essay before it's wrote." I winced and corrected myself. "Written. How am I gonna write a decent essay if I can't even talk right?"

"That's easy," Iris said. "You write it and I'll proofread it for you. My senior year I was the copy editor of the college newspaper. And I used to proof a lot of Warren's writing before his work became top secret."

"Thank you."

"You're entirely welcome." She patted my knee. "I'm so glad you're getting this opportunity, Ruby. This is the kind of experience that will really help you when it's time to go to college."

"I like the way you say when, not if." Not one member of my family ever went to college. Shoot, I don't reckon one member of my family had even seen a college.

"Of course you'll go to college." She set down her coffee cup and jostled Baby Sharon on her lap. "You know, yesterday Eva said to me that my college education was wasted. 'Why do you need a degree to change diapers?' she said. Eva didn't go to college; she just went to one of those fancy ladies' finishing schools." Iris rolled her eyes. "But I told her my college degree was absolutely not wasted. I learned a lot and had a great time, and won't it be an advantage for Sharon to have a mother who knows about a few things besides pouring tea and folding napkins?" She smiled. "Plus, I met Warren in college."

"You went to school with him?"

Iris smiled wider, a pink flush creeping onto her cheeks. "No. He was my physics professor. I thought taking physics would demystify the whole universe for me. It didn't, but I did meet my husband."

"So that explains the age difference," I said without thinking.

"It does indeed. And now that I've let you know what a wicked girl I am, I should probably leave Sharon with you for an hour or so. My errands aren't going to run themselves."

* * *

When Iris came back, I was reading to Sharon from the encyclopedia.

"Does she find baboons interesting?" Iris said, laughing.

"She seems to," I said. "Or at least she likes the sound of my voice."

Iris set down her sacks and started digging through one of them. "I bought you a little present," she said.

"Oh, you didn't have to do that," I said. "It ain't Christmas yet."

"Oh, it's just a little something," she said. She held out a Big Chief writing tablet and a beautiful blue fountain pen. "For writing your essay."

"Thank you, Iris. You didn't have to..."

"Would you stop saying that? I know I didn't have to. I wanted to. I'm proud of your accomplishment, and I wanted to mark the occasion in some small way."

Getting a gift, especially such a thoughtful gift, from Iris made me feel all shy. I wasn't used to that kind of attention, and when she paid me my babysitting money, I couldn't look her in the eye.

"Ruby," she said, "did I offend you in some way? I've not broken some unspoken code of the mountains or something, have I?"

"No," I said, but it came out choked. "You make me real happy."

"Oh, you," she said and threw her arms around me and hugged me close and long. It felt so good I hated to let go first, but I did so I could say bye and run out the door before she could see my tears.

* * *

When I got home, everybody had already sat down to eat. Mama made a move to get up, but I said, "Stay where you are. I'll fix my own plate." I went to the stove and dipped from the pots of beans and greens, neither of which, I saw from fishing around with the ladle, had a trace of fatback in them. It didn't matter, though. I was just about too excited to eat.

When I sat down at the table, Daddy said, "You're awful smiley this evening."

"Yeah," I said, taking a hunk of cornbread. "I had a good day."

"Them don't come around too often," Mama said. "What was good about it?"

"I bet a boy asked her on a date," Opal said.

"I bet she found some money on the sidewalk," Garnet said.

"I bet she got invited to a party with cake and ice cream," Baby Pearl said.

I laughed. "Nope. It's not about boys or money or parties. There's this writing contest, and Miss Connor was supposed to pick the best girl writer out of her class to enter it." I paused dramatically. "She picked me."

"Oh," Opal said, like she was disappointed I didn't have more exciting news.

Everybody kept right on eating and didn't say congratulations or kiss my foot or anything, until after a couple of minutes, Daddy said, "Well, if you're gonna write something, maybe you ort to write about cowboys and Indians and that kind of thing. Zane Gray makes a pretty penny with them Westerns he writes."

"Well," Mama sighed, "I don't reckon I've got no quarrel with you writing as long as you don't write nothing about our family where anybody can read it."

"I won't," I said, but I was thinking about this diary and how full it is of family stuff. But I don't write it for anybody to read, unless they're reading after I've been dead a long time. "I'm supposed to write about what America means to me."

"Huh," Mama said. "Well, I reckon times have changed that girls get asked to write about such as that. Your granny used to say there was just three times a lady's name should be in print: when she was born, when she got married, and when she died."

I had heard Granny say this myself, and it always struck me as sad. If the only times you did something worth writing about were when you got born, got married, and then died, what was the point of having been born at all?

NOVEMBER 19, 1944

I spent last night at Virgie's. They just moved from the trailer camp to a new apartment where there's more room. I didn't understand why her family needed more room than mine, since there are only two West kids. But Virgie said it was on account of her and Aaron being the opposite sex. Apparently the government figures if a family has a boy and a girl, they've got to have a place with three bedrooms since the kids can't sleep together. But if a couple has three or four kids of the same sex, the government will just shell out for a two-bedroom place, figuring that all the kids can cram into the same bedroom. Isn't it funny that there's somebody in the government whose job it is to think of these things?

When I found Virgie's apartment, she opened the door just as soon as I knocked.

"Come on in," she said, grabbing the paper sack I'd brought to hold my nightgown and change of clothes and toothbrush. "We'll eat supper when Daddy gets home, and after that, we'll go to the show."

"Sounds good to me," I said.

I tried to look around the place without staring too much. The apartment was roomier than our place but nowhere near as spacious as Iris's house. Still, it had bright white walls, and the newness of the place made the Wests' old blue couch and rocking chair look downright shabby.

"Ma's in the kitchen if you want to say hidy," Virgie said. "It's untelling where Aaron is, but he'll be here when supper's ready. The boy can smell Ma's biscuits from clear across town."

Sure enough, Mrs. West was in the kitchen, rolling out biscuit dough. I had met her a few times before, but it never ceased to amaze me that she and Virgie could share the same blood. Mrs. West's hair was so dark it was almost black, and so were her eyes. There wasn't a freckle to be seen on her.

"Hidy, Ruby," she said, looking up from her rolled-out dough. One thing she and Virgie did share was that big, friendly grin.

"Hey, Mrs. West. I like your new place."

She was cutting out circles of dough using the mouth of a jelly jar. "Well, it ain't nothing more than a cracker box, really. But since we was living in a sardine can before, I reckon a cracker box is an improvement." She cut out another circle. "Supper'll be ready soon. You ain't never tried my Saturday-night catheads before, have you?"

I tried not to look shocked. I'd eaten plenty of country vittles back home—rabbit, squirrel, even possum with sweet potatoes. But cat's heads?

Virgie laughed. "I can see from your face that you don't say catheads where you come from."

Mrs. West laughed, too. "It means big biscuits—big as a cat's head."

"Oh," I said, "that sounds a lot better then." And of course, I had to join in laughing.

"Come on," Virgie said. "I'll show you my room."

The bedroom was smallish, but it was all Virgie's. She had a little iron-frame bed with a crazy quilt on it and a chest of drawers with a hairbrush and a Bible and a little china cat on it. It was one of those times when it seems like you're thinking something, but you're really saying it out loud. "What's it like?"

"What's my room like?" Virgie looked at me like I was crazy. "Well, you tell me. You're looking at it."

"Oh!" I said, surprised that I had spoken. "What I mean is… what's it like to have your own room?"

"It's nice," she said, sitting on the bed and patting the spot next to her. "My room back home was bigger, though. And I wish I could put my pictures on the wall, but Daddy'd die if he knew about them." She reached under the bed and pulled out a Sears-Roebuck shoebox. "See?" she said, taking off the lid. Inside were dozens of pictures cut out of magazines: Tyrone Power, Clark Gable, Rita Hayworth, Veronica Lake, and plenty of others I didn't even recognize.

I scooted back on the bed next to her. "I've never had a place that was just mine. I can barely imagine it. On weekend nights I could just stay up and read…or something…without bothering anybody." I almost said "read or write," but I stopped myself. I didn't want to tell Virgie about my diary, maybe because it's the only thing I can think of that really is just mine.

"See, and I've always thought it would be fun to have a sister to share a room with," Virgie said, "and stay awake half the night whispering and giggling."

"I love my sisters," I said, "but sometimes it would be nice to have a door I could close."

"That's how it is," Virgie said. "We always want what we ain't got."

Soon the apartment smelled of baking biscuits, and I heard the front door open. "That'd be Aaron," Virgie said. "He comes and goes without making a sound. I reckon the rest of us talk so much he finally had to give up on getting a word in edgewise."

"Is your daddy a talker, too?" Mr. West had always been at work when I'd gone to visit Virgie at the trailer.

"He's the loudest one of us," Virgie said. "When he hits the door, you'll hear him."

She was right. Mr. West came up to the door whistling some old fiddle tune, and I thought of how Francie's daddy in *A Tree*

Grows in Brooklyn always came into the apartment singing. "I could smell them catheads plumb outside," his voice boomed.

Virgie and I went out into the living room to meet him. He had a big voice, but he was a stout little man, making me wonder how Aaron had gotten so tall. It was no mystery where the kids' coloring came from, though. What little hair Mr. West had was bright orange, and his ruddy face had been planted with a field full of freckles. "And who is this beautiful young lady?" he asked.

He was looking in my direction, so I looked over my shoulder to see if somebody better-looking might be standing behind me.

Virgie elbowed me. "He's talking about you, silly." She grabbed my hand. "Daddy, this is Ruby Pickett from Kentucky, the girl I was telling you about."

Mr. West took my hand in his big, meaty one. "Welcome to our home, Ruby. I'm tickled that Virgie's finally found herself a running buddy. She was real lonesome for a long time after we moved."

"Thank you, sir," I said. "I'm glad I found Virgie, too."

When we sat down to eat, Mr. West said the blessing. It was a long prayer—he thanked the Lord for every item on the table, the biscuits and the grits and the eggs and the bacon and the gravy. He asked for the Lord to shower His blessings on each person at the table, giving me special mention as a guest, which embarrassed me. He prayed for a swift and victorious end to the war so our boys could come back home safe to their mamas.

The only time my daddy said a blessing was at Sunday dinner and on holidays. And when he said it, he always kept it short and sweet. He said the Lord didn't want you praying so long your biscuits got cold.

Once she started passing the plates, Mrs. West said, "Ruby, I bet you think we're right peculiar having breakfast food of a night."

"Not peculiar," I said. "Just different."

"It's habit I got into Saturday nights after we moved here," Mrs. West said, splitting a biscuit and dousing it with gravy. "We go to the show on Saturday nights, so we're kindly in a hurry. One night, I didn't have time to cook up a full supper so I cooked breakfast instead. Everybody liked it, so I just kept right on doing it."

"I like it, too," I said. I especially liked the bacon, which was a rare treat these days. "And the catheads is real good."

After Virgie and I helped Mrs. West clear the table, we all walked to Townsite to the show. Virgie wanted to sit in the front row, and I was the only one who'd sit there with her. I believe she would've sat touching the screen if she could have. Watching Virgie watch the show was almost more interesting than the show itself. Through the newsreel, the Daffy Duck cartoon, the Western serial, and the main feature, she sat with her eyes open wide, almost as if she was willing herself not to blink. She leaned forward in her seat, getting even closer to the screen, and her mouth gaped the way that would've made my mother ask if she was "catching flies." Virgie wasn't sitting next to me, not really. She was in the world on the screen.

I poked her in the arm once to see if she would notice me. She brushed me away absently, as if a fly had landed on her.

Later, when we sat barefoot and Indian-style on her bed, Virgie hugged a pillow to her chest and said, "So, who's your favorite leading man?"

"You know," I said, "I've never really thought about." I racked my brain until an interesting face popped up. "But I do like Humphrey Bogart real good. He's smart. And tough."

Virgie crinkled her nose and stuck out her tongue. "Tough like an old piece of shoe leather. He ain't a bit good-looking. What about Tyrone Power?"

"He is real handsome, but I don't guess I find handsome to be that interesting. For some reason, I always notice women in movies more. I guess I like to pick out who I want to be like."

"I do that, too, sometimes," Virgie said, resting her chin on her pillow. "So what actresses do you like?"

"Well, I love Barbara Stanwyck because she's such a good actress. She's a different person in every single movie she's in, you know? But my all-time favorite had got to be Bette Davis."

"Are you kidding?" Virgie's eyes were wide with shock. "Barbara Stanwyck's as scrawny as a goat, and Bette Davis looks like one of them pop-eyed little dogs people bring back from Mexico. I can't believe you'd rather look at them than Rita Hayworth."

"I didn't say nothing about their looks. I was thinking about being like them—smart and confident and nobody's fool, you know? There ain't much point in picking out what movie star I want to look like. I look how I look, and it sure ain't like Rita Hayworth."

"No, you don't," Virgie said. "But I've got red hair like she does. Too bad I've got all these freckles, though. Rita wouldn't be wearing them strapless gowns if she had freckly shoulders like mine."

Virgie didn't shut up about movie stars until I fell asleep. Of course, I'm just assuming she shut up then. For all I know, she could've chattered on all night with me sleeping beside her. As it was, though, I didn't hear a thing till she was shaking my shoulder and saying, "You'd better get dressed for church."

"Oh, are we going to church?" I asked, confused for a minute to be waking up in a strange place.

There's one main church in Oak Ridge. Mother and Daddy have taken us there a few times, but we didn't really feel much at home there. It's called the United Church Chapel on the Hill, and they have services for all kinds of religions, Baptist or Methodist or Catholic. I've heard tell the Jews even have services there on Saturdays.

"We ain't going to the big church," Virgie said. "Daddy says the people there ain't right with the Lord. They'll let anybody have church there, even the Catholics, and they ain't even real Christians on accounta them worshipping the Pope, so we don't go to the church. The church comes to us."

I thought about telling her I was pretty sure she was wrong about Catholics worshipping the Pope, but I was so confused by what she'd said about the church coming to us that I didn't really know what to say.

I soon found out what she meant. No sooner than we'd had time to dress and have a glass of milk and a cold biscuit apiece, people started knocking on the door: young men in overalls, young women with babies on their hips, a couple of older fellows in guard uniforms. A skinny-necked, buck-toothed boy who was probably just a couple of years older than Virgie and me came in carrying a guitar. Soon there were a dozen people besides the Wests and me crammed into the living room.

Mr. West stood up, holding a fat Bible in his hand. "Now brothers and sisters," he said, "we ain't supposed to shout on accounta the other people living in this building. We ain't supposed to wake up the sinners that likes to sleep late of a Sunday. But I tell you what—I feel like shouting this morning!"

"Amen!" the buck-toothed boy with the guitar called.

Mr. West was pacing back and forth, holding his Bible high. "I feel like shouting because I've got the Lord in my heart this morning!"

Amens.

"I feel like shouting because I am happy in the Lord!"

More amens.

"I feel like shouting because I am sanctified!"

"Preach it, brother!" one of the guards said.

"Now I've got to tell you," Mr. West said, his eyes scanning over his listeners. "They's people in this town that thinks they're safe in the arms of Jesus. But they ain't! They think they can go to a fancy white church on a hill once a week and do what they want to do the rest of the week, and the Lord won't mind. But the Lord has His eyes open every day of the week, and He sees all and knows all."

Somebody said, "That's right."

"He sees all and knows all," Mr. West said, "and He knows the ways of the world is wicked." He shook his head and repeated, "Wicked. I went to the picture show last night, brothers and sisters. And do you know what I seen?"

"What did you see, Brother?" Buck Tooth asked.

"I seen sin and degradation! I seen women in low-cut dresses drinking liquor and smoking cigarettes and running around with men that wasn't their husbands..."

Virgie nudged me and whispered, "Daddy goes to the show Saturday night so he'll have something to preach about Sunday morning."

"Why does he let you go?" I whispered back.

"He says if I see what sin looks like up on the screen, I'll know what it looks like in person and run the other direction," she whispered back; then she grinned.

I wondered how Mr. West would feel if he knew about the shoebox of movie star photos that Virgie opened far more often than she opened her Bible. Or if he knew that Virgie had talked to me in worshipful tones about Tyrone Power and Rita Hayworth, but never about Jesus. At the movies, Virgie had sat in a trance, her eyes fixed on the screen. During her daddy's sermon, though, she was as fidgety as she was at school. Mr. West might think the movies are teaching his daughter how not to be, but here's what I think: The movies are Virgie's religion. She might get more interested in Jesus if Tyrone Power was to play him.

NOVEMBER 24, 1944

The Knoxville *News-Sentinel* today was full of pictures of dirty, tired-eyed U.S. servicemen squatting in trenches and bombed-out buildings eating chunks of Thanksgiving turkey out of tin plates. The caption described each soldier as "enjoying his Thanksgiving dinner." I couldn't help wondering, if I was eating my dinner crouched alone in rubble and in danger of being shot at, would I really be enjoying it? And would I feel thankful? I guess our boys should be thankful they have the freedom they're trying to get for people in other countries, but I don't know if I'd be able to feel too grateful if I was thousands of miles from my family on a big holiday. I must be too selfish to be a soldier.

Or maybe, like so many people in this country, I'm just ready for this war to be won and over with. FDR has called for the time between now and Christmas to be a national period of thanksgiving and prayer in hopes of victory overseas. I guess the Republicans are thankful they got to celebrate Thanksgiving at the regular time instead of the earlier date FDR had set for it the past few years. Franksgiving, the Republicans called it.

My family's taking the prayer and thanksgiving seriously. Daddy said a blessing at dinner, though it wasn't as long as Mr. West's (The biscuits were still warm when he finished). And after dinner, Mama brought out the family Bible and read the verse about turning swords into plowshares. She says she's going to read us a Bible verse a day until the war's over.

I have to say looking at the pictures of those soldiers made me thankful. Sure, I was thankful not to be them—not to be scared and dirty and in danger—but I was also thankful to them for giving up their safety and comfort to help people they didn't even know. I'm thankful for the soldiers, and I'm thankful to FDR, too, and in the spirit of thankfulness, I'm going to close this entry with a list of some other people and things I'm thankful for.

My family: I'm the odd duck in the group, but I know they love me even if they don't always understand me.

Iris: not just for giving me a job, but for being my friend and treating me like I have a brain even though she's older and smarter and more educated and sophisticated than me.

Baby Sharon: for all those gummy grins she flashes at me. Her smiles are special because she doesn't dole them out to just anybody.

Miss Connor: for choosing me for the essay contest and looking me in the eye and saying "*when* you go to college."

Virgie: even though she can't shut up for two seconds.

The Oak Ridge Public Library: because it's the best thing that ever happened to me.

This town: Because sometimes everything's so new and wonderful I feel like Dorothy in the Land of Oz, but I'm not like Dorothy because I got to bring my family here and so except to visit Granny and Papaw, I don't want to go back home at all.

NOVEMBER 27, 1944

Iris offered me some work this weekend—not because she and Warren were going out but because they were staying home and entertaining. "I need that extra pair of hands," she said as we sat in her living room, "to help with the house and the dinner and Baby Sharon and"—she shook her head, all in a tizzy—"You wouldn't happen to have an extra-extra pair of hands hidden somewhere, would you?"

"How many people you got coming?" I asked.

"Eva and her husband and Hannah and her husband."

"Just four besides you and Warren. Shoot, that's nothing. My mama cooks for that many people every night of her life."

"Yes, but your mother can probably cook, unlike some people."

"You'll do fine. Just cook up a big pot of something that stretches a long way—soup beans or squirrel and dumplings or something."

Iris laughed. "I'd just about do it to see the look on Eva Lynch's prim little face when she hears that squirrel and dumplings are on the menu."

Saturday afternoon I went over to Iris's and saw that all the ashtrays had been emptied, all the books had been shelved, and all the newspapers and magazines had been put away. Baby Sharon was crawling around on the clean, swept floor, and a spicy smell was coming from the kitchen which was surprisingly good to be Iris's cooking.

Iris came out of the kitchen wearing her frilly pink apron over her skirt and sweater. The apron was splashed with orange stains. "Looks like somebody else's house, doesn't it?"

"It looks nice," I said. "I don't know if you need this extra pair of hands after all."

"I do so need them," Iris said, taking my hands and squeezing them. "Do you really think that fussy girl here is going to settle down and go to sleep with all these people in the house? I'll need your hands to tend to her while I tend to the company. Right now, though, I'm going to sit down and smoke a cigarette. I'm a nervous wreck." Iris flopped down on the couch, and I flopped beside her.

"What are you nervous for? Mrs. Lynch and Mrs. McGill come over here all the time with your house looking like it usually does."

"Yes," Iris said, lighting up and taking a puff. "But they don't come with their husbands. Warren works under Eva's husband at the lab, so this is one of those occasions where the wife has to make the home nice to welcome the husband's boss. I don't play these kinds of games very well, I'm afraid."

"You'll do fine," I said. "Anybody in his right mind would be impressed by you."

"Thanks, Ruby. That's the real reason I asked you here, you know. You always make me feel better. I knew I could get through tonight if I could look over and see your face."

Iris was leaned against the back of the couch, and she turned her head and smiled at me. The smoke around her face made a sort of veil, and her blue eyes shone behind it, blurred and dreamy. I felt like there was something I needed to say to her, but I didn't know what it was.

"Oh, I took your cooking advice," she said, sitting up straighter. "Not about the squirrel and dumplings, but about cooking a one-pot meal. I found a recipe for chili in the cookbook Warren's mother gave me for a wedding present. Subtle, eh? But the recipe makes what little meat I could buy go a long way, and it was so imprecise it seemed nearly impossible to ruin."

"It smells good," I said. But then Iris hit herself in the forehead. "What's the matter?"

"Crackers! I forgot crackers. We hardly have any, and the ones we have are so stale only Sharon will eat them. You can't have chili without crackers."

"Sure you can. Chili's just a fancy pot of beans, ain't it? You can make cornbread instead."

Iris raised an eyebrow. "*I* can make cornbread?"

"Okay, I can make cornbread. And I'll teach you how to make it while I do it." I stood up, reached out my hand to help Iris from the couch, then stooped down to pick up Baby Sharon to take her to the kitchen with us.

"See, I told you I needed that extra pair of hands," Iris said.

* * *

The cornbread was a big hit. I had my doubts at first because everybody was dressed so fancy they didn't look like the cornbread-eating type at all. Mrs. Lynch and Mrs. McGill both had on black dresses with pearl necklaces. Dr. Lynch—that's what Iris called him—was a salt-and-pepper-haired gentleman in a fancy suit and tie who put me in mind of Clifton Webb a little bit. It wasn't that he looked so much like Clifton Webb; I guess it was more that he had a prissy manner and a mustache. Mr. McGill was younger and stouter and had black slicked-over hair like men in magazine advertisements. When Iris called him Dr. McGill at first, he was quick to say, "Nope, just Mr. McGill. All I've got is a lowly B.S. degree—and we know what 'B.S.' stands for!"

"That's all I've got, too," Iris said, laughing politely.

"Same here," Mrs. McGill said.

"So I guess I've got a degree that qualifies me to sit around and talk to the wives," Mr. McGill said. "Seriously, though, everybody call me Tom."

Dr. Lynch didn't tell anybody to call him by his first name.

"Who'd like a cold beer?" Warren said. His almost too-cheerful tone made it obvious that he was as nervous as Iris.

I figured if these folks were going to get liquored up, I should probably get the baby out of the room. I said, "Say good night, Baby Sharon," and let all the ladies cootchie-coo at her before I took her to her room.

From then on I stayed in Sharon's room, but I managed to eavesdrop on a lot of the conversation. The women chattered about their children, and the men talked about sports. Everybody talked about the new Oak Ridge Symphony and how wonderful it was to bring some culture to this isolated part of the country. This led them to talk about the cities they came from and what they missed about them: the theatres, the ballet, the restaurants.

Once everybody settled down to eat, I heard Mrs. Lynch say, "Well, Iris, you're always saying you can't cook, but this chili is delicious."

"And the bread is wonderful," Mrs. McGill said. "It's crispy on the outside, but inside it has the texture of cake. I've never had anything like it."

"I can't take credit for the cornbread, I'm afraid," Iris said. "Ruby made it."

"Oh, your little babysitter?" Mrs. Lynch said. "Well, that makes sense. Cornbread is native to the people of the Appalachians."

The way she said "the people of the Appalachians" made us sound like some tribe you'd see in a Tarzan movie.

It got harder to follow the conversation after they finished eating. The women stayed in the dining room, and the men moved to the living room, so I only caught dibs and dabs of the overlapping conversations without being able to tell which person was saying what. From the dining room: "Yes, not too bad, just a little queasy in the morning...ginger ale and soda crackers are my salvation." From the living room: "Now that we're away from the ladies, how about another round of beers, Warren…more of a football man myself…about what you'd expect from the Japs…"

I tried to listen to the men more than the women in hopes that one of them might say something about the work they did all day. But nobody did. The only secret I found out from eavesdropping was that Mrs. McGill is expecting a baby.

After a while, the women and the men begged Warren to play something on the violin. I figured he was happy to oblige since small talk wasn't exactly a specialty of his. Baby Sharon had been sitting up in her crib wide-eyed, eavesdropping like me, I reckon, but as soon as she heard her daddy's violin, her eyelids got all droopy. She lay down on her belly, stuck her diaper-padded behind up in the air, and went right to sleep.

Before Warren had even finished his song, Iris pushed the door open. She was carrying a tray with a bowl of chili, a hunk of cornbread, and a glass of milk. "Oh, good. She's out," she said, glancing at Sharon. "You can eat in peace." Iris looked around. "I guess I'll just set your tray on the floor. Putting it on the changing table doesn't seem very appetizing."

"Thanks."

"Well, I can't let you starve, can I? Listen, I think the evening's starting to wind down"—she mouthed but didn't say the words "thank God"—"I'll drive you home after everybody leaves." She gave me a little wink, like we were both in on the same joke, and left, softly shutting the door behind her.

Once all the goodnights were said, Iris opened the door of the nursery. "I'll take you home now if you're ready. Warren doesn't like to drive at night."

After we were in her car, Iris said, "Well, the best thing I can say about that is that it's over."

"It seemed to go fine."

"You think so?" Iris pulled out of the driveway and into the road.

"Yeah, I do." I watched the way the headlights brightened the dark street. I had never ridden in a car at night before, and something about barreling down the road in the darkness was kind of thrilling.

"I think it did, too," Iris said. "I'm just exhausted from the smiling and the chit chat and all the things I had to do to make the right impression—clean all the ashtrays, hide my copy of *Forever Amber*..."

"You're reading that book?"

Iris looked away from the road long enough to grin at me. "I am indeed. And I'm entertained, though I can't say it's up to my exacting literary standards."

Forever Amber is far and away the most scandalous book in anybody's remembrance. Preachers denounced it from pulpits all the time, so I wondered if Virgie's daddy had read it to know what sin looked like on the page. "Is the book as"—I struggled for a way to ask my embarrassing question—"dirty as people say it is?"

"You bet it is," Iris said, laughing. "Dirty enough to turn Eva Lynch's hair snow white."

I laughed at the image.

"Maybe sometime when you're babysitting, you might find my copy of *Forever Amber* lying around. I won't send it home with you, though. Your mother would be scandalized."

"My mother would have my hide," I said. "Mostly she don't pay attention to what I read, but everybody knows about that book." We had left Snob Hill and were coming to the muddy, low-lying land where us common folks live. "Oh, turn here," I said.

When we came up on the camp—all those ugly little boxes planted close together in the mud—I suddenly wished I'd walked home.

"Is this your neighborhood?" she asked. If she thought it was ugly or pitiful, she had the good manners not to say so, and for that I was grateful.

"Yes," I said.

She stopped the car and turned around in the seat to look at me. "Ruby, it really helped to have you at the house tonight and not just because you're an extra pair of hands. I'm never any good at these kinds of gatherings where I have to wonder how I seem all the time. I don't want to think about how I seem. I just want to be what I am, you know?"

I nodded.

"That's what I like about spending time with you, Ruby. You accept me the way I am."

I didn't even think before I said, "I like the way you are."

Iris smiled. "I like the way you are, too."

She leaned over and gave me a quick, light kiss on the cheek. Nobody besides family members had ever done that to me before, and it made me feel all funny and fluttery. I blurted out goodnight, then ran inside, grabbed my diary, and tried to use my pencil to catch all the words that started tumbling out of me.

DECEMBER 4, 1944

It feels like I haven't written in here in a month of Sundays. But really, you can't blame me. It's the end of the semester, and I had to write a ten-page paper for English literature (I wrote about Samuel Pepys, naturally), plus I had to study for tests in biology and history and algebra. I never had to work so hard in school in Kentucky, but then I never learned this much there either.

Today was our last day of school before Christmas vacation, and nobody felt much like working. We had drawn names in homeroom, so we gave our presents to the people whose names we got. It seemed like just about everybody got a box of stationery or chocolate-covered cherries. I ended up with cherries, which was the same thing I'd bought for the person whose name I'd drawn. I was happy, though, because I had really struggled with not letting my sisters eat the cherries I'd bought and not eating them myself. But this box was mine free and clear. There are twelve cherries in the box, so each person in my family can have two.

In English lit we wrote Christmas cards to soldiers and ate sugar cookies Miss Connor brought from home. "It's hard to believe," Miss Connor said, "that when I see you in class next time, it will be a whole new year."

"I wish it was a whole year before we had to go back to school," Virgie whispered to me.

"Not me," I said. "I'd miss it."

"Yeah, but you're weird," Virgie whispered back.

On the way out of the classroom, I set a candy cane on Miss Connor's desk. "Merry Christmas, Miss Connor," I said.

She smiled her little gap-toothed smile. "Merry Christmas to you, too, Ruby. And remember to spend plenty of time during your vacation working on your 'What America Means to Me' essay. It needs to be ready as soon as you come back to school so I can submit it to the contest."

"Yes, ma'am," I said. But I thought, boy, it's a good thing Samuel Pepys wasn't in school because if he had been, he never would've had time to write in his diary!

DECEMBER 16, 1944

Iris is beside herself, and I'm pretty upset, too. Glenn Miller's plane went down yesterday—well, I say it went down, but nobody knows for sure what happened to it. Iris said it's hard to imagine living in a world without any more of Glenn Miller's music. I tried to cheer her up. "He might be all right," I said. "The reports ain't saying he's dead. They're saying he's disappeared."

But he's dead. People don't just disappear, here one second and gone the next. Glenn Miller is—or was—a musician, not a magician. And as much as I'd like to think he landed safely on a sunny island and is drinking coconut juice on the beach with Amelia Earhart, what I really believe is that he, like so many less famous men, ended up sacrificing his life for his country in this long, hard war.

The reason I sat down to write today was to see if I could come up with an idea for the essay contest. At first I told myself I wouldn't write in my diary at all for a while—that I'd turn all my thoughts to my essay instead.

Well, that idea was a miserable failure. I haven't written a word of the dadblamed thing.

So now I'm thinking if I'm writing in my diary, at least I'm writing something. And something's better than nothing, right? Also, maybe while I write in my journal, I can jot down some ideas for my essay:

What America Means to Me

Shoot, what does America mean to me? And why should it matter to anybody what America means to some ignorant, sixteen-year-old hillbilly girl?

But maybe that's one of the important things about America—that somebody would even ask a nobody like me what America means to her. In America, it matters what you think. You can bet that Hitler's not asking his people what Germany means to them. He's telling them what it means to him, and if it doesn't mean the same thing to them, they get shipped off to prison.

Here at least a person has the right to complain and to vote and to complain some more if the fellow they voted for doesn't win. Our country doesn't have to be made up of one big "we" where everybody thinks and acts the same way. But we can come together as a "we" when we need to, like with the war effort. I keep thinking of that picture of Rosie the Riveter showing her arm muscle and saying, "We Can Do It!" The American people have come together as a "we" to be strong and make sacrifices. The soldiers have made the biggest sacrifices, but everybody on the homefront has pitched in, too, with smaller sacrifices that make a big difference. All the Rosies picking up the slack in the factories, all the women who have set aside their vanity and gone without new outfits or stockings, all the people who have done without the foods they like because of rationing or planted Victory Gardens or collected scrap metal or bought war bonds.

Oak Ridge may be one of the greatest examples of people coming together to make sacrifices for freedom. Here we have people of all kinds, from physicists to factory workers, from chemists to construction workers, from generals to janitors— all far from home, many away from loved ones and living in less than comfortable conditions—all working together, each contributing in his own individual way to the war effort. It's that spirit of daring and cooperation and hard work and sacrifice that built America in the first place, and it's the same spirit that will win us the war.

* * *

I just read back over what I wrote, and I guess I must be much better at writing than I am at thinking. When I told myself I wasn't going to write for a while because I needed to think up ideas for my essay, I didn't think up a dang thing. But when I sat down with my pencil a few minutes ago, it just started racing across the paper. I didn't feel like I was thinking while I did it. But when I read back through it, there were my thoughts, right there in front of me. So now that I've seen what I think, maybe I'll try to write the real essay.

DECEMBER 27, 1944

On Christmas Eve morning, everybody woke up happy. Mama had already packed us each a change of clothes in the big cardboard suitcase she'd bought for the trip. Daddy had bought a roll of bologna, a loaf of white bread, and six bottles of orange pop for our lunch on the bus. Baby Pearl was dancing around the room while we were trying to get ready to go and singing, "Home! Home! Home! We're going home!"

"Well, we've got to go home for Christmas," Daddy said, "so Santy Claus'll know where to find you. If we stayed here, he wouldn't know how to pick out your little house from all the others that look just like it."

"That's right," Mama said, laughing. "Now sit down with your sisters, Baby Pearl, and eat your breakfast. It's gonna be a long ride today."

"And I ain't gonna be willing to break out the baloney sandwiches till it's at least noon," Daddy added.

Mama was right about the bus ride being long. It wasn't bad, though, because the bus was full of happy people—construction workers, factory workers, janitors, and their families, all of them mountain people, all of them going home for Christmas. After a while we got to singing Christmas carols, which made the time pass faster, at least for those of us doing the singing. The bus driver never joined in, and I wondered if he wished we'd hush.

The driver needed to concentrate, I reckon, because at every little town—Lake City, Caryville, Lafollette, he had to stop and let people off. Sometimes he'd stop where there wasn't even a town. He'd just let somebody off, and they'd start wandering down a holler.

When some of the kids started saying they had to go to the bathroom, the driver pulled off at a wooded place by the side of the road. The women and children took off to one edge of the woods, and then men went to the other. It was a pain to get my coat and skirt pulled up and my drawers pulled down, and I was so cold with my behind out in the open that my pee felt as hot as coffee. "This is just one more area where boys are luckier than girls," I said to Opal, who was squatting beside me.

"Yeah, and they can write their name in the snow," she said, giggling.

Garnet was standing beside us. "I'm not going," she said. "I'll wait till we get home."

"It's just an outhouse we've got at home," Mama said. She was helping Baby Pearl with her clothes so she wouldn't pee on them. "I don't know why you're acting like you're the Queen of Sheba all of a sudden."

"At least in an outhouse, there's a place to sit," Garnet said. "You don't have to squat down in the dirt like a dog."

On our next bathroom break, two hours later, Garnet wasn't so proud. She dropped her drawers and squatted with the rest of us.

After the bus dropped a few passengers off in Jellico, we crossed the Kentucky state line, and everybody left on the bus cheered. "Ain't you glad we got rid of all them Tennessee hillbillies?" Daddy said. "Now we're all aboard the Briar Hopper Express!"

The bus dropped us in downtown Morgan, and Papaw was waiting for us, standing propped up against his farm truck, working on a big chaw of tobacco. His weathered face looked freshly shaved, and his silver hair was slicked back with Brylcreem. He had probably decided that since he was coming to town, he might as well pay a visit to the barber shop. As always, he wasn't wearing an overcoat. Papaw dressed the same whether it was December or August: in layers consisting of a pair of overalls, a plaid flannel shirt, and long johns. He said the combination of clothing was perfect for keeping out the hot air and the cold air both. "There's my girls!" he hollered, stretching out his arms. "Come give your papaw some sugar!"

We all ran to Papaw, but Garnet got there first. She's always been Papaw's girl. I hung back and let my sisters get their kisses first, then Papaw looked at me. "Well, look what a fine young heifer you've turned into!" he said, around his chaw of tobacco.

"Why, Papaw, if I didn't know you thought cows was pretty, I'd be insulted," I said.

Papaw laughed. "You've still got a mouth on you, I see. You ain't got too big to hug your papaw's neck, have you?"

"Of course not," I said. I wrapped my arms around Papaw and breathed in his special old-man scent: tobacco, coffee, and dried apples.

Mama and Daddy got in the cab of the truck with Papaw, and we girls climbed in the back, which was full of straw. It was cold, but Granny had sent us a quilt to cover up with.

When we walked into Granny and Papaw's little house, I breathed in two other happy smells: the cedar Christmas tree and Granny's chicken and dumplings simmering on the stove. At the moment, though, I was more excited about the chicken and dumplings than the tree. It was past our usual suppertime, and the baloney sandwich I ate on the bus had worn off hours before.

Granny came bustling out of the kitchen, flour all over her apron and dress. "Well, look at you'uns," she said.

Baby Pearl ran for her and wrapped her little arms around Granny's thick middle.

"There's my baby," Granny said. "You know what me and your papaw did today? I kilt a rooster to make you some chicken and dumplings, and your papaw chopped you down a Christmas tree."

After Granny hugged us and fussed over us, we sat down and ate her good chicken and dumplings till I was sure I couldn't eat another bite. But then she brought out an apple stack cake, which is my favorite thing in the world, so I had to eat a big piece of it, too.

After we ate, Papaw and Daddy said they were going to look at the barn, which probably meant they were going to take a nip or two of moonshine. Garnet and Opal and Baby Pearl got busy stringing popcorn and making paper chains to hang on the Christmas tree, and I helped Mama and Granny with the dishes.

"So," Granny said, handing me a plate to dry, "I reckon every young feller in Tennessee is after you now, Ruby."

"Not hardly," I said, laughing.

"Well, as nice as you're filling out, they soon will be," Granny said. "You know, I was your age when I married your papaw." She handed me another dish. "It's your job to give me a great-grandson before I die."

"I'll see what I can do," I said, but I only said it because I love Granny and didn't want to disappoint her by saying that I don't want to be a mother till after I've gotten an education, and I don't want to be a wife ever.

After the tree was decorated and Granny had made us sticky-sweet popcorn balls out of the popcorn that didn't get strung, it was time for Mama, Daddy, my sisters and me to go back to our little house so Granny and Papaw could rest. It was strange to be in our two rooms again, and even though Granny had dusted and swept there regularly, there was still something stale about the air. Everything looked so bare and untouched, it was almost like being in the house of someone who'd died. But when we girls settled down on our pallets on the floor and Mama and Daddy snuggled down in their bed, Mama said, "Lord, it's good to be home," and Baby Pearl said, "Amen."

It seemed like everybody but me was asleep within seconds. But I lay there a long time, listening to the quiet.

Christmas morning at Granny and Papaw's, my sisters and I found each of our stockings stuffed with peanuts and an orange and a candy cane. There were unwrapped Santa Claus presents under the tree of the younger girls: a baby doll for Baby Pearl and a cute stuffed puppy dog for Garnet which I knew she'd want to keep on her bed. There were wrapped presents for Opal and me: pretty fake fur winter hats with matching muffs. And Granny had knitted a cream-colored sweater for each of us girls and one for Mama, too. We ate biscuits and gravy and sausage, and eggs fresh from the henhouse. After breakfast, Daddy and Papaw went off to shoot their shotguns—a Christmas tradition that's never made much sense to me. And Mama and my sisters settled around the fireplace, listening to Granny talk about what people they knew who had had babies or gotten sick or lost a family member in the war.

I put on my coat and new hat and muff and went for a walk. Even though we'd been there for such a short time, I was still gripped by my old restlessness. There was nothing to read, nowhere to go. But everybody else seemed so happy. I wondered, not for the first time, what was wrong with me.

About five o'clock, after a late dinner of ham and sweet potatoes, Daddy said, "Well, Papaw, I reckon you'd better drive us on into town soon. The bus is picking us up at six o'clock."

"Mercy," Granny said, "it seems like you'uns just got here."

Baby Pearl let out a high-pitched wail the likes of which we hadn't heard since she was a toddler. "No!" she screamed. "No! You said we was going home!"

Mama picked her up and cuddled her. "I said we was going home for a visit, honey. We ain't coming home to stay till the war's over."

Sobs shook Baby Pearl's small body. She cried until she couldn't catch her breath, then she hiccuped and cried some more. Papaw offered her candy and pennies, but nothing would comfort her. She cried in the truck. She cried on the bus until she cried herself to sleep, and as Mama held her, I could see tears in her eyes, too. I knew she felt the same way Baby Pearl did, even if she was too grownup to show it.

I felt so sorry for both of them I almost cried myself. But here's what I'll never tell anybody: I loved seeing Granny and Papaw again, but the whole time I was in Kentucky, I felt like a visitor. Going back to Oak Ridge, I felt like I was going home.

JANUARY 1, 1945

People say whatever you do on New Year's Day is what you'll be doing for the rest of the year, so I figured I'd better write some to make sure I stay in the habit. I'm just glad what you eat on New Year's Day isn't what you have to eat for the rest of the year because I'm no fan of black-eyed peas and hog jowls, but Mama says we have to eat them for good luck.

Iris got special permission from my mama for me to sleep over at their house on New Year's Eve. Iris and Warren wanted me to keep Baby Sharon while they went to a party where everybody was going to stay up late and watch the New Year come in. Mama was fine with me staying over, though she said to me, "I don't see no sense in staying up to watch the New Year come in. It don't look no different than the old one."

I went over to Iris and Warren's around seven o'clock, and Iris answered the door wearing her black dress and pearls. "Come on in," she said, clipping an earring onto her earlobe. She had on more makeup than usual—some black liner on her eyelids and extra-bright red lipstick. "You look real pretty," I said, but as soon as I said it, I had to look away from her.

"Oh, pshaw," she said, grabbing my hand and pulling me into the house. "Get in out of the cold."

Baby Sharon was sitting on a blanket on the floor, shaking a rattle like it was a very important job she had been given to do. When she saw me, her face lit up, and she said, "Gah!"

"Gah right back at you," I said and sat down next to her on the floor.

"Oh, let me show you this," Iris said, grabbling some papers off the coffee table. "But you'll probably want to keep it out of the reach of Sharon's spitty little fingers." She held out the papers. The top page was blank except for the typed words in the middle that read:

A Spirit of Sacrifice
by Ruby Pickett

"Thanks for typing it," I said. "I like seeing my name in print like that."

"Well, I'm thinking this may be the first of many times your name appears in print," Iris said. "Your essay is excellent."

Warren came in, tying his tie, and Baby Sharon greeted him with, "Da!"

"Warren read it, too," Iris said. "He was impressed."

"What was I impressed by?" he asked, letting Iris take over fixing his tie.

"Ruby's essay," Iris said.

"Ah, yes, it was very good," Warren said. "I had no idea Sharon had such a literary babysitter."

"Thank you," I said. I could write off Iris's compliment because she was my friend. But Warren's was harder to dismiss because I'd never heard him compliment anybody before, not even Iris. He seemed to lack whatever part of the personality that makes most people say nice but meaningless things just to get along with others.

"Sharon will probably pass out in about an hour," Iris said, shrugging into her coat, "so feel free to read and eat us out of house and home. I left a blanket and pillow on the couch in case you get sleepy before we get back."

Once Iris and Warren left, I noticed Baby Sharon was still dutifully shaking her rattle. I wondered if she'd cry if I took it out of her hand, but instead she looked relieved, like she was thinking, "Thank the Lord I can stop now. That thing was wearing me out."

I put on a record—one of Warren's classical albums with lots of slow, swoony strings—picked up Baby Sharon and danced her around the room. Soon she was asleep with her head on my shoulder, and I put her down in her crib.

I couldn't believe I had the evening all to myself in this nice house full of books and music and even food and drink if I wanted it. I took off my shoes and padded into the kitchen. There were six cold Cokes in the icebox, so I figured there was no harm in taking one. The music was still playing, so I danced through the house, sipping my icy Coke and pretending to be lucky enough to live there.

And then on the coffee table I saw the two items that would make my whole evening: a box of chocolate-covered cherries which Iris had labeled with a tag reading "for Ruby" and right next to the cherries, the big, fat, and supposedly shocking novel *Forever Amber*. I set my Coke on the coffee table, lay down on the couch with the open box of cherries on my belly, and opened the book.

And then time just melted away because I was in old England with Amber St. Clare, who was living in the same time as Samuel Pepys, but my Lord, nobody was ever going to teach this book in a high school literature class! Amber St. Clare is a saucy wench who lets a variety of men have their way with her and lives a life of glamour and intrigue. As I was reading, I knew it wasn't great literature—it wasn't exactly nourishing my mind, but I kept on reading, just like the chocolate-covered cherries weren't exactly nourishing my body, but I couldn't stop eating them. Lying on the comfy couch with a whole box of candy and *Forever Amber* all to myself, I felt deliciously wicked, and I wondered if Virgie's father could see me if he'd say, "This is what sin looks like."

Eventually, though, I must've fallen asleep because the next thing I remember is hearing the door open and feeling that

I'd left the copy of *Forever Amber* lying open on my chest. "My word, she started reading it and passed out from the shock," Iris said, laughing.

"Oh, no, I must've just dozed off," I said, sitting up and straightening my skirt.

"What did you think?" Iris said, nodding toward the book.

"Well, it's not boring, I'll say that for it," I said.

"That's true." Iris stepped out of her high-heeled shoes. "Still, it is a kind of spiced up, watered-down *Moll Flanders.*"

"Defoe for dullards," Warren said. "Though you're not a dullard, Ruby. As a matter of fact, I think that you, like the heroine of that potboiler, will rise above your original station in life. Of course, unlike Amber Saint Clare"—he said the name with a silly, mock-English accent—"you'll get ahead by using your mind, not your…your…"

Iris clamped her hand over Warren's mouth. "We'd better get you to bed," she said, giggling.

Right then it dawned on me why they were so loud and silly and friendly. It was the same reason Daddy and Papaw had been so silly when they came back from the barn on Christmas Eve. I wondered what Iris and Warren had been drinking.

"Good night, Ruby," Iris said, pulling Warren toward the bedroom. "And Happy New Year."

I lay back down on the couch, this time with my head on the pillow and the blanket pulled up to my neck the way I like it. A few minutes later, I heard sounds coming from the bedroom—Iris was giggling again, and then there was a few minutes of quiet followed by squeaking bedsprings and other sounds that took my mind back to the pages of *Forever Amber*. But what was fun to read about a saucy wench doing in Old England was mortifying to hear my friend doing in the next room.

As soon as the morning light shone through the windows, I grabbed my typed essay and my coat and sneaked out the door. I knew what I'd heard the night before was a natural, normal thing that married people like Iris and Warren do—the very act that was responsible for the existence of Baby Sharon. But I still wasn't going to stick around and sit at the breakfast table with them.

JANUARY 4, 1945

Yesterday was our first day back at school, and all morning I was waiting for English literature class so I could see Miss Connor and give her my essay. I knew she'd be proud of me just for writing it, and I was dying to know if she—like Iris and Warren—would think it was good.

But when we filed into the English literature classroom, it wasn't Miss Connor at the front of the room, but a gangly young man with glasses and an Adam's apple which bulged over his bowtie. I took my seat, figuring Miss Connor must be out sick for the day and this Ichabod Crane-looking fellow was substituting.

But then he said, "My name is Mr. Masters, and I will be your English literature teacher this semester."

There was a lot of whispering about where Miss Connor might be, but I didn't say anything. I felt too sick.

Mr. Masters called the roll, and when he got to my name, he said, "Miss Pickett, I was instructed to give this packet to you."

I rose, and he handed me some papers clipped to an empty envelope. The top page was a letter. I sat back down at my desk and read

> Dear Ruby,
> The reason you are looking at some other teacher's face instead of my own is that like so many other young men, my fiancé Robert lost his life in the Battle of the Bulge. Right now I'm too devastated to even contemplate teaching, so I've gone to stay with my parents in Buffalo. I might look for a new teaching position in the fall, but to be honest, it's difficult to imagine my future now that it doesn't include John.
> Even if I can't imagine my own future, I can imagine yours, Ruby, and a bright future it is. I have attached your entry form and a stamped, addressed envelope for your essay, which is no doubt as distinguished as your writing always is. Enter your essay in the contest, stay in school, and keep reading and writing. While I don't know what I believe about many things anymore, I still believe in you.
> Sincerely,
> Maureen Connor

I was up on my feet before I even knew what I was doing, still holding the letter in both hands.

"Miss Pickett?" Mr. Masters said. "Are you all right?"

"I...I need to be excused," I managed to say, then I ran out of the room, down the hall, and into the girls' bathroom. I kneeled in front of one of the toilets and threw up so hard it felt like my body was ripping itself apart. Then the tears came, along with big, racking sobs because of Miss Connor's loss, because of my loss, because no matter who wins a war, it's really all about loss.

I don't know how long I'd been sitting in the bathroom floor sobbing when Virgie finally found me.

"There you are!" she said. "Mr. Masters sent me to check on you." She sat down on the bathroom floor beside me. "Are you sick? You kindly smell like vomick."

I handed her Miss Connor's letter and watched her lips move as she read.

When she finished, she said, "That's sad. I reckon now she'll be an old maid schoolteacher sure enough."

Her tone wasn't sad, just matter of fact, which infuriated me. I snatched the letter out of her hand. "I can't believe you can't muster up even one tear for Miss Connor. You cry buckets at the least little sad thing that happens in some silly picture show."

Virgie shrugged. "I said it was sad, didn't I? But Miss Connor's just a teacher. It's not like she was a friend or a member of my family or anything."

"Well, she was my friend," I said, and then another wave of sobs rushed over me.

Virgie put her arm around me. "Shh," she said. "Shh, it's all right. I know she was your friend. Listen, if we go see the school nurse and tell her you throwed up, she'll let you go home for the rest of the day. Why don't we do that?"

I let Virgie help me off the floor and lead me to the nurse, who wrote me an excuse and told Virgie to help me gather my things.

Virgie walked me to the front door. "Shoot," she said, "I wish I could go home. Maybe I orta throw up, too." She made a motion like she was going to stick her finger down her throat.

"Listen," I said, "I'm sorry I yelled at you. I'm upset about Miss Connor, is all."

Virgie grinned. "You've heard my Daddy get all fired up preaching. You think a little yelling bothers me?"

And so I walked out of the school, into the slate-gray January cold. I could've taken a bus, but for some reason, I wanted to walk. The weather matched my mood, I guess, and I kept having the picture of the tears that were flowing from my eyes freezing to my skin, so that by the time I got home, my face would be covered with icicles.

I had meant to go straight home, but when I passed the post office, I stopped and took Miss Connor's stamped envelope, the entry form, and my essay out of my school satchel. I folded up the pages, stuck them in the envelope, and dropped it in the mailbox.

I didn't care one way or another about the essay contest anymore. But I knew Miss Connor wanted me to enter it. And I knew I couldn't help Miss Connor or comfort her—knew, really, that I'd never see her and her sweet, gap-toothed grin again. The one small thing I could do for her was drop that envelope in the mailbox.

JANUARY 10, 1945

When Iris came back from the grocery store, she found me holding Baby Sharon and singing "In the Pines," tears streaming down my face.

Iris knocked a pile of magazines off the coffee table so she could set her bag on it. She scooted up next to me on the couch. "Why the tears, my lady?"

"Just sad."

"Mm," Iris said and reached out her hand. I thought she was going to reach for Baby Sharon, but instead she started stroking my hair. It felt nice, but something about the gentleness of it made me cry harder.

We didn't say anything for a while. Baby Sharon had fallen asleep, and I felt the sweet weight of her little head on my shoulder. After a while, I said, "Iris?"

"Hm?"

"Have you lost anybody in the war? Anybody close to you, I mean?"

"No one too close." She was still stroking my hair. "Jimmy was the closest, I guess. He'd been my brother Bob's best friend from the time they were little kids. When Jimmy was twelve and I was seventeen, he had the worst crush on me. His face would turn bright red when I talked to him, and he was always looking for some excuse to touch me—just to brush against my sleeve or something. The crush passed, of course, and Jimmy grew up and married a girl his age. But it's strange...when Bob told me Jimmy had been killed, it wasn't Jimmy as a man I saw in my head. It was that little twelve-year-old kid, blushing behind his freckles."

"Miss Connor's fiancé got killed," I said. "She left town and moved back home."

"I'm glad I married a scientist and not a soldier," Iris said.

"Do you think it's fair...asking somebody to die like that?"

"No," Iris said, "it's not fair. But maybe it's inevitable. Is there any way to get the tyrants of the world out of power except by meeting their violence with equal force?"

"I don't know." I wondered if I was a bad person for even thinking of these things. "Do you think it's unpatriotic of me to ask questions like this?"

"In America," Iris said, "it's never unpatriotic to ask questions."

"Knock, knock!" a ringing female voice called from outside. The door, which Iris never locked, swung open. It was Eva Lynch, wearing a leopard-print fur hat that matched the collar of her overcoat. Little Helen was hiding behind her and peeked out, then disappeared again. "Iris, I thought I'd pop by with some hand-me-downs Helen's outgrown. Sharon's probably not big enough for them yet, but she'll grow into them in no time." She looked from Iris's face to mine. "My, don't you two look serious! I hope I'm not interrupting some important conversation," she said with a tone implying that nothing a lowly babysitter said could ever be important.

"Of course not," Iris said, making her voice sound bright. "We're just fighting off a case of the winter doldrums. I know what will perk us up. A nice cup of coffee. Eva, why don't you sit down, and I'll start a pot while I get these groceries put away."

"I'll help you," Eva said. She peeled little Helen off her leg and said, "Why don't you play with the nice girl while Mother helps Mrs. Stevens in the kitchen?"

Once Eva disappeared, Helen started screaming, which woke up Baby Sharon. Only a few minutes before, Iris and I had been having a soft-spoken but meaningful conversation, and now my ears were full of screams that, unfortunately, weren't quite loud enough to drown out the sounds of Mrs. Lynch's meaningless chatter in the kitchen.

JANUARY 14, 1945

"How come you ain't ever asked me to spend the night at your house?" Virgie asked me in biology class one Friday.

We were paired up as lab partners, and we were supposed to be looking at stuff under the microscope, but I couldn't get the hang of it. Every time I looked into the danged thing, all I could see was my own eyelashes. "I just figured you'd rather have me over at your place," I said, turning the knob on the microscope, like I could adjust it for a better signal like the dial on a radio. "I mean, you've got a room of your own. I have to sleep with a passel of sisters."

"Maybe I'd like to sleep with a passel of sisters for a change."

I wasn't sure why she'd want to crowd in with my sisters and me, but I said, "You can come over tomorrow night if it's all right by my folks and yourn."

"Can I?" Virgie said loud enough that the biology teacher shot her a mean look. She got busy with the microscope for a minute, then whispered, "Shoot, I can't. Tomorrow's Saturday. I've got to be home early Sunday morning for church. Say—

what if I come home with you after school today? If your mama says I can't stay, I'll go."

"Don't you need to tell your mama?"

"We'll stop at my place on the way to yourn. I'll need to get my toothbrush and pajamas anyway."

Sometimes being friends with Virgie was like being pulled onto a fast-moving train. You had to forget you're out of control and don't know where you're going and just enjoy the ride.

On the bus we sat down with Aaron, who only looked up at us by way of greeting. "How you doing, Aaron?" I said.

"Awright," he mumbled, looking down at the lap of his overalls.

I could never decide if it was a kindness to speak to him despite his intense shyness, or if it would've been more of a kindness not to speak to him at all.

When the bus stopped, Virgie told the driver, "Wait here. I'll be right back."

"You better be," he said. "I run on Uncle Sam's time, not yours."

In less than three minutes, she was back on the bus, out of breath and carrying a paper sack. "Mama says I can go," she panted.

Once we got to my house, I asked Mama, who was hanging up the wash, if Virgie could stay all night.

"I don't see why not," Mama said, smiling. "What difference would one more girl make?"

I think Mama was pleased. Opal and Garnet brought over girlfriends all the time, but this was the first time I had.

Even though Virgie and I are too old to jump rope, we spent an hour before supper turning the rope so Opal, Garnet, and Baby Pearl could jump all they wanted. The ground was frozen enough to jump on now. In the fall, it had been so muddy that when Opal tried jumping in it, she got mired up past her ankles.

When we came in out of the cold, Mama had made hot chocolate to go with our supper. Hot chocolate and soup beans is a strange combination, but everything's better with chocolate, in my opinion. Baby Pearl must think so, too, because she crumbled up her cornbread into her hot chocolate instead of her soup beans.

"How's that cornbread taste with that hot chocolate there, little bit?" Daddy said.

"It's dee-licious," Baby Pearl said, and everybody laughed.

Once we finished eating, Daddy said, "Well, ladies, I'm even more outnumbered than usual, and I know a hen party when I see one. I reckon I'll go on out to the rec center and see if I can't get up a card game."

After Daddy put on his coat and tipped his hat to us on the way out the door, Virgie put some hillbilly music on the radio, and we danced around the kitchen, helping Mama clear the table and wash and put away the dishes. I kept grabbing Mama's hand and trying to get her to dance with me, but she play-slapped me away, saying, "You know I don't dance. I was raised a Baptist."

"Shoot, we dance in my church," Virgie said. "Except we don't call it dancing. We call it getting happy."

When the last dish was put away, Mama said, "Any of you girls want pin curls in your hair?"

Everybody but me shouted, "I do! I do!" I've never found having my hair messed with something to get excited about. But even Baby Pearl wanted pin curls, and her hair's as curly as Shirley Temple's in her heyday. Mama fixed our hair, and we listened to some funny programs on the radio, and Baby Pearl dozed off with her head in Mama's lap and had to be carried off to bed.

When Mama came back from tucking in Baby Pearl, she said, "Who wants to help me make some fudge?"

"But what about having sugar for your coffee?" I asked. Since sugar's rationed, Mama won't usually throw a bunch of it away making something as sweet as fudge.

"I'll do without it," Mama said. "I'd rather have fudge right now than sugar in my coffee later."

We all clambered into the kitchen, giggling and getting in Mama's way and probably not being much help at all. Virgie took an apple from the bowl on the table. "You know," she said, "if you twist the stem of an apple while you say your ABCs, the stem'll pop off when you get to the first letter of the name of the man you're gonna marry."

"Really?" Garnet said.

"Sure," said Virgie. "It's scientific."

"Try it," Opal said.

Virgie twisted the stem and said her letters. The stem popped off at R. "Dang it," she said. "It was supposed to hang on till I got to T so I can marry Tyrone Power."

"One time when I was around your age," Mama said, grinning. "This girl I knew told me if I spread out some cornmeal on the back porch and set a snail on the edge of it, then by morning the snail would write the first letter of the name of the man I was gonna marry."

"What happened?" Virgie said.

"Well, her and me decided we'd both try it. I found me a snail and laid out the cornmeal, and the next morning when I got up, there was a long, straight line going right through the middle of the cornmeal. So I said, it's an I! I'm gonna marry a man whose name starts with I! When I saw my friend who'd done it, too, she told me she was gonna marry somebody whose name started with an I. And every girl that tried the snail and cornmeal thing, it came out the exact same way. The trouble was there was only one boy in the whole school whose name started with an I—Isaac Dockins. He was real popular there for a couple of weeks."

Mama laughed and stirred the fudge, and I saw something in her I'd never seen before. In this house full of just girls, she didn't seem like the grown woman who was always hanging out wash or cooking supper or mopping mud off the floor. She seemed like a girl, too. And for a minute, I could see what she'd been like before there was a me—before she knew Daddy, even, before she had to spend all day taking care of other people. I liked seeing that part of her. Mama may not understand me as well as she could, but maybe there's a lot about her I don't understand either.

JANUARY 20, 1945

"We shall strive for perfection. We shall not achieve it immediately—but we still shall strive. We may make mistakes—but they must never be mistakes which result from faintness of heart or abandonment of moral principle." That's what FDR said in his inauguration speech on the radio today. For such a short speech, he said a lot. He talked about how his favorite teacher used to say that sometimes life will take a downhill turn but that in the big picture things are always moving upward.

Mama and my sisters and I were sitting around the radio, and I was trying to write down everything important the President said—maybe because I was remembering what my own favorite teacher had said—that FDR being elected for a fourth term was "unprecedented." But then FDR said something that threw my sisters into a state of confusion: "We have learned that we must live as men, not as ostriches, nor as dogs in the manger."

"How can a man be an ostrich?" Garnet asked.

"Ostriches stick their heads in the sand when they're in danger," I said. "He's saying we shouldn't be cowards."

"What about the dogs in the manger?" Garnet asked.

"They put Baby Jesus in a manger," Baby Pearl said.

By the time everybody got finished talking about ostriches and dogs and Baby Jesus, FDR's speech was over, and I hadn't written down another word of it.

But at least I got to hear FDR say that even if things are going downhill, it's only temporary. I've been feeling a little downhill myself lately. I miss Miss Connor something awful. I didn't realize until she was gone how much of my enjoyment of school was because of her and the way she taught English literature. Now, with Mr. Masters, we still read great stuff. Our class is in the middle of *A Tale of Two Cities* (I finished reading it a week ago). But the way he teaches, he just sucks all the juice out of whatever we're discussing until it's like the hollowed-out husk of an orange with the delicious parts all gone and nothing left but the pips.

Also, there's something else that's been bothering me since Christmas, but I would never say it anywhere but here. I really want the war to end. I want both victory and peace, like FDR was saying in his speech. But—and this is a big "but"—there's another part of me—the selfish part, I guess—that worries about what's going to happen to our family after the war is over. If Oak Ridge was just built because of the war, then after the war, the city will have no reason to exist. And the people who came here will have no reason to stay.

So my family will pack up our few belongings, get on the bus, and head back home, with a little more money in our pockets so Daddy can build on to our little house. And everybody will be happy except for me. Because I can't even imagine going back home and living like I did before, now that I know how different life can be. I'm not the same girl I used to be. My eyes have been opened up to the whole, big world, and if I could barely stand the long, dull days of country life before, I know I couldn't stand them at all now. I do want the war to end. It's just that I know that when it does, the sacrifice I'll have to make will be far greater than giving up a little meat and sugar for war rationing.

I've been reading *Forever Amber*—slurping it down like ice cream—every chance I get when I'm sitting for Baby Sharon, but since finishing *A Tale of Two Cities*, I've been out of something respectable to read at home. After the radio broadcast, I wandered down to the library, already feeling sad because when we move back to Kentucky, there won't be a library in walking distance. Is it possible to feel nostalgic for something you haven't even lost yet?

I browsed through the fiction shelves, hungry for something good but not quite sure what that something might be. Mrs. Harris, the librarian, came by with an armload of books. "Are you out of reading material, Ruby?" she asked. She'd stamped my books so many times it would have been impossible for her not to have known my name.

"Yes, ma'am," I said. "Got any recommendations?"

She set down her stack of books on a table. "Well, what kind of story are you in the mood for? Suspenseful? Sad? Funny?"

"Maybe funny. I could use a laugh."

"Got the winter drearies, too, eh? Hmm…" She scanned the shelves and pulled out a book. "You might like this one."

I took it from her and looked at the cover: *Cold Comfort Farm* by Stella Gibbons.

"It's about a young woman not much older than you," Mrs. Harris said. "She's very clever and urbane, and she goes to stay with her relatives in the country who are quite the opposite of urbane. It's a sort of comedy of manners. I laughed a lot when I read it."

"Well, I guess I'd better take it, then. Thank you. There's one more thing I need to do, though, before I check it out."

One way I try to learn is by building my vocabulary, so when somebody says a word I don't know, I always write it down so I can look it up in the dictionary when I'm in the library. Mrs. Harris had just used two terms I wasn't familiar with, and I figured since I was already in the library, I'd proceed straight to the dictionary.

First I looked up *comedy of manners: comedy that satirically portrays the manners and fashions of a particular class or set.* Then I looked up *urbane: notably polite or finished in manner.*

It was strange, though. The page on which the word "urbane" appeared had been worn so thin it was shiny and almost transparent. The letter "U" on the guide tab of the dictionary had been fingered so much the gold of the lettering was faded and dull. It seemed odd that the letter "U" would generate such interest. Compared to other letters, there aren't very many words that start with it.

I took *Cold Comfort Farm* home and spent the rest of the day reading it and laughing. Apparently country people in England aren't that different from country people in Kentucky. Mama said she felt like she was living with a crazy person. Who else would spend a whole evening sitting alone in a corner, laughing to herself about things that nobody else could understand?

JANUARY 25, 1945

When I went over to keep Baby Sharon this afternoon, Iris wasn't even dressed. She had on blue pajamas that looked like they might be an old pair of Warren's with a pink bathrobe over them. Her hair was uncombed, and she was sitting on the couch, smoking a cigarette, while Baby Sharon played on a blanket on the floor.

"Hey," I said, noticing Iris's red nose and puffy eyes, "you feeling under the weather?"

"I'm feeling," she said, her voice tight, "like I'm under a ton of concrete blocks. But I'm not sick or anything. I'm just having a bad day."

"I'm sorry," I said, sitting beside her.

"Oh, no need for you to feel sorry for me, too. I'm doing a more than adequate job of feeling sorry for myself." She half laughed, but there were tears in her eyes. "It's hard sometimes. Being here."

"I reckon so." To me, Oak Ridge feels like a big city full of excitement, but to Iris, it must feel like the rear end of nowhere.

"When Warren and I moved here, it felt like such an adventure. I was sure it would bring us closer together, but"—she stopped to blow her nose—"he can't talk to me about what he does all day. And why would he care about what I've been doing here all day?" She swept out her arm to indicate the house. "Why would anybody care? Hell, except for making sure Sharon's all right, *I* don't even care."

"What you do at home's important, though." I was trying to make her feel better, even though I knew staying home all day would drive me as crazy as it was driving her.

"I know," she said. "But it's repetitive and boring and lonely. And it doesn't exactly make for any lively topics of conversation. Though you couldn't prove that by women like Eva and Hannah. When we get together for coffee, they can talk for ages about stain removal and floor waxing and meatloaf." She looked at me like she was searching for something. "Ruby, sometimes I feel so different from other women I wonder if I'm even a member of the same species."

"I've felt that way as long as I can remember," I said. When I looked at her, it felt like I was looking at myself. Then I felt embarrassed, almost like we were seeing each other naked, so I put on a cheery voice and said, "You know, you don't need to be cooped up in the house for so long on such a cold, gray day. Why don't you go out to the show?"

She ground out her cigarette. "I don't feel like going anywhere by myself."

"Do you want me to go with you?"

Her eyes looked a little more lively all of a sudden. "What about Sharon?"

"We'll take her, too. It'll be a girls' afternoon on the town. And if we go to the four o'clock show, you'll still get home before Warren."

Iris went to dress, and I took Baby Sharon into the kitchen and looked around for something I could fix ahead for Warren's supper. I found a can of tuna, mixed it with some mayonnaise and pickle relish and salt and pepper and set it in the icebox. Warren would probably be expecting a hot meal when he got home, but I figured it wouldn't kill him to eat a tuna fish sandwich just this once.

We bundled up Baby Sharon in her snowsuit, which made her arms and legs stick out as stiff as a gingerbread man's. The theatre was empty except for the three of us. For a while, Baby Sharon entertained herself by pulling herself up to standing on the armrests of the theatre seats. But then she settled on her mama's lap and watched the movie, too, looking up wide-eyed at the giant faces on the screen. Iris turned to look at me as I was watching Baby Sharon and leaned toward me with a little smile. "Thank you for getting me out of the house," she whispered.

JANUARY 30, 1945

Mama's sick. On Sunday after dinner, she took to her bed with a headache, and there's only two reasons I've ever seen Mama get near a bed in the daytime: to strip the bedclothes or to have a baby. Sunday evening she said she still felt pretty poorly and asked me to bake a pone of cornbread and just give everybody bread and milk for supper.

Yesterday morning she got up to fix breakfast, but she was hollow-eyed, and her color wasn't good. By the time I got home from school, she was burning up with fever. I opened a can of Spam and fried it and some eggs for supper, but because I was worried I didn't eat much. Neither did Daddy.

Before he left for work this morning, Daddy said, "Ruby, I want you to stay home and look after your mama. Watch Baby Pearl, too, and make sure she lets your mama get some rest. I'm gonna stop in town and see if I can get a doctor to come take a look at her."

The doctor came in the early afternoon. He was a serious-looking gray-headed fellow and not a bit friendly. He didn't pay a bit of attention to Baby Pearl, not even when she asked him what he was carrying in his black bag. You can tell a lot about a person from how he acts around children and animals.

He took his black bag into Mama's room and stayed in there with her for around ten minutes. When he came out, he looked at me and said, "Are you the oldest girl?"

"Yessir."

"Well, I need you to listen to me carefully. Your mother has influenza. It's been going around the trailer camps and the hutments and all the less hygienic areas."

I didn't like the way he curled his lip and said "less hygienic." Mama keeps our little house so clean you'd never know it was sitting in a giant mud puddle. But I knew my job was to say nothing but "yessir," and even if I didn't like the fellow, if he was going to tell me how to take care of Mama, I was going to listen.

"Except for taking care of her bathroom needs," the doctor said, "your mother should not get out of bed until Saturday at the earliest. She should be given juice and clear fluids and aspirin for her aches and fever. Do you understand?" He said every word slowly and carefully, as if he was talking to a two-year-old.

"Yessir."

"It is also vitally important," he said, "that you keep your mother isolated from your siblings and especially from your father. Influenza is highly contagious, and we certainly don't want an epidemic among our war workers."

He was already headed for the door when I said, "Sir? I have a question."

He looked at me in puzzlement, as if he was amazed that a person like me in a place like this could possess enough intelligence to ask a doctor a question. "Yes?"

"If Mama can't get out of bed till Saturday, that means I'll have to miss the rest of the week at school to take care of her. I don't mind doing it, of course, but I was wondering…could you write me a note I could show to my teachers explaining why I'm missing so much? Maybe that way they'll let me make up my work."

His expression softened. "School is important to you?"

"Yessir. I want to go to college after I finish high school."

"Well, in that case"—he opened up his black bag and took out a notepad and pen—"what's your name, dear?"

"Ruby Pickett, sir."

He scrawled something down on a piece of paper and handed it to me. "Take good care of your mother, Miss Pickett," she said, "and send for me if you need me."

"Thank you." I looked down at the note he had given me. I hoped my teachers could read his handwriting because I sure couldn't.

FEBRUARY 5, 1945

Well here it is Monday, and Mama's not out of bed yet. The doctor came back today and says she has bronchitis on top of everything else. He gave her some medicine and told her to stay in bed for three more days.

Mama's got company in the bed now, though. Opal and Garnet and Baby Pearl all have the flu, too, and they've piled in with her. The doctor said to especially keep an eye on Baby Pearl, since the flu hits the very young and very old the hardest.

Daddy and I are the only healthy ones in the house. He's been sleeping on the living room floor in front of the stove, and I've been lying in bed, half-asleep and half-awake, listening to Mama's cough through the thin bedroom wall. Daddy and I are just waiting to get sick, too.

The past couple of mornings, Daddy's gotten up, poked his head in the door of my room, and said, "I feel fine. How about you?"

"Fine, too," I've said.

Daddy says the two of us must have the strongest constitutions in the family.

I've needed my strong constitution for the past week. All of Mama's work has become my work: cooking meals, washing dishes and clothes, keeping the house clean—all that, plus looking after four sick people who are always needing drinks or medicine or something to blow their noses on.

I'm glad that I'm healthy and can take care of them, but I'll be much gladder when they're healthy and can take care of themselves. In the past week, all the normal things I love about my life have disappeared. I've not been to school. Iris and I have had to do without each other. Even if I didn't have to take care of Mama and my sisters, I wouldn't keep Baby Sharon in case I'm carrying flu germs. And I've had no time to spend with Virgie, to just act silly and be girls together. I've not even had time to go to the library to return *Cold Comfort Farm* and get something else to read.

I've not said one word of complaint, though, because people have to take care of each other and do the best they can. Here on these pages is the only place I've let myself complain a little.

I'll tell you one thing I know for sure now, though. A life of cooking for and cleaning up after other people is not for me. Like Iris said, it's boring and repetitive and lonely. I don't know where my adult life will take me, or else I might just let the dust on the furniture get so thick I can take my finger to it and write, "From dust we are born, and to dust we shall return."

This evening, Daddy and I sat down to some tomato soup that had come from a can. We've been relying on canned soup a lot lately because it's something sick people can eat, and fixing it takes a minimum of cooking effort. Daddy took a slurp of soup, a bite of cracker, and a sip of milk, then said, "Ruby, I'm right proud of the way you've took charge of the house with your mama sick. I've had my doubts at times, but now I'm thinking that when you're a little older, you'll make a good little wife and mama yourself."

"Thanks, Daddy." I wasn't about to tell him I still had no plans to become anybody's wife. No use starting an argument with somebody who's just paid you a compliment.

FEBRUARY 14, 1945

Thank the Lord and the doctor, everybody's healthy again. I didn't get back to school till Friday, and since then I've been buried in books and papers, trying to catch up on my work, which is why my journal hasn't been getting much attention.

But today something happened that I just have to write down because it's the kind of thing that never happens to me. Or, I guess, it's the kind of thing that's never happened to me before, but now it's happened to me once. See? I can't even write about it without getting all flustered.

Here's what happened.

We were changing classes, and I went to my locker like I always do. When I opened it up, though, this red, heart-shaped piece of paper fell out onto the floor. I picked it up fast, slipped it into my history book, and scurried off to the girls' bathroom so I could look at it in private.

Behind the closed bathroom door, I opened up my history book and took out the paper heart. White lace had been glued neatly along its edges, and in the middle, in letters that looked like they'd been cut out of a newspaper or magazine, it said,

Happy Valentine's Day
To Ruby
A real jewel
From your secret admirer

My first thought was that if my name hadn't been on it, I would've thought somebody had put it in the wrong locker by mistake. My second thought was what if this was some kind of cruel joke meant to hurt my feelings? Maybe some of the rich girls who ignored me had made me a fake Valentine so they could watch my reaction and laugh at me. But then again, why would girls who didn't seem to know I existed go out of their way to be so mean to me?

My mind kept turning through reason after reason. It wasn't till the final bell rang that I let myself consider the most obvious reason—that somewhere in the halls of Oak Ridge High School, there might be a boy who actually liked me. This thought made walking through the crowded hallways nearly impossible because I had to look at the face of each boy I passed and think, is it him? Could it be that short, pimply-faced freshman whose family just moved to town? It surely couldn't be that movie-star handsome Kleen Teen whose dad was a high-ranking general. Or could it be Cal, the black-haired boy who always said hey to me and whose daddy worked on the same construction crew as mine did?

The strange thing is, I do want to know who my secret admirer is, and at the same time, I don't. Because if he did reveal himself to me, it would mean I would have to do something— reject him or go out on a date with him, and both of those options scare me so bad I want to throw up. I never thought I'd be in a situation like this because I never thought I was the kind of girl a boy would like. A flat-chested, freckle-faced country girl with mouse-brown hair and her nose stuck in a book all the time. Whose type is that?

Here's something else about me, too. If Opal or Garnet or Virgie had gotten a card like mine, they'd tell every other female in creation about it. They'd be giggling and blushing and jumping up and down at the thought that some boy liked them. And maybe that's the way it should be, too, but it seems silly to get all excited when you don't even know who you're getting excited about. Maybe the boy who likes me stinks or has cooties.

I know that Opal and Garnet and Virgie would never understand why I'm not acting the way they would in the same situation. And so I haven't told them about the card. I haven't told anybody. I folded up my heart and tucked it inside my journal where only I can see it.

FEBRUARY 20, 1945

"Bee!" Baby Sharon squealed as soon as Iris let me into the living room. "Bee!"

"Oh," Iris said, looking at Sharon and then at me. "A mystery has just been solved. These weeks you've been gone, Sharon's been saying 'Bee? Bee?' all the time and looking around all over the place, even under the coffee table and behind the couch. Apparently, you're Bee, and she's been trying to figure out where you've gone."

Sometimes with babies, all you can say is "awww" and then pick them up and cuddle them, which is what I did with Sharon right then. "I'm sorry it took me so long to come back," I said. "Once everybody was finally healthy, I was so behind in my schoolwork…"

"Bee!" Baby Sharon squealed triumphantly and petted my cheek with her chubby hand.

"You should be pleased," Iris said. "You're her second word after 'Mama.'"

"I am pleased," I said, taking Sharon's little hand and kissing it.

"Well, Sharon wasn't the only one who missed you," Iris said.

She looked better than the last time I saw her. She had dressed without being told to, and her hair was clean and combed. But there was still sadness in her eyes. "I missed you, too," I said. "A lot." I took Iris's hand and squeezed it.

"And you can see what a state the house has fallen into," she said, gesturing around her. "I don't know if it's because having you help with Sharon a few hours a week gives me more time to tidy up...or if it's because knowing you're coming over in the afternoon gives me a reason to tidy up."

The living room did look especially lived in. The usually-full ashtrays were now overflowing, spilling ashes and butts over the top of the coffee table. The unswept, unmopped floor was cluttered with magazines and newspapers and Baby Sharon's toys. Half-empty coffee cups sat abandoned on every flat surface in the room. "You know," I said, "this is what I want my house to look like when I grow up. Women like my mama waste too much time trying to keep everything spotless."

"Well, it's fine to be a slob if you're a single girl," Iris said, "but heaven help you if you're married. Apparently in most women's minds there's some kind of correlation between the cleanliness of their homes and their love for their husbands." She suddenly winced. "Damn, I forgot! It's my turn to have 'the girls' over for coffee in the morning. If they see the house looking like this, they'll tar and feather me!"

"I'll help you clean it up."

"Ruby, you're not my maid. I don't pay you to clean."

"But I want to help you."

It was true. As tired as I was of cooking and cleaning for my family, at that moment there was nothing I wanted to do more than help Iris empty her ashtrays and clean her floor. It was strange. But I'm a strange girl, I reckon.

"Okay, you've convinced me, but only because I'm desperate." Iris walked over to the record player. "If we're going to clean, though, we have to have music, and that means we have to play Baby Sharon's favorite song, 'Rum and Coca-Cola.' I suppose some teetotalers would object to my playing my child a song with booze in the title, but it's not like I'm putting rum in her baby bottle. Do you like it?"

"Rum in a baby bottle?"

Iris laughed. "No, the song, silly."

"I ain't heard it."

Iris rolled her eyes. "Ruby, 'Rum and Coca-Cola' is the number-one song in the country. You're a teenager—you're supposed to keep up with these things." She dropped the needle on the record, and the Andrews Sisters' happy harmony filled the room. Even though we were cleaning, it sounded like we were having a party. Baby Sharon laughed and clapped to the music—the three of us must've listened to the song a dozen times, and by the last few times, we were singing along with it: Iris on-key, me off-key, and Sharon in baby babble.

With the Andrews Sisters urging us along, we had emptied the ashtrays and dusted the furniture and swept and mopped the floor within an hour. Maybe because of too much rum and Coca-Cola, Baby Sharon passed out for a nap, and Iris and I collapsed on the couch.

"It's good to have you back," Iris said, "and not just because you helped me clean."

"It's good to be back," I said, "and not just because you pay me for helping you."

All of a sudden, a picture of the red paper heart flashed into my mind. I knew I could talk to Iris. She wouldn't tell anybody, and she wouldn't make anything silly out of it. "Iris...can I talk to you about something?"

"Sure," she said, folding up her legs on the couch like she was settling in to listen.

Even though I wanted to talk about it, I couldn't make any words come out for a couple of minutes. Finally, I took a deep breath and said, "The other day—well, it was Valentine's Day, really..."

"Mm-hm?" Iris prompted when I trailed off.

"Somebody left a card in my locker, and I don't know who it was." I was talking like I was in a race to see who could finish a sentence the fastest.

"What did it say?"

"It said, 'Happy Valentine's Day to Ruby, a real jewel, from your secret admirer.'"

"That's sweet. Do you have any idea who might have sent it?"

"Nope. There ain't a boy at school who'll even give me the time of day."

"And the handwriting on the card isn't familiar?"

"There isn't any handwriting. The letters looked like they'd been cut out of a magazine or something."

"Very sneaky." Iris smiled.

"Yeah. You're the only person I've told about it. Have you ever had a secret admirer?"

Iris looked down, then gave a shy smile. "I've never had one, but I've been one. When I was Warren's student, I used to leave notes and poems in his faculty mailbox. I even scented them with my perfume. I was a bit melodramatic in those days."

"Is that how he found out it was you—because your notes smelled like your perfume?"

Iris lit a cigarette. "No. I guess he'd never been close enough to me to smell me. He figured it out by comparing the handwriting in my notes with the handwriting on my mid-term exam."

"So you weren't as sneaky as my secret admirer."

"I'm afraid not." She let out a puff of smoke. "Of course, I did kind of want to get caught."

"I've been a nervous wreck ever since I got the card," I said. "What do you think I ought to do?"

Iris ashed her cigarette. "You don't really have to do anything. Just enjoy the fact that you have a secret admirer. He'll let you know who he is when he's ready."

I wasn't sure how to ask my next question without sounding like a terrible person. "And when he does, what if he's...he's..."

"Not up to your standards?"

I nodded. Iris could always find a nice but accurate way of putting things.

"Well, then, you let him down gently. Even if he's not to your liking, he's still paid you a lovely compliment."

"So I just wait and see, then?"

"Yep." She stubbed out her cigarette. "And enjoy it. You should always enjoy it when someone—no matter who they are—thinks you're special. And Ruby, whoever it is who thinks you're special"—she reached out and patted my arm—"is absolutely right."

I knew my face was red as a Valentine.

FEBRUARY 22, 1945

Virgie's been acting real strange around me lately. She's been almost quiet—or as close to quiet as Virgie can get—and has seemed kind of far away somehow. Yesterday when the final bell rang, I said, "Are you going over to the Red Cross to roll bandages?"

"I'm going," she said. "You can come if you want to."

Virgie and Aaron and I walked to the Red Cross in silence. For Aaron, silence is the norm, but for Virgie, it's downright spooky. Once we got to the door of the Red Cross, Aaron left us like he always did. When Virgie and I were sitting with a stack of bandages in front of us, I said, "Are you mad at me or something?"

Virgie started folding a bandage in a fury. "No, I'm not mad. I just keep waiting for you to talk to me, and you don't say nothing."

"I talk to you all the time. What do you mean?"

"I mean, to talk to me about something that happened to you last week. On Valentine's Day. You know what I'm talking about."

I knew, but I didn't know how she knew. "How do you know about the card? You didn't give it to me, did you, as some kind of joke?"

Virgie threw down her bandage. "I can't believe somebody could have so much book sense and not a lick of common sense! Can you honestly tell me you don't know who gave you that card?"

"Of course I have no idea who gave it to me. Why—what do you know about it?"

Virgie rolled her eyes like my stupidity both annoyed and exhausted her. "I swear, how could you not know?"

Neither of us was folding bandages now. "Stop torturing me and tell me."

Virgie looked around. The room was empty. "It was Aaron."

"Aaron?" I wouldn't have been any more surprised if she had told me it was Douglas MacArthur.

"You seem like you've got eyes and ears," she said, going back to her folding. "Ain't you seen the way he looks at you? Ain't you heard the way he talks to you?"

"But he doesn't look at me! He looks down at the ground. And he doesn't talk to me unless I talk to him first, and when he does, he just mumbles under his breath."

"That's because he likes you," Virgie said, finally giving me a smile.

"But ain't he like that with everybody?"

"Well, yeah, but with you, it's worse." She scooted her chair closer to me and spoke in a whisper. "See, he didn't know how to tell you how he felt, so I gave him the idea of giving you a Valentine and signing it from a secret admirer. I even helped him make it since boys ain't no good at that kind of thing. We cut the letters out of one of my movie magazines. Of course, I thought you'd have enough sense to know who it was from as soon as you seen it." She shook her head.

"Well, I'm sorry I'm not too bright."

"That's all right," Virgie said. "It sure is hard trying to get people together when one's too shy to talk and the other's got her nose stuck too deep in a book to know she's in the world."

Poor Virgie. Here she was, acting as director in a movie of her own making, and she couldn't get either Aaron or me to play our roles the way we were supposed to. I still didn't—still don't—know how to act. Until Virgie spilled the beans, I had never thought about Aaron at all, except in passing. "Are you gonna tell Aaron I know?"

"I might as well," Virgie said with a sigh. "It'll take him so long to get his nerve up to say anything to you that I reckon I should speed things up a little by telling him. And I'll tell you something, too. He wants to ask you to that dance they're having at the teen rec center next month."

"The March Hare Hop?"

"That's the one."

The dances at the rec center were frequented by Kleen Teens in shiny penny loafers and spotless saddle shoes. At school I heard one girl say she always wore galoshes over her saddle shoes to protect them from the mud until she got to the dance. "Virgie, I don't go to them dances."

"That's because you've never had a boy to take you."

"Well, Aaron don't go either, does he?"

Virgie smiled like she had all the answers to all the questions in the world. "That's because he ain't never had a girl to take." She leaned close and whispered, "Of course, Daddy would have a fit if he knew Aaron was taking a girl to a dance with godless music and godless people. So I'll think up some way to cover for him. Me and Aaron would never get to do nothing if we hadn't figured out how to cover for each other with Daddy."

I could see the movie in Virgie's mind just like it was being projected on a screen in front of me. Aaron was a Hollywood version of Romeo, and I was a movie star Juliet, and Virgie was one of the sympathetic friends trying to help us get together. Virgie was forgetting that *Romeo and Juliet* was a tragedy.

FEBRUARY 26, 1945

"After school today, me and you and Aaron are going to the drugstore for a Coke," Virgie said.

"All right," I said because I knew it was an order, not an invitation. A heavy weight dropped into my stomach and stayed there all afternoon while I tried to pay attention in my classes. Do most people really feel like they have butterflies in their stomachs when they're nervous? I felt like I had a lead cannonball in mine.

On the way to the drugstore, Virgie chatted happily about some movie that was coming to town on the weekend, but Aaron and I were both quiet, dragging our feet like we were walking to the gallows. Once we got to the soda fountain, Virgie jabbed Aaron with her elbow, and he said, "Uh…let me buy your Coke, Ruby…on accounta you buying me one that time."

"All right," I said.

We sat down with our Cokes, and Virgie kept looking at Aaron, then at me. At first she was smiling, but after a while she started squirming and rolling her eyes. "Aaron," she said, "wasn't there something you wanted to *ask* Ruby?" She spoke in the same tone she'd have used if she'd been asking a two-year-old if he needed to go potty.

Aaron's face turned so red his freckles disappeared. He looked down and mumbled to his Coke glass something that sounded like "joogo pants."

"Ask *her*," Virgie said. "And loud enough so she can hear you."

Aaron didn't look up from his Coke glass, but he did manage to blurt out, "Ruby-you-wanna-go-to-the-dance-with-me?"

"All right," I said.

He nodded and drained his Coke in one gulp. I'm sure that in the soundtrack to the movie in Virgie's mind, violins were playing.

But no violins played in my head. No bells rang. I didn't feel much of anything except nervous and uncomfortable. And part of the reason I was so uncomfortable was because I knew that if Aaron wasn't Virgie's brother, I would've said no. Not for any personal reason, just because boys aren't a priority for me right now. But Virgie had gotten it in her head that I was going to the dance with Aaron, and saying no to Aaron would've meant saying no to Virgie's and my friendship. And so to keep from losing a friend, I gained a date.

MARCH 2, 1945

It took me the rest of the week to get my nerve up, but I finally told them. We'd just finished supper, and I figured my chances were best if everybody was full and happy, so I said, "Mama, Daddy, I need to tell you something."

"All right," Daddy said, sounding worried.

I looked down at the table while I talked. "This boy asked me to go to a dance at the teen rec center on March seventeenth, and if it's all right with you, I think I'll go."

As soon as I said "boy," Opal and Garnet started squealing like hogs at killing time. Baby Pearl joined in, too, just to be sociable, I reckon.

"Hush, girls!" Mama said, then she looked at me hard. "Who's the boy?"

"Aaron West," I managed to choke out. "Virgie's brother."

This set my sisters to squealing again, but Mama's eyes softened a little. "Oh," she said, "well, what do you think, Daddy?"

"Aaron's daddy's a right good feller," Daddy said. "I reckon it'd be all right for my little girl to go to a dance with his boy."

"I think so, too," Mama said. She laughed. "To tell you the truth, I'm downright relieved. I thought one of them fast-talking boys from Up North might be after you."

"No, Mama." Nobody could ever accuse Aaron of being a fast talker. Or a talker, period.

Opal and Garnet had started whispering to each other and were giggling up a storm.

"Now, girls, you know it's rude to whisper," Mama said. "Anything you got to say, you can say it to everybody at this table."

Garnet hollered—at least it sounded like a holler to me— "Opal says Ruby's gonna have her some red-headed, freckle-faced babies!"

"Nobody around here's having any babies any time soon. Ruby got asked to a dance, not proposed to," Mama said. "Do you girls want to give your daddy a heart attack?"

From where I was sitting, it looked more like Daddy was about to bust out laughing than have a heart attack. My heart didn't feel so good, though.

While we washed the dishes, Opal and Garnet asked me so many questions about Aaron that I felt like I was being interrogated about selling secrets to the Japanese. After I dried and put away the last dish, I waved the dishtowel in the air and said, "That's it! No more questions! Here's my white flag! I surrender!"

Mama and Daddy laughed. They were happy, I could tell. Happy that I was finally going out with a boy and happier because it was a nice country boy to boot. For the first time in a long time, I was doing something they thought they understood.

MARCH 6, 1945

The past few times I've sat with Sharon, Iris had run to the grocery store or the doctor's office or the beauty shop, so we didn't have much of a chance to talk. Today when I got there, though, she said, "All I've done the past four days is chase Sharon around the house and make sure she doesn't crack her head when she pulls herself up on something to stand. She's so…mobile all of a sudden."

"Just wait till she's walking," I said.

"Knowing Sharon, she'll skip walking and start off at a dead run," Iris said. "You know what sounds absolutely delicious to me right now?"

"What's that?"

"To stretch out on the bed with a Coke and a chocolate bar and a cigarette and read this silly *Cosmopolitan* magazine. I've had it for days, but every time I pick it up to read it, I have to drop it again to rescue Sharon."

"Go read. I'll rescue Sharon for a while."

As soon as Iris left the room, Sharon looked at me, squealed, "Bee!" then took off crawling, hell for leather, toward the kitchen, laughing like a little lunatic. I chased her the same as I reckoned Iris had been doing all day. She scooted over to one of the kitchen cabinets, opened the door, and yanked out a box of baking soda. She inspected it, then held it up to me. "Dis?" she asked.

"This?" I pointed to the box. "This is baking soda."

My answer seemed to satisfy her. She reached back into the cabinet and pulled out a dark blue container. "Dis?"

"This is salt."

An hour passed, with Sharon grabbing various household objects, asking "Dis?" and me answering her and trying to clean up after her at the same time. It was like she was giving me some kind of test, grilling me on the contents of her home. Sometimes I'm pretty sure she'd trick me to make sure I knew what I was talking about, asking me "dis?" about an object I'd already identified to make sure my answer was the same.

Iris came out of the bedroom, stretched, and said, "That was almost as good as a week-long vacation."

Sharon had worked her way back to the living room and was grabbing books off the lower shelves of the bookcase. "We're playing 'Dis,'" I said.

Iris grinned. "I knew you would be. It's all she does right now. It wears me out, but at the same time, I love her curiosity and watching her catalog all this information. Sometimes I can almost see the little wheels in her brain turning."

"She's a smart baby," I said. "Of course, she would be since she's got such a smart mama."

Iris rolled her eyes and sat down on the couch. "If she's smart, it's because of her daddy. I'm just smart enough to know that in the big picture, I'm not that smart at all." She shrugged. "Of course, that does make me smarter than some people."

"Than a lot of people," I said.

Sharon held up a book of Emily Dickinson's poems. "Book!" she proclaimed.

"Very good, Sharon," Iris said, and we both applauded her. "Sometimes," Iris said, looking at her daughter, "I wonder what it would be like for everything to be so new—for every day to seem like this big, exciting surprise."

Iris's voice sounded sad, so to distract her, I said, "Speaking of surprises, I found out who my secret admirer is."

"Really?" She sounded cheerier right away. "Do tell."

I took the Emily Dickinson book out of Sharon's hands and mouth and gave her a rattle instead. "It's Aaron, my friend Virgie's brother."

Iris scooted forward on the couch. "So…tell me about him."

I almost said "there ain't much to tell," but that didn't sound nice, so instead I managed to get out, "Well…he's a year younger than me and about a foot taller. He's real quiet…and he's got red hair."

"Oh, I like red hair," Iris said. "Redheads always seem so full of life somehow…vibrant."

Vibrant wasn't a word I would've thought of to describe Aaron. It did sort of describe Virgie, though.

"So do you like him?" Iris asked, lighting a cigarette.

"I don't know." I sighed. "I guess I don't not like him."

Iris laughed. "Well, that's certainly a passionate declaration of feeling."

I laughed, too. "I know it sounded bad. It's just…I guess I don't know Aaron well enough to know how I feel about him. And then…he asked me to go to this dance with him, and I don't really like dances…"

"Have you been to dances before?"

"No."

"Then how do you know you don't like them?"

"I know because I can't dance. You don't go to a swimming hole if you can't swim, and you don't go to a dance if you can't dance. The only difference is at one you drown, at the other, you die of embarrassment."

Iris laughed. "Well, I can prevent one of those catastrophes, anyway."

"What do you mean?"

"Well…when's the dance?"

"A week from Saturday. Why?"

Iris hugged her knees to her chest. "I was just thinking that between now and then, I could give you a couple of dancing lessons."

I couldn't understand why Iris said she wasn't that smart. It seemed like there was nothing she didn't know. "You'd do that?"

"Sure. I mean, I'm no Ginger Rogers, but I'm all right. Is Aaron much of a dancer?"

"I'd be surprised if he was. He's from the country like me, and Virgie says he ain't never been to a dance before."

"Okay," Iris said, stubbing out her cigarette. "So it's not a matter of turning you into a Ginger to match his Fred. It's more like teaching you how not to trip over your own feet and knock over the punchbowl."

"That's about right," I said, grinning.

"Well, I think I can handle dance instruction on that level. Let's see...I have to run errands on Thursday, but when you come over on Tuesday, I'll put on some records, and we'll trip the light fantastic."

"I thought you was gonna teach me how not to trip."

"I am. 'Trip the light fantastic' is just an expression for dancing."

It was almost suppertime. "Well, I reckon I'd better head on home. Thanks for"—I felt like I had so much to thank Iris for I didn't know where to begin—"being so good to me."

"Thank you, too," Iris said. She scooped up Baby Sharon in her arms and said, "Say bye-bye."

Baby Sharon said, "Bee" instead.

"Well," Iris said, seeming almost shy for a second, "remember to bring your dancing shoes next week."

"Lord, I don't have any special shoes! Will I need them?"

"That's just an expression, too, Ruby. You really are a nervous wreck about this dance date, aren't you?"

She was right. I was. I am.

MARCH 9, 1945

"Ruby, come outside a minute and help me get these clothes off the line," Mama said.

It was a strange request. Mama had never asked for help getting clothes off the line before, but I did as I was told. And as it turned out, she didn't need help getting clothes off the line this time either. She'd just wanted to get me away from my sisters.

"I bought you something in town today," she half-whispered, taking one of Baby Pearl's dresses off the line. "I thought it might help you get ready for next Saturday night."

"Well, uh, thank you," I said, not sure what I was supposed to say.

"I tucked it under your mattress so your sisters wouldn't see it," she said. "They're not old enough for such things."

It was all I could do not to run straight to my bedroom, but since I didn't want to arouse suspicion, I walked instead. I felt around underneath the mattress and pulled out a thin book, the cheap paperback kind you can get at the drugstore. It was called *How to Get Along with Boys*.

Of course, I was curious to start reading it, but I didn't want my sisters to catch me at it. Their giggling would ring in my ears for weeks. Finally, I got the idea of putting the book inside my history textbook so it would look like I was studying. I'd seen kids in school do the same thing with comic books.

I opened *How to Get Along with Boys* with no idea what to expect. I wondered if it was a book about the facts of life. My mother had never talked to me about those things, except to explain how to keep clean when my time of the month came around. Other than that, it was just what I could figure out on my own. But between watching the animals and Granny and Papaw's farm and reading *Forever Amber* at Iris's, I had a pretty good idea what went where and how.

As it turned out, *How to Get Along with Boys* didn't have anything to do with what might happen in a barnyard or to a saucy wench in eighteenth-century England. I read the whole danged book, and honestly, it made me feel like a visitor to a foreign country trying—and failing—to understand the local customs. Here are some of the things I learned from the book:

Boys don't like girls who endlessly chatter about clothes and movie stars and parties. Instead, the girl should let the boy take the lead in conversations just as he takes the lead in dancing. If the boy is slow to begin a conversation, the girl should ask him a question about *his* interests, such as, "Are you fond of football?"

I figure that if I let Aaron take the lead in conversation, it's going to be a silent night. Unless Virgie comes to the dance with us, which I wish she would. I don't reckon the author of *How to Get Along with Boys* would like Virgie much since she never lets anybody but herself take the lead in conversation—or get a word in edgewise.

Boys don't like girls who insist on having a great deal of money spent on them. Instead of asking to be taken to a fancy restaurant, the girl should offer to make sandwiches so they can go on a picnic at the park.

When it comes to money, I figure Aaron's got less than I do, so I'd come closer to being able to take him to a restaurant than he would me. Of course, he didn't even like me buying him a Coke that time, so I guess a restaurant meal is out of the question.

Different hairstyles are flattering to different face shapes. A girl with a heart-shaped face, for example, should wear bangs; whereas bangs are unflattering to a girl with a square face.

Now this one is just stupid. Who has a heart-shaped face? Or a liver-shaped face or a kidney-shaped face, for that matter? It's ridiculous, and in my opinion, anybody whose face is in the shape of a heart or a square is going to be so strange-looking that no boys are going to want to date her no matter what she does with her hair.

A girl should never be seen to have a large appetite. Even if she is famished, she should still leave some food on her plate uneaten. Also, asparagus should be picked up with the fingers and eaten. To cut it with a knife looks common.

Honestly, with rationing going on, isn't it downright unpatriotic to leave food on your plate? Mama may have bought me this book, but I know she'd disagree with this piece of advice. If my sisters and I don't eat all of our supper, she always says the same thing: "They's people in this world that's starving to death who'd be glad to get what you're letting go to waste." And when it comes to the part about it being common to eat asparagus with a knife…well, I've never eaten asparagus before in my life, so how common does that make me?

I know Mama was trying to help me by buying this book, but honestly, if I acted the way it says to act around Aaron, he'd think I was putting on airs or that I'd gone plumb crazy. And besides, I disagree with the idea that a girl has to act a certain way just because she's around a boy. I see it with girls at school all the time. They'll be having a perfectly normal conversation, then a pack of boys will walk by, and all the girls turn into these giggling, eyelash-batting, hair-flipping fools.

Maybe "how to get along with boys" is not to act any way at all—just to be your natural self. I guess that's how I caught Aaron's interest—by being natural and not even trying. The trouble is, now that I've got his interest, I don't know what to do with it.

MARCH 13, 1945

"Here's my dancing partner!" Iris said after she swung the door open. She was wearing rolled-up blue jeans and one of Warren's old shirts and had her hair pulled back in a ponytail. She wouldn't have looked out of place in the halls of Oak Ridge High School.

"I've never seen you wear blue jeans before," I said.

"Well, I figured if I had to play the boy when we dance, I might as well look the part. See? I made us a dance floor."

The coffee table had been cleared off and set on top of the sofa, and the rug was rolled up. I asked, "Where's Baby Sharon?"

"I put her down for her nap late, so we'd have time for our lesson."

"You didn't have to do that. I'm supposed to look after her and let you have a break."

Iris lit a cigarette. "Not today you're not. Today you are a dance pupil at Mrs. Stevens' Finishing School for Young Ladies." She struck a pinup pose. "And don't I look the proper teacher with my blue jeans and cigarette?"

I laughed.

"Oh, I have the perfect record for us to dance to," Iris said, heading over to the record player. "Warren hates it. He says it's sentimental pap. But I don't think there's anything wrong with music being sentimental. It's supposed to be about feelings, right?" She held up the cover of the record so I could see it.

"Frank Sinatra," I said. "I've seen him on the newsreels. Girls just scream their heads off for him even though he looks like a half-starved hound dog."

Now Iris laughed. "It's his voice. It would make any girl swoon. As far as his looks go, well, most of the young men those girls would date are overseas now, so I guess even the scrawny fellows are looking pretty good."

Iris put on the record. First the strings swelled; then there was the sound of Frank Sinatra's voice, as thick and rich and smoky as molasses syrup. Iris came to stand in front of me, her bare feet with red polish on the toenails almost touching my saddle shoes. "Maybe you should just dance in your socks at first," she said. "That way, if you step on my toes, it won't hurt so much."

I slipped out of my saddle shoes, happy to be given something to do. I was feeling shy all of a sudden, as if I didn't spend several hours a week with Iris, as if I didn't consider her my best friend (though I'd never tell Virgie this). Maybe it was because Iris was so close I could smell all her smells: her cigarettes, her perfume, her shampoo, her own natural smell—a little spicy—underneath. "I don't guess you'll be jitterbugging if your boyfriend isn't much of a dancer…"

"He's not my boyfriend." I said it so fast it sounded almost snippy.

"Your potential boyfriend, then," Iris said. "So what he'll do is put his arm around you so this hand is touching the small of your back."

Her hand felt warm. I don't think anybody had touched me there before. I tried to imagine Aaron's hand on the small of my back and couldn't.

"And then you'll put this arm around him, though you'll touch him higher on his back, around his shoulders."

I put my left arm around Iris, cupping my hand over the little hill of her shoulder blade.

"And then we grasp these hands together in the air, like this."

I was surprised to feel that her hand was smaller than mine. Small and soft—a lady's hand. Not like my big rough peasant paws, made for hard work and calluses.

"Now," she said, softening her voice—we were so close she could've whispered—"The box waltz is the inexperienced dancer's best friend. Follow my lead now—two steps at a time—we're going to make a box with our feet."

One, two; one, two; one, two; one, two...I didn't step back in time and we both stumbled a little, but I kept counting in time to Frank's voice, and soon we were moving in time together.

"Ruby, you're good at this," Iris said.

"You're a good teacher," I said, my face feeling warm.

The music stopped. "Wait—let me turn the record over." Iris let go of my hand and my waist, leaving me feeling strangely alone.

But then there was music again, and Iris slipped right back into my arms. She was only a couple of inches taller than I am. I was having a hard time imagining how tall, gangly Aaron and I would manage to fit together. One, two; one, two—we were getting smoother.

"It feels strange to be leading," Iris said after a while.

"You're good at it," I said. "You know, it seems like it'd be more fun if the fellow and the girl took turns being the leader and the follower. It'd make things more interesting, don't you think?"

"Sure it would." Iris gave my hand a little squeeze. "But it doesn't work like that. In dancing or in life. It's too bad, though. Some girls—like you—are natural leaders."

We danced our way through Frank Sinatra, through the Andrews Sisters, through some classical waltzes. Maybe because of the soft, soothing music in the background, Sharon didn't wake up.

"Since you're doing so well, let me show you a few flourishes," Iris said. "A couple of things that look fancy but are easy to do. If you want to spin out like this"—she ducked under my outstretched arm and twirled—"it looks really pretty, especially if you're wearing a dress. Blue jeans kind of ruin the effect. You try it."

The first spin looked like something out of Abbott and Costello, but the second time I did it, Iris said, "Beautiful!" when I moved back into her arms. "Ruby," she said, "you're going to be the belle of the ball."

"Not hardly."

We danced some more. I didn't know how I'd feel dancing with Aaron in a room full of sweaty kids, but dancing with Iris in her living room, I felt wonderful. I wondered if she liked it, too, but I wasn't sure how to ask her. Finally, I heard myself saying, "Does it feel uncomfortable to be dancing with a girl?"

"On the contrary," Iris said, smiling. "Warren's so tall that when I dance with him I spend the whole time staring at his necktie. With you, though, I can look right at your pretty face."

She was looking at me then—really looking at me—and I was looking at her, too: her green eyes, the elegant bridge of her nose, her bow-shaped lips.

"Ruby." She said it so softly I could barely hear it, but I saw her say it—saw her wet red lips forming my name, and somehow I felt a big wave of happiness and sickness at the same time, and I stumbled and stepped on her toe.

"Sorry," I said.

"It's okay. I was just…I was just going to say maybe we should stop after the next song. If I don't wake Sharon from her nap, she'll be up all night."

"Okay."

We glided across the floor—I didn't need to count anymore. The rhythm came naturally now. I spun out and then back into Iris's arms.

The front door must have opened, but I didn't hear it.

"It looks like a tea dance at Wellesley in here," Warren said.

Iris laughed and pulled away from me. "Ruby's got a date for a school dance on Saturday, and she's never been to one before. I was showing her some steps."

"Let's see them, then," Warren said.

We took a few turns across the floor, and I did fine, but somehow it wasn't the same with Warren watching.

"Very nice," he said, then excused himself to go work at his desk.

"Well," Iris said, "I guess I'd better get dinner on the table. Oh, I almost forgot..." She reached into her pocket and handed me some money.

"You don't need to pay me for today. I should be paying you."

"What? And make me feel like a cheap, dance-hall floozy? Nonsense. Take the money. You do help me so much, Ruby, and I know your family counts on you to bring in some cash every week."

I couldn't look at her. "Thank you."

She put her finger under my chin to tilt up my face. "Are you feeling more comfortable about going to the dance now?"

Without thinking, I blurted, "I'd feel a lot more comfortable if I was going with you instead of Aaron."

She laughed, but it was different from her usual laugh, higher and less natural. "Don't be such a silly. You'll go with Aaron, you'll have a wonderful time, and you'll tell me all about it."

MARCH 17, 1945

When I sat down to breakfast this morning, Mama already had on her second-best dress. She saves her best dress for weddings and funerals. Her hair was pulled up in a neat bun, and her lips were stained with a touch of pink lipstick. "You look nice, Mama," I said. "Where you going?"

"*We*," she said, "are going to town."

Even though we live in a town now, Mama still says "going to town" when she means "going shopping."

"You done bought groceries this week," I said.

Mama poured herself a cup of coffee. "I ain't buying groceries. I'm buying you a new dress to wear to that dance tonight."

"A store-bought dress?" Except for socks and underwear, Mama made all my sisters' and my clothes.

"A store-bought dress," my mother repeated. "I talked to your daddy about it, and it's all right with him as long as you don't pick out the most expensive one in the store."

"Did Daddy say it was all right for all of us to have new dresses?" Garnet asked. Her eyes were narrowed, and I could tell she was getting her back up.

"No, he didn't," Mama said.. "But as soon as you're old enough to go to a dance, then the good Lord willing, Daddy'll buy you a dress, too."

"I don't want no dress," Baby Pearl said. "I want a puppy."

Mama laughed. "How did we get from a dress to a puppy? Ruby, go get cleaned up as soon as you're done eating. Opal, you watch your sisters till me and Ruby get back."

"We don't even get to go to the store and help her pick out her dress?" Opal said.

Mama shook her head. "I think three extra girls in the dress department is more help than anybody needs."

* * *

Dillard's department store is so fancy I felt nervous walking around in it. Somehow I was afraid I'd knock something down—one of the lady mannequins in a smart spring suit or a stack of shoeboxes. I could tell Mama was nervous, too, by the way she hunched her shoulders and gripped her pocketbook with both hands. In the young ladies' department, we were approached by a woman with chic curled bottle-blonde hair and bright red lipstick. Her dress was solid black—a color I'd never worn—and her heels were so high I wondered how she walked in them. "May I help you ladies?" she asked. She had a voice like the ladies in detective movies who smoke a lot of cigarettes.

"My daughter's going to a dance tonight," Mama said, a quiver in her voice. "We're looking for a dress."

"Is it a formal event?" the saleslady asked.

For a moment I pictured myself decked out in a big satin ball gown like the kind Amber St. Clare favored. "No, ma'am," I said. "It's just a regular kids' dance."

"Well, you still should look your best," the saleslady said. "What size do you wear, hon?"

My face was hot. "Uh…I don't know, really. Mama always just measures me for her sewing." I was embarrassed to have let it slip to this glamorous lady that my mama sewed my clothes. But then again, she could probably tell by looking at me.

"Well, I'll just measure you, too, then." She grabbed a cloth measuring tape from behind the counter. "Let's start with the waist, then." She wrapped the tape around me. "Well, you're no bigger than a minute, are you?" she said.

I stiffened when she wrapped the tape around my bust. It felt strange to be standing in the middle of a store with somebody messing around with that area of my body. She must've been able to tell I was embarrassed because she said, in a light, chatty tone, "Have you thought about what color of dress you'd like?"

I looked at her elegant dress. "Maybe black."

"Black isn't nice on young girls," Mama said, then she added to the saleslady, "It looks real nice on you, though, honey."

The saleslady smiled. "Well, black is very slimming, which is great for us grownup gals. You girls, though, don't have so much to hide." She looked at me, harder than I was used to being looked at by a stranger. "I was thinking a nice blue might set off your eyes," she said. She crossed over to a rack and pulled out a simple dress in a dreamy shade about halfway between sky blue and navy. "This is called Eleanor Blue because it's Mrs. Roosevelt's favorite shade," she said, holding the dress out for me to see. "Though now that I think on it, why any young girl would want to go to a dance looking like Mrs. Roosevelt is beyond me."

I reached out and touched the soft fabric. "I love Mrs. Roosevelt," I said. "And I love the dress. Can I try it on, Mama?"

Mama glanced at the price tag. "You can try it on," she said.

I stood in front of the mirror looking at the dress while Mama and the saleslady looked at me. "She looks darling," said the saleslady.

I did look a lot better than I usually looked. The blue did go with my eyes, and while the dress wasn't tight, it was fitted, and it made me aware of feminine things about me I hadn't really noticed before—my tiny waist, my bosom—which wasn't a big, heaving Amber St. Clare bosom, but it wasn't flat as a plate either.

"Why, Ruby, you've growed into a woman without me hardly noticing it!" Mama said, sounding like she might cry.

"Well, I hadn't hardly noticed it myself until I put this dress on," I said.

We bought the dress. And I spent all afternoon doing things to get ready for the dance with my sisters hovering around me like ladies in waiting who occasionally got into arguments with each other. I took a long bath and shampooed my hair. I painted my fingernails with clear polish so they'd shine. I let my sisters arrange my hair in all kinds of ways—some of them downright silly—until I found a style I liked, with the front of my hair pulled back in a barrette and the rest hanging free down my back.

After supper, which I didn't eat much of, Opal zipped me into my dress. "I bet you can't wait to see Aaron," she said.

But the truth was, I hadn't really thought about Aaron much at all. I'd been too busy playing dress-up with my sisters, a game that had nothing to do with boys.

When Aaron did show up, his red hair was slicked back with so much grease it looked brown. He was wearing a brand-new pair of overalls that were so stiff they could've stood up just as well without him. Aaron wasn't any more talkative than a pair of overalls either. He just stood in the doorway saying nothing.

Finally, Daddy said, "Now, Aaron, I want her home by ten o'clock."

Aaron nodded and mumbled, "Yessir."

Aaron was quiet, too, on the long walk to the teen rec center. I tried to make conversation. I said, "This mud sure is ruining the polish I put on these shoes," and he nodded. After a while, though, I shut up for the simple reason that I couldn't think of a word to say to him.

The teen rec center was decorated with streamers and balloons and pictures of rabbits that somebody had drawn and cut out. A big hand-lettered sign read, *The March Hare Hop*. There was a real band, too, that looked like it might be made up of people's dads. They were playing "String of Pearls," and it sounded real good. The dance floor was full of Kleen Teens, kids who never would've spoken a word to kids like Aaron and me, kids whose dancing ability went way beyond the box waltz.

Aaron gripped my forearm in his hand and led me, more like he was leading a cow than a girl, to the chairs on the side of the room. We sat. We sat through three songs, though my feet were doing a tiny version of the box step on the floor.

Finally, Aaron nudged me. "You want something to drink?"

"That would be nice," I said.

He left for a minute and came back with two cups of punch. We sat and drank. After that, we just sat. Finally, I decided to forget everything I'd read in *How to Get Along with Boys* and said, "Are you going to ask me to dance?"

"Naw. I don't know how to dance."

"Oh. Well, I don't want to sound mean or anything—really, I'm just curious—but why did you ask me to a dance?"

"It was Virgie's idea."

"It was Virgie's idea for you to ask me on a date?"

His ears turned as red as candy apples. "Naw. I wanted to ask you to go to the show. But Virgie said I had to ask you to the dance. Said it'd be more romantic. Or somethin."

I had to give Aaron credit. He'd just said more words at one time than I'd ever heard him say. "Well, that's all right. We can just sit and enjoy the music."

We sat for another hour, then he walked me home. At the door, I broke the silence long enough to say, "Thank you for a nice time, Aaron."

"Well," he said. "Bye."

As soon as I walked in the door, Opal and Garnet pounced on me, spilling out questions faster than I could follow them: How was the dance? How was the music? How were the decorations? Was Aaron a good dancer? Did I feel like Cinderella?

"It was nice," I said. "The decorations were pretty, and the band was good, and I had a nice cup of fruit punch."

I didn't have the heart to tell them that for my money, getting ready for the dance had been a lot more fun than the dance itself.

MARCH 20, 1945

Today Mr. Masters, the Ichabod Crane lookalike who can never truly replace Miss Connor, smiled at me when I sat down in class. He had never smiled at me before, and it made me notice how tiny his mouth was. It was like being smiled at by a chipmunk. "I believe I have something that might be of interest to you, Miss Pickett," he said. He picked up a piece of paper from a stack on his desk and handed it to me. I looked down at it and read:

Dear Miss Pickett,

The East Tennessee district of the Society of American Clubwomen is pleased to announce that your essay, "A Spirit of Sacrifice," was selected as the first-prize winner in our annual essay contest. Your winning essay has been entered in the state contest representing the East Tennessee district. As the author of the winning entry, you will be awarded a certificate of achievement and a $10 savings bond to be presented at a special awards luncheon held at the Wemberley Hotel in Knoxville at 12:00 noon on Saturday, April 21. Please accept our most sincere congratulations.

Cordially,

Mrs. Louella Dobson

President, Society of American Clubwomen,

East Tennessee District

Who I really wanted standing by me was Miss Connor. I would've hugged her then and there, but I couldn't very well put my arms around a man teacher like Mr. Masters. Not that I'd want to anyway—he's so skinny I would have had to wrap my arms around him twice.

But I had to hug somebody, and I had to jump up and down and squeal even though nothing had ever made me jump up and down and squeal before. Lucky for me, Virgie walked in right then, so I hugged her and jumped up and down and squealed, and so did she, even though she didn't know what she was jumping up and down and squealing about.

After a minute, Mr. Masters cleared his throat and said, "Students, the cause of the jubilation you are now witnessing is that Miss Ruby Pickett was just informed that she won the East Tennessee district of the the Society of American Clubwomen's annual essay contest. Perhaps we should give Miss Pickett a round of applause before she takes her seat."

Everybody clapped—most of them softly, but Virgie, standing beside me, clapped extra loud and yelled, "Woo-hoo!"

I sat back down at my desk, glowing with a strange mixture of happiness and embarrassment. Most people, I reckon, would've been thinking, I can't wait to tell my folks. But I was thinking I couldn't wait to tell Iris.

As soon as the final bell rang, I was out of the building. I ran all the way to Iris's house with the letter in my hand. As soon as she opened the door, worry flashed across her face. "Ruby, what's the matter? You're all flushed..."

"Look," I said, holding the letter out to her.

She took it, and as she read, I watched the clouds of her worry part to make way for a radiant smile. And then her arms were around me in a hug. "I knew you'd win," she said.

"Really? Why?"

"Because you're brilliant. That's why."

I had said thank you so many times to Iris, and it was never enough, so we just kept on hugging each other, right there in the doorway. It was a long hug, like neither of us wanted to be the first to let go.

MARCH 23, 1945

I waited a whole day before I told anybody in my family about winning the contest. Sometimes when you're real excited about something and you tell somebody who doesn't think it's exciting at all, it kind of takes away some of your excitement. It's like thinking a joke is absolutely hilarious, and then when you try to tell it to somebody, they say "I don't get it," and suddenly the joke's not funny anymore.

I didn't want to lose any of my excitement yet. I wanted to keep it for a little while as my secret—mine and Iris's—and so I said nothing, but every once in a while I'd sneak off to read the letter again.

I finally spilled the beans when we were eating our beans on Wednesday evening. "You'uns remember that essay contest I entered back in the winter?" I said. "I got a letter saying I won it."

"That's good, honey," Mama said, but her expression didn't change, and her voice wasn't any more excited than if she was talking about the weather report.

"That is good, Ruby," Daddy said. "Would you pass me that dish of sweet onions, honey?"

"Here's the letter saying I won." I placed it on the table. Nobody made a move to look at it.

"Did you win any money?" Opal asked.

"A ten-dollar savings bond," I said.

"Whatcha gonna spend it on?" Garnet asked.

"Nothing yet," I said. "I've got to wait till it matures."

"Oh," Garnet said. She and Opal turned their attention back to their supper, now that it was obvious I wasn't going to have any wealth to spread around any time soon.

"There's a luncheon," I said, "on April twenty-first at the Wemberley Hotel in Knoxville. That's where they'll give me my certificate and savings bond. I thought maybe you and me could go, Mama."

Mama pushed her plate away. "Now, you know that ain't the kind of thing country folks like us do. I probably couldn't even find my way to that hotel, and even if I could, I wouldn't know what to wear or how to act or what to say. And neither would you."

I stood up and grabbed my letter. "Mama, that's not true, and you know it. I could wear the blue dress I wore to the dance, and when it comes to how to act, I can read Emily Post as well as the next person. And as for what to say, well, I reckon some people think I've got some pretty interesting stuff to say, or else I wouldn't have won this contest."

My sisters were all staring at me with their mouths hanging open. They had never seen me mad like this before. Shoot, I had never been mad like this before.

"Now don't go getting the big head just 'cause you won something," Mama said. She looked at me with narrowed eyes, like I was somebody she didn't know and didn't quite trust.

"I'm not getting the big head. I just want to go get my award. If they're having a luncheon on account of me, then I should go to it."

"Well, I ain't taking you," Mama said.

"Then I'll take the bus and go by myself."

"No, you won't," Daddy said. "A girl your age can't be going to the city by herself."

Hot tears of frustration flooded my eyes. "Then what should I do?"

"What you should do right now," Daddy said, "is go sit in your room and think about the way girls is supposed to talk to their mamas. I never have to call you down, Ruby. I don't know what's got into you."

As I turned to go, I heard Mama say, "Town's got into her."

But Mama's wrong. I'm the same person I've always been. It's just that Mama and Daddy are seeing me for the first time. I want what they see to make them proud, but it just makes them confused and scared.

MARCH 27, 1945

I spent the whole weekend sulking about not getting to go to the awards luncheon. I went to the library and checked out *Jane Eyre* and read it again because like Jane, I felt misunderstood and ill-treated. Maybe I should've read *Pollyanna* instead. Pollyanna would've played the Glad Game and would've been glad about winning the contest instead of sad about not getting to claim her award. But Pollyanna always did get on my nerves. I'm definitely more of a Jane than a Pollyanna.

If I was a Pollyanna, though, I probably would've been optimistic enough to see that there was a solution to my problem instead of just moping about it. Instead, the solution had to hit me over the head before I noticed it.

Today at Iris's, I was on the floor, playing blocks with Baby Sharon, when Iris said, "So are you going to wear your Eleanor blue dress to the awards luncheon?"

I don't know what got into me, but I started to cry. Baby Sharon looked at me in alarm, like she was thinking, hey, I'm the baby here; I'm the one who's supposed to cry, not you.

Iris sat down on the floor next to me. "My goodness, what's wrong?"

Between big, hiccuping sobs I told her about Mama's refusal to go the awards luncheon, about how she said things like that weren't for people like us.

Iris gave me a hanky. "Did she forbid you to go?"

"No. She just said she wouldn't take me, and Daddy won't let me go by myself."

"Well, then, that's easy to fix," Iris said. "I'll ask Hannah or Eva to watch Sharon that Saturday, and I'll take you."

It was obvious, it was perfect, but it hadn't occurred to me. "You'd do that?"

"Of course I would. In my heart I may not be the proper club lady type, but I know how to fake it. I can make chit-chat and delicately pick at each course of a meal with the appropriate utensil. I'll even stick out my pinkie when I drink my coffee if you like."

I laughed. "Don't stick out your pinkie on my account." I took her hand and squeezed it. "Thank you."

"No need to thank me. It'll be nice to get out of town for a couple of hours and go to what passes for a city in this part of the world—"

The front door swung open, and a voice trilled, "Helloooo?" It was Eva Lynch, decked out in a blue dotted dress with white gloves and a funny little hat perched on top of her head. She looked at us for a second. I'm sure we looked strange, both of us sitting so close together on the floor with the baby. Then she said, "Oh, good, your sitter's here. Are you ready to go to the Woman's Club meeting?"

"I'm ready," Iris said. "Just let me get my hat and purse."

The tone Iris used talking to Eva was completely different than her tone talking to me. With Mrs. Lynch she sounded deliberately cheerful, and I could tell she had no interest in the Woman's Club at all, that Mrs. Lynch had pressured her into it, and Iris was just being a good sport. After all, Iris had just said she wasn't a proper club lady in her heart. Somehow it made me feel good to know that Iris was real with me and fake with Eva Lynch—that Iris might let Eva burst into her house without knocking, but she would never let Eva into her heart.

MARCH 30, 1945

Apparently it's possible to be dating somebody without even knowing that's what you're doing.

Wednesday morning this boy named Bob who's in my English class waved me over to his table at the school library. He said, "Ruby, I was wondering if you could read this paper over for me so I can fix my spelling mistakes before it's time to turn it in."

Since Mr. Masters had announced that I won the essay contest, a lot of people have been asking me for help with their English papers. So I sat down at the table with Bob who, I saw after one glance at his paper, couldn't spell his way out of a wet sack.

I didn't give helping Bob another thought. But that afternoon, Virgie hissed, "I need to talk to you," and dragged me to the girls' bathroom.

"Are you okay?" I asked once we were alone.

"Yeah, I'm okay," Virgie said, "which is more than I can say for my brother."

"What's the matter with Aaron?"

Virgie rolled her eyes as though I should've known good and well what was the matter with him. "What's the matter with him is that he saw you sitting in the library with Bob Davenport and he's fit to be tied."

I tried in vain to make sense of what she'd just said. "Why would Aaron care if I help Bob with his English paper?"

"'Cause he didn't know that's what you was doing. He just saw you sitting with Bob and got mad 'cause you're his girl."

This was news to me. Aaron hadn't said two words to me since the dance. "I am?"

Virgie let out a huff of breath. "I swear, Ruby, I never will figure out how a person can be so smart and so dumb at the same time."

That afternoon, Aaron followed Virgie and me silently as we walked to the Red Cross. Finally, Virgie said, "Ruby, wasn't there something you wanted to say to Aaron?"

It was more like something Virgie wanted me to say to Aaron, but to smooth things over, I said, "Aaron, I don't know Bob Davenport from Adam's housecat. The only reason I was sitting with him was I was helping him with his English paper."

"All right," Aaron said, without looking at me.

"Now, Aaron," Virgie prompted, "wasn't there something you wanted to say to Ruby?"

He blurted out, barely above a whisper, "You-wanna-go-to-the-show-with-me-this-evenin?"

"All right," I said, without looking at him.

* * *

Going to the show with Aaron was better than going to the dance because nobody was expected to do anything but sit quietly. Virgie came, too, because she wanted to see the new picture, but she made a big deal out of not sitting with us so we could be "alone together." Instead of sitting beside us, she sat in the row behind us, occasionally reaching over us to grab fistfuls of our popcorn.

APRIL 1, 1945

Easter is the only Sunday my family always goes to church. Usually we girls all get new dresses, but this year Mama didn't make me one. It was fair enough. I had my new store-bought dress to wear, and fabric is scarce. In fact, Mama could only find enough of one color to make dresses for all my sisters, so they were all decked out in yellow dotted Swiss. I was just as glad to have my Eleanor blue. Mama's sewing is real pretty, but yellow makes me look like a poisoned dog.

"Look at all that yeller!" Daddy said when he came in from shaving. His face was red from the razor's scraping, and he was already tugging at the collar of his dress shirt. "You'uns is my sunshine girls."

"What am I? A storm cloud?" I said.

Daddy looked at my dress. "No, you're my blue sky girl," he said. "And this here," he said, going to Mama who was wearing her best floral print dress, "is my rose."

We went to the ten o'clock Baptist service at the Chapel on the Hill. The Methodists were just finishing up when we got there, and the Catholics had been there before them. After the Baptists left, the Presbyterians would have their service, then the Episcopalians. I had no idea how many kinds of church folks there were until we moved to Oak Ridge.

I like that all kinds of people with all kinds of beliefs use the same church house, even if Virgie and her family don't feel the same way. "Daddy says you can't have Catholics using the same church as Christians," Virgie told me one day when we were at the Red Cross. "They drink blood and worship Mary."

"They don't drink blood," I said. "They drink wine and think it's Jesus's blood."

"What difference does that make?" Virgie said. "Thinking it's the same as drinking it. And you know on Saturdays at that place they let the Jews come in and do whatever it is they do?"

"They oughta let the Jews in," I said. "That's why we're the U.S.A. and not Germany."

"I ain't got nothing agin the Jews," Virgie said, "but they ain't Christians, and you can't argue with that."

I couldn't, so I did what I usually did when Virgie started spouting religion: I changed the subject to movies.

Brother Simmons, the Baptist preacher at the Chapel on the Hill, spits a lot less fire and brimstone than our preacher back home. He uses good grammar and big words and talks about his days at the seminary. He sounds more like a teacher than a preacher.

Even though the grammar was better, the content of Brother Simmons' sermon was pretty much the same as the Easter sermons I'd heard my whole life. Most of the time was spent on Jesus's horrible suffering—the nails driven through the hands, the mouthful of vinegar when he cried out for water, the mocking crown of thorns. Then there was the sword that pierced his side, proving he was dead, and then after three days, the discovery of the empty tomb and hallelujah, He is risen.

Here's what I get out of the Easter story: Jesus was good and only wanted to help people, but then mean, powerful people tortured and killed him because they felt like he threatened their power. It's a smaller version of what the Nazis are doing in Germany.

But I have a secret thought—so secret I'd never say it out loud, and my hand is shaking even as I write it here: I don't believe Jesus rose from the dead. I don't believe anybody can. Yes, the tomb was empty, but wasn't there such a thing as grave robbers even back then?

I can't even imagine how Mama and Daddy and my sisters would react if I was to say such a thing out loud. Would they be mad at me? Would they cry because they feared I'd go to hell?

But I don't believe in heaven or hell, either one. It's comforting to think of just floating out of your body when you die and being in heaven with all the people you've lost to sickness or accidents or war. It's even comforting in another way to think of really bad people like Hitler winding up in hell. I'd like to believe in all that, but somehow I just can't. I look at the world, and I know that the good are often punished and the evil rewarded. And I want to be good and be the kind of person Jesus would want me to be, but I don't want to do it to win the prize of heaven or avoid the fires of hell. I just figure the best thing we can do in this life is to be good to each other, especially because this life is probably the only one we've got. I'd never tell anybody in my family, and I certainly wouldn't tell anybody in Virgie's family, but this is what I believe. Amen.

APRIL 5, 1945

"God, I'm glad it's spring," Iris said. I was sitting on the front steps of Iris's house and Iris was walking in the grass with Sharon, holding onto both of her hands as she took lurching steps forward.

"Me, too," I said.

"Some of those long winter days cooped up in the house—I thought they'd never end. Going so stir crazy that I had to get out for a while, then having to mummify Sharon in her snowsuit and blankets to take her out in the cold."

"Well, now it's the season of rebirth," I said. "Or at least that's what the preacher said at church on Sunday."

Iris let Baby Sharon drag her forward. "Oh, yes, this past Sunday was Easter, wasn't it? Warren and I ignored it as usual. I don't know what we're going to do once Sharon's bigger, though. I'm fine with celebrating the non-religious aspects of the holidays—Easter baskets and Christmas stockings and the like. But Warren is adamant that we shouldn't teach her about Santa Claus and the Easter Bunny and the Tooth Fairy and things like that. He says, what kind of lesson does it teach your kids if you start lying to them right off the bat?"

"I guess I never thought of those things as lies," I said. "Just stories. And I don't know…somehow a story and a lie aren't the same thing to me."

"That's because you're of a literary bent," Iris said. "Warren isn't." Baby Sharon started dragging her in the other direction across the yard.

I stood up. "Why don't I let Sharon drag me for a few minutes? You're gonna break your back if you keep leaning over like that."

"Thanks." Iris held Baby Sharon's hands until I could take them, then sat on the front steps and lit a cigarette. "Of course, the biggest thing Warren and I argue about in raising Sharon is what to tell her about God. To Warren, God is the biggest lie of all. He outstrips even Santa Claus and the Easter Bunny." I must have looked as shocked as I felt because she quickly added, "Oh, I've offended you. I'm sorry."

I tried to wipe the shock off my face. "I'm not offended, just surprised. The way I've been raised, people just know there's God the same way they know there's air to breathe and water to drink." Sharon pulled me forward, and I took silly-looking tiny steps to match her pace.

Iris let out a breath of smoke. "That must be nice. Comforting. See, I don't believe in God either, but unlike Warren, I don't think we should teach Sharon that atheism is the only way. I think she should have choices."

Iris had said *I don't believe in God* out loud. Not only had she said it, but she'd said it where anybody could hear it—said it as though it was a casual, everyday statement like *I don't like lima beans*. "I like your way better," I finally managed to say. "A person should have choices and should be able to ask questions. See, back where I'm from, you didn't get to ask questions about anything in the Bible. You just shut up and do what you're told. I have so many questions, but I'm afraid to ask them. I think about things like what's going on in Germany, and I think if there is a God, how could he let something go on like that?"

"Exactly." Iris ground out her cigarette.

"But then," I said, letting Sharon drag me the other way, "if something makes me feel good, I want to believe it came from God. That verse 'God is love' always kind of made sense to me because how else do you explain how I feel about my family…"

"Or about Aaron?" Iris said, smiling.

But that hadn't been what I was going to say. I was going to say "about you and Sharon," but maybe I would've stopped myself even if she hadn't. "I don't really know how I feel about Aaron yet."

Iris stood. "Well, I think love is all chemistry and instincts. People are just animals with overdeveloped brains and the ability to walk upright. Isn't that right, Sharon?"

I let go of Sharon's hands and said, "Walk to Mama."

She made two shaky steps on her own before she sat down hard on her diapered behind. Iris and I both applauded and hugged Sharon and kissed her. She grinned all over herself, like she knew she had done something big.

* * *

Since I talked to Iris today, I've been feeling like I'm moving toward something, but I'm not sure what it is. Some different way of thinking or feeling about life, I guess. But it's all so new to me that I feel as shaky and unbalanced as Baby Sharon taking her first steps with no help from above.

APRIL 7, 1945

Virgie saw some movie where a couple had a picnic on the grass, and she thought it was the most romantic thing. Yesterday during lunchtime at school, she went on and on about this movie picnic and the beautiful woven picnic basket and the roasted chicken and the long loaf of bread and the grapes the couple had fed to each other. "That's what you and Aaron ort to do," Virgie said. "You'uns can have a romantic picnic tomorrow. I'll come, too."

I laughed. "How's it gonna be romantic if you come, too?"

Her brow crinkled a little. "You don't want me to come?"

"Of course I want you to come." And I did, too. I couldn't stand the thought of a picnic alone with Aaron, where the only sound would be us chewing our food.

"Good. 'Cause Aaron wouldn't know nothing about putting a picnic together. And I figure with food scarce, you and me both ort to bring whatever our mamas say it's all right to bring."

Mama gave me permission to take enough bread and cheese for three sandwiches. I wrapped the cheese sandwiches in wax paper and cut a red apple into lots of thin slices, so it would seem like each of us was getting more than we really were. When I met Virgie and Aaron in our designated spot in the woods, Aaron was spreading a crazy quilt on the ground.

"Hey," Virgie said, "whatcha bring?"

"Cheese sandwiches and apple slices," I said, squatting down to set them on the blanket.

"I brought us a boiled egg apiece," Virgie said, holding up a small paper sack.

But my eye was on what was in Virgie's other hand—a mason jar full of clear liquid. "What's that?" I said. "Moonshine?"

Virgie laughed. "Naw. It's my special war ration lemonade, ain't that right, Aaron?"

Aaron shook his head with a little grin.

"What's in war ration lemonade?" I asked as we sat down on the blanket.

"Well, it's like regular lemonade," Virgie said, "except that sugar's rationed so we ain't got no sugar in it. And fruit's scarce, so there ain't no lemon in it." She grinned wide. "But there's one lemonade ingredient we've still got plenty of."

"Water?" I laughed.

"And if you close your eyes when you drink it and think real hard about lemons and sugar, you can almost taste them."

We ate our boiled eggs first, then our cheese sandwiches, then our apple slices extra slowly to make the sweetness last. And we washed it all down with Virgie's colorless, odorless, tasteless lemonade.

Once we'd finished eating, Virgie hopped up and announced she thought she'd go for a little walk to give Aaron and me some time alone. It was all I could do not to beg her to stay.

So there on the blanket Aaron and I sat. The breeze rustled the leaves on the trees. The birds chirped. The squirrels chattered. Aaron was silent.

Desperate for something to say, I looked at the sunlight shining through the trees and said, "It's pretty out here."

After too much time had passed, Aaron said, "You. Uh... you're pretty, too."

My face was as hot as a coal stove. I managed to say "Thank you," but it was embarrassing, having to accept a compliment I flat-out knew wasn't true. I'm not plug ugly, but I'm as plain as they come, not a bit pretty, and that's fine with me. I didn't feel like I had much choice but to say thank you, though. What was I supposed to do—start an argument?

After another stretch of silence, I became aware that Aaron's hand was creeping close to mine. He was moving it just a little at a time, like he was sneaking up on a shy animal. Finally, once his hand got about an inch away from mine, he grabbed it real fast and held it.

I think he was scared that I'd pull away, but I didn't. I just sat there, feeling how big and rough his hand was and feeling like I should be feeling something else—something like what's in books. A stirring—that's what the books always called it. But I remained as unstirred as Virgie's war ration lemonade.

Actually, holding hands with Aaron was a lot like drinking Virgie's war ration lemonade. It was neither good nor bad. It was just something that happened because we were in a certain place in a certain time.

APRIL 12, 1945

Opal is saying, "I can't believe you're writing at a time like this." But honestly, it's the only thing I can think of to do. Mama and the girls are all crying and hugging each other, and Daddy went out to talk to some fellows and—I'm betting—to have a nip to drink if he can find it. And I guess what I'm doing is setting this terrible day down for posterity, like Samuel Pepys did with the fire in London.

This evening right after supper everybody was listening to Tom Mix on the radio. Well, everybody except me...I was doing my math homework. I don't find math to be the most interesting of subjects, but it's still a lot more interesting than Tom Mix. At least math problems are different from each other. Every episode of Tom Mix is about the same. But then an announcer's voice broke in and said, "We interrupt this program with a special news bulletin."

President Roosevelt is dead.

It feels so strange to write those words and to see them, but it's true. He died of a cerebral hemorrhage at the place nicknamed "the little White House" in Warm Springs, Georgia. The announcer said that even if a doctor had been there, he wouldn't have been able to do anything.

The first feeling that hit me was sadness—the same kind of sadness I'd feel if a member of my family died. Because FDR did feel like a member of the family. With his Fireside Chats and his reminders that we all had to pull together, he was sort of like a wise uncle or, at the very least, a beloved teacher.

And then I thought of Eleanor, a war widow now like so many thousands of others. The agony of being Commander-in-Chief of the war took its toll on FDR just as surely as bullets took their toll on so many of our soldiers.

And there's the fear. I know the man who said "We have nothing to fear but fear itself" wouldn't want his people to be afraid. But how can we not be afraid about what's going to happen with the war and with the world? How can we not worry just a little bit that President Truman, however smart and competent he is, might not be able to fill FDR's shoes? How strange it feels to say "President Truman" when it's been "President Roosevelt" ever since I was old enough to know there was such a thing as a president of the United States.

Mama is crying with my sisters saying, "Oh, girls, how can things go on like they did before?"

It's the only question right now I feel like I might know the answer to: They can't.

APRIL 15, 1945

"You've got to go to church with Aaron and me this Sunday," Virgie said. "Daddy's had him a revelation, and you need to hear him prophesy."

I've noticed that Virgie and Aaron always say "go to church" like their church isn't right there in their apartment. For them, going to church just means walking from the bedroom to the living room. It wasn't as easy for me to get there, but I made the effort. I was curious. I had never heard anybody prophesy before.

The word must've gotten around about Mr. West's revelation because the Wests' living room was packed with men in overalls and women in homemade dresses. Or maybe the crowd wasn't because of the revelation but because everybody was reeling from the President's death and wanted some religion for comfort.

But if comfort was what people wanted from Mr. West's sermon, they were out of luck.

Mr. West's face was flushed and sweaty, and his eyes were wide and wild. Virgie had told me that sometimes when her daddy was being delivered visions and prophesies, he would go days without sleeping or eating. Now, she had said, was one of those times, and to look at him, it wasn't hard to believe. His hands were shaking as he held up the Wests' huge family Bible, and he looked like a man who needed to be fed some biscuits and gravy and then put to bed for about three days. "My girl Virgie's gonna read us the scripture this morning," he said.

Virgie walked up and took the Bible from his hands. Even though Mr. West was of the opinion that females weren't fit to preach, he always asked Virgie to do the reading at his services because he said reading out loud made him nervous.

"This here's from Chapter Eight of the Book of Revelation," Virgie said.

This here is what Virgie read (I just copied it out of our family Bible):

7 The first angel sounded, and there followed hail and fire mixed with blood, and they were cast upon the earth; and the third part of the trees was burnt up, and all green grass was burnt up.

8 And the second angel sounded, and, as it were, a great mountain burning with fire was cast into the sea; and the third part of the sea became blood.

9 And the third part of the creatures which were in the sea, and had life, died; and the third part of the ships were destroyed.

10 And the third angel sounded, and there fell a great star from heaven, burning as though it were a lamp, and it fell upon the third part of the rivers, and upon the fountains of water.

11 And the name of the star is called Wormwood; and the third part of the waters became wormwood; and many men died in the waters because they were made bitter.

After Virgie read this part, her daddy said, "That's enough, honey. Thank you."

She sat back down next to Aaron and me and whispered, "I hope Daddy tells us what that means. None of it made a lick of sense to me."

"There will be no singing today," Mr. West announced. "We ain't got time for singing. There will be no passing of the collection plate because money's no good where we're going.

Brothers and sisters, for seven days and seven nights, I ain't slept a wink. I ain't eat a bite except for a few spoonfuls a day Sister West fed to me like a baby. But it don't matter. I won't need my body where I'm going."

"Amen!" a young man in overalls hollered.

"Amen is right," Mr. West said. "When you say a prayer, 'amen' is what you say when you get to the end. And brothers and sisters, we are getting to the end. The End of Times where every soul will be judged and found worthy or wanting."

Mr. West rubbed his bloodshot eyes. "I have seen it all. It has been revealed to me. The great beast has risen from the earth, and his mark is the swastika. And his land and the other lands that have risen up with him is the land of Babylon, the painted harlot who lures men to their doom."

I looked around at the other people in the room. Mr. West had their attention, that was for sure. But people's expressions were hard to read.

"But we—America—we are Jerusalem the holy, and we will smite the wicked and the unrighteous. We will rain down fire on their islands and mountains, on their cities and villages, and they shall be cast off this earth! But the righteous of Jerusalem will rise tall and strong to sit at the throne of God."

Brother West kept at kept at it like that for a long time until he finally said amen, staggered backwards, and fell down, dead asleep. Mrs. West ran to his side and hollered, "Could some of you boys help me get him to the bed?"

That was the end of the service.

Virgie asked me to stay for Sunday dinner, but I couldn't. I didn't understand how a person could sit for two hours listening to somebody talking about the end of the world and still have an appetite for fried chicken. But I guess Virgie and Aaron are used to that kind of thing.

I took the long way home from Virgie and Aaron's, and I spent the afternoon trying to concentrate on my studies. But I found myself opening up the family Bible and reading through the Book of Revelation and trying to make some sense of it. The words were scary and beautiful, but I kept having the blasphemous thought that they sounded like something a crazy person would say. And then I thought of Mr. West's wild eyes and sleeplessness and wondered if he might be a crazy person himself. But I felt bad for thinking it because I knew he was a good man who meant well.

When I finally decided I needed to stop brooding and be with my family, everybody was gathered around the radio listening to Edward R. Murrow talking about Buchenwald, the Nazi camp he visited after Americans liberated it. What he said he saw was at least as bad as anything in the Book of Revelation: starving little boys with death in their eyes and numbers tattooed on their arms; men too weak to clap their hands in welcome for Mr. Murrow; a doctor who said that people at Buchenwald had died at a rate of 900 a day; and the corpses to prove it, naked, bony, and stacked up like kindling.

Even though I was just hearing all this on the radio, the picture burned in my mind as sharp as photographs. I had to run outside for air. The image of those starved, stacked bodies filled my head, and bile filled my throat. I fell to my knees and vomited in the mud.

APRIL 21, 1945

Except for my schoolwork, I haven't written a word all week, and I've barely eaten or slept. You'd think I was Mr. West getting ready to prophesy, but really, it's because I've been so nervous and excited about the Society of American Clubwomen luncheon.

I told Iris I'd walk over to her house this morning, and we could leave for Knoxville from there, but she insisted on picking me up at my house. She wanted to talk to my mama, she said, so she wouldn't worry about her daughter being taken off to the big, bad city. Sitting at the kitchen table, waiting for Iris to knock on the door, I saw the house as she would see it: thin sheets of plywood tacked together to make a flimsy shack. I was aware, too, how worn out Mama's housedress looked and how few belongings we had to personalize the place. I hoped Mama would just talk to Iris at the door, that she wouldn't let her in.

When Iris knocked, I jumped like I hadn't been expecting it.

After Mama opened the door, she said, "You must be Mrs. Stevens. Ruby talks about you like you hung the moon. Come on in."

I felt heat rise to my cheeks.

Iris looked pretty. She had on a light green spring suit with a matching hat that perched on top of her curls. Her pink lipstick was a little smeared, but that was just Iris.

Mama shrugged. "It ain't much to look at."

Iris smiled. "What house in this town is? We live where Roane-Anderson tells us to live. There's not much room to be house-proud in Oak Ridge."

"Ain't that the truth?" Mama said, and I could tell that Iris had won her over.

"Are you ready for your big day, Ruby?" Iris held out a white-gloved hand, and I stood up, walked to her, and took it. My hands were so sweaty I was probably soaking her glove. "Now, Mrs. Pickett, if it's all right with you, I may run a few errands after the luncheon is over, but I should have Ruby back to you no later than six this evening."

"That'll be fine," Mama said, "as long as she's no trouble to you."

"Oh, Ruby is never any trouble," Iris said. "Ruby is a treasure."

Once we were in the car, Iris turned to me and said, "Nervous?"

"As a long-tailed cat in a room full of rocking chairs."

She smiled. "It'll be fine. Anyone who meets you is going to like you instantly. And it'll do us both good to get out of this place for a day."

We rode away from our little settlement of shacks, past the business area and the nicer houses, and up to the gatehouse at the edge of the city. Iris rolled down the window for the soldier who came to meet us.

"Leaving the reservation this morning, ma'am?" he asked. He didn't look like he was much older than me. He was so baby-faced I bet he didn't need to shave every day, even though he probably did anyway.

"Yes, sir," Iris said. If she thought it was funny to call such a young boy "sir," she didn't show it. "Just for a few hours. We're going to a luncheon in Knoxville."

"Let me see your badges, please."

We took off our badges, and he stared at them for a minute. "Now, Mrs. Stevens," he said, "you wouldn't have any of your husband's paperwork in the car with you—nothing of a confidential nature?"

"No, sir."

"No copies of the *Oak Ridge Journal*? Those are supposed to stay on site."

"No, sir. Feel free to have a look around my car if you like."

He handed back our badges. "That won't be necessary, ma'am. Drive safely."

As soon as the gate opened, Iris lit a cigarette. "Being questioned always makes me nervous." She smiled. "Even when I'm being questioned by a twelve-year-old playing soldier."

Our case of nerves seemed to fade once we were on the open road. Iris turned on the radio and hummed along with the Andrews Sisters. "God, I love to drive like this," she said. "Sometimes when I get behind the wheel on a pretty day with the radio playing, I feel like I don't want to stop—that I just want to keep on following the road to wherever it takes me. Don't worry, though. I'm not kidnapping you or anything."

"I'm not worried." But a little thrill shot through me. What if Iris really did just keep on driving? Where would we go? What adventures would we have? But even as I thought it, I knew it was silly. Neither of us could just drive away from our families who loved us.

Oak Ridge called itself a city, but it wasn't that big, and all its buildings had been slapped up over a short period of time, like a city a little kid would build out of blocks. Knoxville was a city with both size and history, and as Iris drove us down Gay Street, my stomach tied itself into strange knots of joy and fear.

"Have you ever been to the Tennessee Theatre?" Iris said as we passed the golden movie palace's lighted marquee.

"Uh-uh."

"Maybe we can make a matinee once the luncheon's over. It's beautiful in there, like a Faberge egg. Oh, the hotel's up here. See?"

The Wemberley was an elegant yellow brick building with carved stone lions' faces in the molding. "Lord, this is too fancy for me," I said, feeling sick. "I don't think I can do this."

Iris pulled the car into a parking space. "Don't be silly, Ruby," she said in the same firm voice she used to tell Baby Sharon to stop climbing the bookcase. "This is an opportunity for you, and I'll be damned if I'm going to let you miss it just because you're scared."

"But the ladies in there all have money and breeding and education, and here I am, wearing my only store-bought dress."

Iris looked straight at me. "And since that dress is Eleanor blue, I feel compelled to quote our dear former First Lady: 'No one can make you feel inferior without your consent.'"

There was no arguing with Eleanor, so I took a deep breath and got out of the car.

Grand is the only word I can think of to describe the lobby of the Wemberley Hotel. I had never seen a crystal chandelier except in the movies, and the one hanging over our heads was even more beautiful than in the movies because it was in full color. My eyes wandered from the chandelier to the bustling hotel workers in their gold-braided black uniforms and then down to the thick crimson carpet at my feet.

I don't know how long I stood there gaping before Iris said, "Isn't the luncheon in the Dogwood Room? We'd better go find it." She took my hand and led me away from the spot on the carpet where I'd been frozen. One woman in a fur stole stared at us, probably thinking Iris was my keeper instead of my friend.

All the tables in the Dogwood Room were covered with white tablecloths. In the center of each tablecloth was a bowl of daisies. A few ladies already sat at the table, but most of them were mingling, chattering and tittering amongst themselves. The younger ladies wore floral print dresses or light suits with little straw hats and white gloves. The older ladies, who tended to be a little broader across the beam, wore more somber colors but still with the obligatory white gloves. I've never understood why ladies feel the need to wear those silly white gloves when they go out. Are they afraid the sight of their naked fingers will drive men wild? Or do they just want to look like Mickey Mouse?

"We should look for your place card," Iris said, leading me to the tables and saving me from standing and staring once again. To my horror, Iris found my place card at what could only be called "the head table." It was right next to the podium where, I guessed, I'd have to accept my award. I pictured myself getting up from the table, knocking over my chair, and somehow pulling the tablecloth and sending all the plates and cups and silverware clattering to the floor.

"Would you like to sit, or would you like to mingle?" Iris asked.

I was so terrified it seemed like having to choose between being shot or hanged. "Um, sit, I guess."

We hadn't been sitting for a minute when a big woman with poodle-dog curls and little half-glasses came barreling over to us. She had on a gray suit with a jacket that seemed about ready to pop its buttons under the strain of holding back her enormous bosom. Something about her put me in mind of one of those tanks you see in newsreels.

"Ruby Pickett!" she gasped, clasping her hands together. You would've thought she was meeting Rita Hayworth.

"Yes, ma'am." My nerves made my voice small and squeaky.

"Ruby, I'm Mrs. Louella Dobson, the President of the East Tennessee chapter of the Society of American Clubwomen. Your essay was positively an inspiration to us, and we're delighted you could join us today."

"Thank you," I squeaked.

"And you must be Ruby's mother. I'm sure you're so proud."

In order to be my mother, Iris would've had to give birth to me at the age of eight. But if she was offended, she didn't show it. She beamed right back at Mrs. Dobson and said, "I am proud of Ruby, but I'm not her mother. I'm her friend, Iris Stevens."

"Well, we're glad you could join us, Mrs. Stevens. And now, if you'll excuse me, I must ask the hotel manager if he can do something about making the lighting in this room more of a glow and less of a glare." She marched off on her mission.

"She's a formidable specimen, isn't she?" Iris whispered. "I bet she's got a terrified little milquetoast of a husband at home—the kind with two words in his vocabulary: *yes* and *dear*."

Soon a bell was rung announcing the beginning of luncheon. Mrs. Dobson and a thin reed of a lady named Mrs. Crabtree sat across from Iris and me. Once everyone had found her place at a table, Mrs. Dobson stood and said, "And now Mrs. Betty Richards, wife of Reverend Harold Richards, will lead us in prayer."

Mrs. Richards, a soft-featured lady with pure white hair, stood and commanded, "Let us pray."

And boy, did Mrs. Richards pray! She prayed for the soul of President Roosevelt, for Eleanor in her time of grief, for President Truman in his new position as Commander-in-Chief. She prayed for our boys overseas and for a swift and victorious end to the war. Then she started praying for the poor and the sick and for some specific people by name. I opened my eyes and looked across the table at Mrs. Dobson and Mrs. Crabtree, their heads bowed and their eyes closed. Then I turned to Iris, who looked right back at me and winked, and I felt the excitement that comes with sharing a secret.

When a colored waiter set bowls of soup in front of us, I watched Iris to see which spoon she picked up and imitated her.

"This is mushroom consommé," Mrs. Dobson said, lifting her spoon. "We always have meatless luncheons to support the war effort."

"It's lovely," Iris said.

To me, it tasted like dirt soup.

"So," Mrs. Dobson said to me, "you live in Oak Ridge."

"Yes, ma'am," I said. "So does Iris."

"It must be a fascinating place—with all those people from all over the country and so much activity going on." She leaned forward, putting her gigantic bosom in striking distance of her soup bowl, and half-whispered, "We're all patriotic women here. You can tell me. What *do* they make there?"

Iris set down her spoon. "Well, I think the laborers make about seventy-five cents an hour. The higher ranking scientists and military men are on salary, though."

Mrs. Dobson's smile was less than pleasant. "That was very clever, Mrs. Stevens, but I think you know exactly what I'm asking you."

"Oh, I understand the question. I just don't know the answer," Iris said.

"Oh, really," Mrs. Crabtree broke in. "How can you live there and not know?"

"If the entire U.S. government is working to keep something secret, it's going to take somebody smarter than me to figure it out," Iris said.

"My daddy always tells my little sister they're making lights for lightning bugs," I said. "He says as far as he knows that could be the truth."

The soup bowls were taken away and replaced by what looked like domes of red Jell-O. I took a bite, expecting it to be either cherry or strawberry, but my mouth was shocked by a sour tang. My surprise must've shown because Iris leaned toward me and whispered, "Tomato aspic."

If this food was what ladies ate, then it was one more reason I didn't want to be a lady. The only positive thing I could say about the soup and aspic was that they didn't need to be chewed. I swallowed them like spoonfuls of medicine, and they slid right down.

The program after lunch consisted of Mrs. Dobson calling on different ladies to sing songs or talk about the club's community projects. Nearly an hour had passed by the time Mrs. Dobson got around to saying, "And now I am pleased to present the awards portion of our program."

I scooted back from the table in preparation for getting up (hopefully without taking the tablecloth with me), but Mrs. Dobson wasn't ready to give up the spotlight yet. She had to make the declaration that in These Trying Times, the Flame of Youth shone like a Beacon of Hope in the Darkness. Eventually, she got around to mentioning that in this case, I was the Flame.

I managed to get up without falling or knocking anything over, accept my certificate and my ten-dollar bond and choke out, "Thank you." Somehow the moment wasn't as exciting as I'd imagined it in my head.

I guess when people look forward to things and imagine what they'll be like they blow them up in their heads until what's in their imaginations is bigger and better than the thing itself could ever be. Maybe it's the unexpected things we don't have time to anticipate that bring the most pleasure. Like when Iris and I were walking out the hotel's front doors and she said, "I'm all for war rationing, but that consommé and aspic wouldn't have been enough to fill Sharon's little tummy. Why don't we go get some ice cream?"

We sat at the counter at the soda fountain, digging up spoonfuls of gooey chocolate sundae and laughing about how we were nothing like the ladies at the luncheon. Afterward, we sat in the Tennessee Theatre and watched the red and gold Wurlitzer organ rise onto the stage. I don't know if it was the award or the gilt and velvet beauty around me or Iris beside me, but the swelling music from the organ felt like it was coming from my own heart.

APRIL 25, 1945

It happened Monday night, but I've not been able to bring myself to write about it until now. At about eleven o'clock when we were all in bed, there was a knock on the door that sounded like somebody was fixing to kick it in. I heard Daddy get out of bed and the rustling of his clothes as he got dressed. Once he opened the door, I heard voices for a minute, and then Daddy hollered, "Ruby, it's for you!"

I didn't even think to put on clothes. I went to meet whoever it was barefoot and in my nightgown.

Standing in the doorway were Virgie and Aaron, their red hair shining like halos in the moonlight. Aaron's face was a blank mask, but Virgie's was blotchy and swollen. Something was bad wrong. "Y'all want to come in?" I said. "Everybody's in bed, so we'll have to whisper."

Virgie took a step into the house, then flung herself into my arms, sobbing. I held her and stroked her hair and said "Shh, shh" even though what I wanted to say was, "Tell me what in the Sam Hill is going on."

After her sobbing slowed down, Virgie slipped out of my arms and held both of my hands in hers. "We're leaving," she said. "But we couldn't go without saying goodbye."

I could barely catch my breath to speak. "Leaving? What do you mean?"

"Daddy got called in for questioning," Virgie said. "The army fellers that questioned him say he's been giving out all kinds of government secrets in his sermons—secrets that are a security threat. Daddy said he didn't have no secrets to tell, but they didn't believe him. They're kicking us out firs' thing tomorrow morning."

Now I was crying, too. "But what will you do? Where will you go?"

"Back to West Virginia, at least for now. Daddy's gonna look for work."

My hands were probably squeezing hers too hard. Maybe if I held tight enough, I wouldn't have to let go. "You'll...you'll write to me, won't you?"

"I'll write you, Ruby, but that don't mean you'll ever see the letters. You know how it is. This place ain't even on the map, so it's hard enough to get the mail here. And then the government opens up every letter that gets sent here. Do you really think they're gonna let a letter from somebody who got kicked out of this town get through?"

"Virgie, this ain't right. The government can't do this to you."

"Sure they can," Virgie said, wiping her eyes. "They can do anything they damn well please." She threw her arms around me. "I'm gonna miss you, Ruby."

"I'm gonna miss you, too." I choked. "You're a sister to me, Virgie."

"You're a sister to me, too."

We held each other for a minute, and when we pulled apart, I saw Aaron staring right at me. He stood facing me and took both my hands in his. "Ruby," he said, looking at me more directly than he'd ever looked at me, "I can't believe this dadblamed war is tearing us apart like this. But one day when all this is over, I'll come and find you."

Those two sentences were the most he'd ever said to me at one time, and before I could say anything back to him, he pulled me to him and kissed me, long and hard on the mouth, the way Rhett kissed Scarlett, the way Humphrey Bogart kissed Lauren Bacall.

It was my first kiss, and all I really felt was surprised— surprised because shy Aaron would do such a thing, surprised because while I'd known Virgie was living in a Hollywood-created fantasy, I'd had no idea that Aaron was a romantic hero in the movies in his own mind. I guess he was the strong, silent type.

"We'd better get back," Virgie said. "Mother and Daddy'll throw a fit if they find out we snuck off."

I couldn't make myself say goodbye, so I threw my arms around both of them, and we stood for a minute in a quiet, three-person hug. "I love y'all," I sobbed.

"I love you, too," Virgie said.

Aaron said, "I love you, Ruby," and I knew he meant it in a different way than I had. If I loved Virgie as a sister, then I loved Aaron as a brother, but as much as we were all hurting, I figured there was no harm in letting him interpret my words however he wanted to. Virgie was who my heart was breaking over, but during a war it's surely not a crime to let a boy think you're in love with him when the odds are you'll never see each other again.

APRIL 27, 1945

"I could say it's okay, but I know it's not," Iris said. "I hate when people try to comfort me by telling me everything's fine. If everything were fine, I wouldn't need comforting."

I sat on Iris's couch, dabbing at my eyes with the hanky she had given me. I had been running though the hankies even though I'd been trying my best to save my tears for private. Sometimes I couldn't help crying in public, though. Walking into English class yesterday and seeing a new girl—a stranger—sitting in the desk that had been Virgie's was more than I could stand. As I ran out of the room, Mr. Masters called my name, which made me think of the day I walked into the classroom to find that he had replaced Miss Connor. People I loved disappeared and were replaced as though they had never been there at all.

"I feel guilty for being so sad," I said to Iris. "I think about how many people have lost sons or brothers or husbands or boyfriends. And I think of the pictures coming out of Germany, of starved bodies in piles like garbage, and I think here I am, feeling sorry for myself when compared to so many people I've lost nothing."

Iris sat down next to me. "War tears people apart. Your losses, my losses, other people's losses, they're all an effect of the same cause." She took out a cigarette, studied it for a couple of seconds, then lit it. "I know what you mean, though, about feeling guilty. The way things are now with Warren and me— how we only seem to be able to make polite chit-chat with each other—that's because of the war, too. And because we live in this place, where the war is absolutely inescapable. But then I think, why am I so sad? Two of my girlfriends from college have lost husbands, so better I should be in a less-than-ideal marriage than be a war widow."

"I don't think Virgie's dad gave out any government secrets," I said. "I don't think he knew any to give out."

"He probably didn't," Iris said, exhaling smoke. "I know that loose lips sink ships, like all the signs around here say, and that the general attitude for the purpose of security here is that you can't be too careful. But maybe sometimes they are too careful. Or at least too suspicious. But that's another thing about war: innocent people get hurt."

She put her free arm around my shoulder, and I scooted closer to her, comforted by her warmth and her smell of smoke and perfume. "Iris," I heard myself saying.

"Hm?"

I wanted to say *don't ever leave me*, but I knew this was a promise she couldn't make. We were in a temporary place, after all, brought here by temporary circumstances that were way, way beyond our control. But maybe that's the way it always is with people, and when a person promises she'll never leave, it's just the same thing as when somebody says everything's okay even when it's really not: a lie meant to make somebody feel better.

"Nothing," I said. "I'm just glad you're here."

"I'm glad you're here, too," Iris said, her fingertips lightly brushing my cheek.

"Mama!" came a voice from the next room.

"Sounds like somebody's up from her nap," Iris said, stubbing out her cigarette and running to Baby Sharon's room.

When Iris came out Baby Sharon's fuzzy hair was sticking out funny, and her eyes were still droopy with sleep. When she saw me, her face opened up into a grin and she said "Bee!" and spread out her arms for me to hold her.

I got up and took her in my arms. She was still warm from her nap and I held her close, inhaling her sweet baby smell, holding her tiny fat feet, trying to memorize her babyness because I knew that it, like so many things in life, was too sweet to last.

MAY 1, 1945

April was a month of loss. Our country lost its leader, and I lost my friend. But yesterday, on the last day of April, there was a loss that might turn out to be a gain. We were in student assembly and had just finished saying the Pledge of Allegiance when the principal said, "Students, I have an important announcement which impacts the future of the war and the future of our country." He paused dramatically and pushed his glasses up on his nose. "It has just been announced on the radio that Adolph Hitler is dead."

You know that part in "The Wizard of Oz" when the Munchkins first see that Dorothy's house has squashed the Wicked Witch? It was just like that—everybody cheering and laughing and hugging. If everybody had burst into song, I wouldn't have been surprised.

After a few minutes of whooping and hollering, people started to talk. "However the old bastard died, it was too good for him," said a Kleen Teen in a letter sweater.

"I wonder if this means the war's gonna end so we can all go home," said a girl with poodle-curly hair.

"It ain't over yet," said a country boy in overalls. "Not while we've still got the Japs to deal with."

Even after we went back to our classes, the mood was giddy. I don't think anybody got much work done. The teachers seemed just as distracted as the students.

When I got to Iris's, she met me at the door holding Baby Sharon, who was wearing a frilly light pink dress. They were both all smiles.

"Baby Sharon, you look like a princess," I said, kissing her chubby cheek.

"It is a fancy dress, isn't it?" Iris said. "Her grandma sent it to her, and I thought she should get dressed up since it's a special occasion."

I figured surely Iris wasn't dressing up the baby because of Hitler being dead, so I said, "What's the occasion?"

"The occasion," Iris said, "is that Miss Sharon is one year old today. She's my May Day girl."

"Oh, I wish I'd known!" I said. "I would've brung her something."

"Oh, I don't think she's old enough to get the concept of birthday presents yet anyway," Iris said. "But we'd love it if you'd celebrate with us. With the hours Warren's been working lately, Sharon'll be asleep by the time he gets home."

"I'd love to help celebrate."

Iris set Sharon down on the floor, and she toddled toward a pile of wooden ABC blocks. "Well, it's a good day to celebrate, isn't it? The Führer kicked the bucket. The weather's lovely." She patted my shoulder. "But I'm sure you're still sad about Aaron."

I nodded. "And Virgie." I didn't know how to explain to Iris that I was sadder about Virgie than I was about Aaron. I wasn't sure I could even explain it to myself.

"Well, maybe a modest birthday party will distract you from your heartbreak. Eva's bringing a cake later. I bought the ingredients for it but asked her to bake it because I knew if I did, it would be a disaster. Oh"—she reached for some spools of colorful ribbon on the coffee table—"and I thought we could turn the pole from the clothesline into a Maypole."

I didn't know what a Maypole was, but I said okay.

Outside I helped Iris tie long pink and green and yellow ribbons to the clothesline pole while Baby Sharon played with the empty spools. Once all the ribbons were tied on, Iris clapped her hands and said, "Now we need music. Something light and airy. The Magic Flute, maybe?" She ran into the house and propped the door open, and after a couple of minutes, music filled the air. She picked up Baby Sharon and cuddled her. "We should be barefoot, I think."

She pulled off Sharon's white shoes and tiny socks, then stepped out of her own pumps.

I pulled off my socks and shoes and laughed. "Now what?"

"Now we dance."

Iris grabbed the end of the yellow ribbon and started skipping around the pole. After a minute she set Sharon down, handed her the pink ribbon and said, "Dance! Dance!"

Baby Sharon laughed and toddled around the pole with the ribbon in her hand.

"Ruby," Iris said in a mock stern tone. "You're not dancing."

"Oh, all right." I grabbed the blue ribbon and skipped around the pole. It was the first time I'd skipped since I was eight years old. "I feel like I fool," I said, laughing.

"Me, too." Iris's grin was huge. "Isn't it the best feeling in the world?"

I did feel good. How could I not, hearing Baby Sharon giggle, seeing Iris's honey blonde hair flying out wild behind her, hearing Mozart's music, and feeling the soft cool grass between my toes? Sometimes people need to stop thinking and just feel.

We danced and laughed until the music stopped. Then Iris went in and turned the record over, and when we came back, we danced and laughed some more.

"What is this—some kind of heathen ritual?"

I turned around to see Mrs. Lynch, in a prim little flowered hat and white gloves, holding a pink-frosted birthday cake on a tray. Her little blonde daughter Helen was clinging to her skirt.

"No, just a birthday party," Iris said. "The cake is beautiful. Thank you so much." She leaned down to make eye contact with Helen. "Helen, would you like to dance with us?"

"Can I, Mommy?" Helen asked, tugging on her mother's hem.

"It's 'may I,' not 'can I.' And yes, you may. But just for a few minutes. And keep your shoes on. I don't want you catching cold."

Helen grabbed a free ribbon and started running like she was fleeing Japanese gunfire. It was too bad her mother had made her keep her shoes on because it meant it hurt more when she stepped on my bare foot. "Careful now," I said. "Don't go stomping around too much. Baby Sharon's littler than you."

"I'll just go in and set this cake on the table," Mrs. Lynch said, completely ignoring the fact that her daughter had just broken several bones in my foot.

"Somehow I'm not surprised she chose not to skip around the Maypole with us," Iris whispered once Eva was out of earshot.

"Me neither," I said. "I can't imagine her skipping, not even as a little girl."

"I can't imagine Eva as a little girl, period," Iris said. "I think she was born a lady."

After it became clear that Helen was going to clobber Baby Sharon if we kept up the Maypole dance, we went inside for cake. When we sang happy birthday, Baby Sharon clapped her hands over her ears like the "hear no evil" monkey. Once her piece of cake was set in front of her she slammed both of her fists into it. She lifted a pink frosted fist to her mouth and sucked it.

"What a mess she's making, Iris!" Eva fussed. "Aren't you going to at least make her use a spoon?"

"It's her cake," Iris said. "She should be able to eat it however she likes. And afterward I can always give her a bath."

"Or you could have Ruby give her a bath," Mrs. Lynch said. "That's the kind of thing you pay her for, isn't it?" She set the plate in front of Helen and put a spoon in her hand. "Show Sharon how to eat like a big girl," she said.

When Iris handed me my cake, she cut her eyes toward Mrs. Lynch, then winked at me.

Baby Sharon got more cake on her than in her. Iris had to wipe her hands with a wet washcloth before letting her at her birthday present. Sharon tore into the red tissue paper to find a new teddy bear, then tossed the bear aside to play with the paper.

Iris laughed. "Well, clearly I could've saved some money and just bought the paper. More coffee, Eva?"

"That would be lovely," she said. "Maybe Ruby could get it for us."

Before Iris could protest, I said, "My pleasure," and went to the kitchen for the pot. After I poured, I said, "You know I think I will go run Baby Sharon a bath, Iris. If you don't, your whole living room is gonna be frosted pink."

There's nothing sweeter than giving a baby a bath. Baby Sharon sat up in her little pink tub, looking like one of those baby angels from old paintings. She smacked her hands down in the water over and over again, laughing harder each time she did it. "Who's a splashy girl?" I said, slinging a little water at her round little belly.

"Pash!" she said, sending a big wave to hit me right in the face.

When Iris came into the bathroom, she said, "There's my birthday girl in her birthday suit!" And she looked at me and said, "They're gone. Thank God. I've been dying for a cigarette." She sat on the lid of the toilet like it was a living room chair, sighed, and lit up. "I'm sorry about the way Eva acts toward you…like you're Cinderella and she's your wicked stepmother."

I laughed. "Well, there's no need for you to be sorry about it." I used the washcloth to clean some pink frosting out of Sharon's ear. "Besides, she doesn't bother me one iota. She's not better than me just because she thinks she is."

"You're absolutely right," Iris said. "And if somebody asked me who I'd rather pass the time of day with—you or Eva Lynch—well, let's just say the decision wouldn't be in Eva's favor." She reached over to ash her cigarette in the bathroom sink. "Maybe that's why she acts like she does around you. She's jealous."

I rubbed shampoo into Baby Sharon's thin, fine hair. "Now why in the Sam Hill would somebody like Eva Lynch be jealous of somebody like me?"

"Because," Iris said, "she knows that no matter what she says or does, she'll never be as close a friend to me as you are."

My face must have been as pink as Baby Sharon's when it was covered in cake frosting.

MAY 4, 1945

As soon as I sat down in English class, Mr. Masters said, "Oh, lest I forget, Miss Pickett, I have a piece of mail to deliver to you."

At first I wondered less about what the mail was than I did about the fact that Mr. Masters was the kind of person who could use "lest" in the course of normal conversation. But when I looked down at the envelope I saw the return address was from the Society of American Clubwomen. My hands shook as I tore it open.

I swallowed hard and looked down at the creamy white paper:

Dear Miss Pickett:

Congratulations! Your essay "A Spirit of Sacrifice" has been judged as the second-place winner in the state division of the "What America Means to Me" essay contest. While the second-place prize does not qualify your essay to compete at the national level, it does earn you an invitation to attend the state awards banquet at the Capital Hotel in Nashville on Saturday, September 1, at 6:00 p.m.

Also, through our association with the Tennessee Teachers' College for Women, we are pleased to offer our first- and second-prize winners an exciting opportunity. Tennessee Teachers' College for Women is prepared to offer a full scholarship to each of our winners upon her graduation from high school. While you are under no obligation to accept this scholarship, it is a generous offer, and we do hope you will consider it.

Please accept my most sincere congratulations on behalf of the Tennessee division of the Society of American Clubwomen. Young women such as yourself are the keepers of the flame of American liberty.

Sincerely yours,

Mrs. Alice Nicholas,

President, Tennessee Division,

Society of American Clubwomen

The first thing I did after I read the letter was look over to Virgie's desk. But then I remembered it wasn't Virgie's desk anymore.

"Well, Miss Pickett? What does it say?"

I hadn't realized that Mr. Masters had been waiting while I read. I looked up at him. "I…I won second prize in the state contest. The Tennessee Teachers' College for Women is giving me a full scholarship."

Mr. Masters flashed a small, rare smile. "Well done, Miss Pickett. I imagine that Tennessee Teachers' College isn't exactly Smith or Wellesley. But if they can beat that infernal Appalachian accent out of you, you should make a fine teacher."

It was the closest he had ever come to being warm. "Thank you, sir."

Mr. Masters started writing notes on the board about our term paper, and I copied them down without really thinking about what he said. It was hard enough to stay in my seat, let alone focus on Mr. Masters' droning voice. My heart was beating its wings in my chest, and my feet were dancing under my desk because ever since I was ten years old I'd been saying the phrase "if I go to college." And now that "if" was a "when."

Since today is Friday, I didn't have to go to Iris's to work, but I stopped there after school anyway to show her the letter. I wanted her to be the first to see it because I knew she'd understand what it meant.

She stood in the doorway, reading, and as soon as she looked up, she threw her arms around me. "Oh, Ruby, this is marvelous! I'm so proud of you!" She pulled away from the hug and looked at me, smiling. "I had pictured you walking the halls of Vassar instead of"—she looked back down at the letter—"the Tennessee Teachers' College for Women, but a full scholarship to anywhere is an honor. And who knows? After you finish your two-year degree from the teachers' college, maybe you could go on to pursue your bachelor's somewhere more prestigious." She clapped her hands. "Oh, Ruby, this is so exciting. The world is your oyster." She crinkled her nose. "Though I've never really understood that saying—maybe because I've never really liked oysters."

"I think it's because of the pearls," I said.

"I guess so. Well, speaking of Pearl—and your other jewel-named sisters—have you told your family the big news yet?"

"Not yet. I wanted to tell you first."

"Oh, Ruby, that's so sweet." She reached out and patted my cheek. "And I'm sure your family will be just as proud of you as I am."

I kept the letter to myself once I got home. I lay across my bed and read it till I had it memorized. I held it to my nose and smelled the paper and the ink. I studied every loop and dot in Mrs. Alice Nicholas's signature.

I let myself dream about the Tennessee Teachers' College for Women. I imagined brick buildings and green lawns and neat young women in sweaters and skirts clutching their books to their chests. It dawned on me that I didn't even know where the Tennessee Teachers' College was. Was it in a big city or a small town? It didn't matter. I was going there.

When Mama hollered that it was time for supper, I brought my letter to the table. After Daddy said the blessing, I handed him the letter. He held it up and read it silently, his lips moving. "Well, what do you know," he said, handing the letter to Mama.

She read it, too. "Well, that's good, I reckon," she said, real calm, handing the letter back to me.

"What is it?" Baby Pearl asked.

"It's a letter saying I won second prize in the state essay contest," I said. "And they're offering me money to go to the state teachers' college."

"How come they just give you second prize instead of first?" Opal said.

"I don't know," I said, adding some chow-chow to my bowl of beans. "But second prize in the whole school's still pretty good."

"So," Mama said, crumbling her cornbread, "this here scholarship means that if you was to go off to teachers' college your daddy wouldn't have to pay a penny for it?"

"That's right," I said.

"So you want to be a schoolteacher?" Garnet said, like I'd just announced I wanted to be a murderer.

"I think I might," I said.

Of course, what I really want to be is a writer, but I figure I could write and teach school, too. It worked for Jesse Stuart. Also, thanks to Miss Connor, I knew what a difference a good teacher could make in a kid's life. I wouldn't mind being able to do that for some kid.

"Shoot, if Ruby ends up being a schoolteacher, she'll be an old maid for sure," Opal giggled.

"Well, I reckon that'll be all right as long as the rest of you girls has plenty of grandbabies for me," Daddy said.

When my family looked at me, I was sure they saw a thin-lipped middle-aged woman with weak eyes and thick glasses, a cameo brooch pinned in the center of her high collar—the spinster aunt to her sisters' dozen dimpled babies.

I took the letter back, and now it's in this journal for safekeeping. I know it is a ticket to a world that's very different than my family's, and this knowledge makes me happy and sad and scared all at the same time.

MAY 8, 1945

In the middle of biology, the principal's voice came over the public address system: "A special assembly has been called. All students proceed to the auditorium in an orderly fashion."

We were all at our lab stations about to cut into a cow's eyeball, which wasn't exactly something I'd been looking forward to. Our teacher seemed a little flustered by the interruption but said, "Well, you heard the man. Drop your instruments and form a line. We're going to the auditorium."

The line was orderly, but there was lots of whispering.

"I wonder what this is about."

"They've never called a special assembly before."

"I hope nothing bad's happened overseas."

Once we were in the auditorium the whispering turned into a buzz as everybody wondered out loud what was going on. You could feel the anxiety zinging through the air like currents along an electrical wire. Everybody knew something was going on and feared that whatever it was might not be good.

Principal Davis, a man in his mid-fifties, his hair cut in the super-short style of the former military man he was, strode across the stage and took his place behind the podium. "May I have your attention, please?" he said.

Usually, he had to ask at least a couple of times before he really got all the kids' attention. This time, though, he had it.

"Thirty minutes ago," Principal Davis said, "President Truman announced that the forces of Germany have surrendered to the United Nations. We have achieved victory in Europe."

A cheer rose from the auditorium in a giant wave. I was sitting between two girls who normally wouldn't have given me the time of day, but we hugged each other like sisters.

Principal Davis let us carry on like that for a couple of minutes, but then he waved his hands to signal that it was time for the whooping and hollering to end. It took several minutes for that to happen, though.

Once it had quieted down some, a boy in the front row hollered, "So does this mean we can leave this godforsaken place now and go home?"

"Absolutely not," Principal Davis said. "As our President said this morning, 'our victory is only half-won.' Germany has surrendered, but the war in the Pacific rages on. Only when the last Japanese division has surrendered will the war truly be over." He leaned closer into the microphone. "And that is why, despite the gladness in our hearts, this will not be a day spent in parties and celebration. It will be a day spent working with increased fervor and dedication. As our president has said, the watchword for the months ahead of is 'work, work, and more work.'

"So just as your parents are working even harder to end the war, you must work even harder in school to ensure that here on the homefront we have plenty of young people who are strong in mind and body. And in that spirit, I will ask you to stand and join me in singing the National Anthem, after which you will return in an orderly fashion to your classrooms."

Usually the National Anthem is just something I move my lips along to without thinking about it, in part because I can't hit the notes and in part because the words are kind of hard to understand. But today I sang it and really thought about it, and I got kind of choked up when I got to the part about "the land of the free and the home of the brave" because I thought about all the brave people, some living and some dead, who were brave so that people could be free.

On the way back to class, I heard two country boys talking.

"Well, whatever they're making here it's got to do with whipping the Japs instead of the Krauts."

"I think it's a boat—a boat they'll send to Japan full of soldiers to whup 'em."

A blonde girl in a sweater and skirt walked right between the two boys and said, "You know, you're not even supposed to try to guess what's being made here. It's unpatriotic."

I don't think the boys meant to be unpatriotic, though. They were just curious, which everybody here is whether they admit it or not.

Iris admits it. When I came over to watch Baby Sharon, Iris's eyes shone as she sat down with me on the couch. "Isn't it exciting about the Germans surrendering?" she said. "I mean, I know we're not supposed to be dancing in the streets yet, but I certainly feel like it." She hugged her knees to her chest, looking like a little girl. "Also, this is interesting because it implies that whatever they're working on here must be about Japan rather than Germany."

"I heard somebody else talking about that today, just not so intelligently."

"It feels like a piece of the puzzle, you know? Not that Warren or anybody else is going to show me any of the other pieces. It's strange being here just as a wife...here, but I'm not a part of things."

"It's the same being here as a kid."

"I would think so. Since your dad's in construction, though, he probably doesn't know much more about what's going on here than you do. But Warren has to know a lot. He has this whole other life completely separate from me—a life I don't know the least thing about." She took out a cigarette and lit it. "Of course, this is probably nothing new. I guess wives and children have always been kept in the dark during times of war." She blew out a cloud of smoke. "I suppose our job right now is just to smile and be happy the war's half-won."

MAY 12, 1945

Yesterday Iris asked me if I could come over after school and stay late enough to put Baby Sharon to bed so she and Warren could celebrate their four-year wedding anniversary. She had a special dinner planned for the two of them and wanted me to look after Sharon while she got everything ready. She answered the door wearing a pink chenille bathrobe that matched the pink curlers in her hair. Her face was covered in some kind of white goo.

"Did somebody give you the old pie in the face?" I said.

She laughed. "It's a beauty treatment that Eva recommended. It's got egg white and cucumber in it, and it allegedly will give me a glowing complexion. Unfortunately, the sight of Mommy with stuff all over her face terrifies Sharon. She's hiding from me in her room."

"Well, I reckon I can go play with her while you get gussied up."

"Bee!" Baby Sharon said a soon as she saw me. She was putting her alphabet blocks one by one very carefully into their wooden box. I knew that once she'd filled the box, she'd dump all the blocks back on the floor and laugh hysterically. She can entertain herself playing "Fill and Spill" for hours.

"Bee help," she said, pressing a block into my hand.

I put a block into the box, and so did she. Her face was as serious as a little undertaker's. That was how the game always worked. She'd be all solemn as she filled the box, treating it like a Very Important Job, but when spilling time came, she'd collapse into giggles.

A few minutes later, Iris stood in the bedroom doorway, still in curlers but with the baby-scaring goo washed off her face. "Are we okay in here?" she asked.

"Yep, just filling and spilling," I said.

"Well, I guess I'll go start dinner then. I saved up enough ration cards for meat to make beef stroganoff. It's Warren's favorite—probably because it's one of the few things I can make competently."

By 5:30, when I put Sharon in her high chair to eat her peas and carrots and zwieback, Iris announced that all the stroganoff needed to do was simmer, so she figured she'd go change and fix her hair and face.

After Sharon ate her peas and carrots and then some rice pudding, a lot of which she smeared on her face to look like her mommy's beauty treatment, I put her in the tub and let her splash around until she started yawning. By seven she was asleep in her crib, cuddling her teddy bear.

When I walked out into the living room, Iris was sitting on the couch, smoking a cigarette. Her honey-colored hair fell in soft curls around her face, and her lips were very red. She had on a black dress, high heels and stockings, and her string of real pearls. She looked beautiful, and I told her so before I thought to stop myself.

"Thanks," she said, rolling her eyes like she didn't believe me for a minute. She patted the spot on the couch beside her. "Why don't you sit down and keep me company till Warren gets home?"

"Okay." When I sat beside her, I could smell her flowery perfume.

"I wasn't expecting him till at least seven." Her legs were crossed, and she was shaking her foot. "His days at work just get longer and longer. I worry that Sharon will forget she has a daddy. Sometimes I feel like the U.S. government is the Other Woman in Warren's and my marriage, though I don't suppose that's a very patriotic thought."

"Any wife would feel the same way."

We changed the subject to what we'd been reading. She had just finished *The Human Comedy* and liked it even though it was a little sentimental for her taste. I'd been reading *Pride and Prejudice* because I was writing my term paper on Jane Austen.

"Mr. Darcy," Iris said. "What is it about those silent, taciturn types? We fall in love with them, and then we get all frustrated because they won't talk to us. Aaron was like that, wasn't he? A Mr. Darcy type?"

It was such a ridiculous comparison I had to laugh. "Mr. Darcy in overalls."

After we'd been talking half an hour or so, the phone rang. Iris excused herself to answer it in the kitchen, and I heard her say "I understand" and "No, no, it's all right" and "I love you, too."

When she came back into the living room, she was rubbing her fingers under her eyes. "Warren," she said, with a break in her voice. "Apparently something terribly important's happening at the lab. He couldn't say what, of course, but he won't be able to get away any earlier than nine."

"Oh, Iris, I'm so sorry."

"It's okay. It's to be expected." She sank back down on the couch and slipped her feet out of her dressy shoes. "He was nice about it. He said he'll make it up to me, and I know he'll try to." She wiped her eyes. "I know what he's doing is much more important than a silly little anniversary dinner."

I took her hand. "It's not silly to want to be with your husband on your anniversary."

We sat there for a couple of minutes, holding hands, until Iris said, "Ruby, will you stay and have dinner with me? There'll be plenty left for Warren when he gets home."

"Well, I did tell Mother and Daddy I'd be here till late, so I reckon it's all right."

She dried her eyes. "Good. I really don't want to be alone tonight. But please don't think I'm just using you as a fall-back plan because Warren's not here. I really do love your company."

I couldn't meet her eyes, but I muttered, "I love your company, too."

"Well, then," Iris said. "Let's eat."

She kept the lights off in the dining room but lit the two long white candles she'd arranged on the table. "I figure we might as well make this a celebration," she said. "I mean, friendship's worth celebrating, right?"

I nodded.

"And I've got two bottles of champagne in the refrigerator thanks to placing a special order with the local bootlegger. Maybe we'll open one bottle now, and I'll save the other one for when Warren comes home."

"I don't know. I've never drunk before."

"Oh, you can have just one glass. It won't be enough to make you tipsy."

She took a beautiful green bottle trimmed with gold foil out of the refrigerator and then handed me two long-stemmed goblets. "Now you hold these while I open the bottle."

When the cork popped, I screamed. "Was that supposed to happen?" I asked, once I'd caught my breath.

Iris laughed. "Isn't that how it happens in the movies?" The foaming liquid spilled into the two glasses.

"It's not that loud in the movies."

She grabbed a dishtowel and dabbed where the sticky foam had slopped onto my hands. "It's not this messy in the movies either." She took one of the glasses and clinked it against the one in my hand. "Well…cheers. Happy anniversary to me."

She drank, but I stopped lifting my glass when it was halfway to my lips. "I probably ought not to drink this. I'm just sixteen."

Iris rolled her eyes. "Americans have such Puritanical ideas about alcohol. If you were European, you would've been given a small glass of wine on holidays when you were just a child.

In America we make booze into something that's secret and forbidden until adulthood. No wonder so many Americans drink too much. If something's forbidden and secret, that just makes it more tempting." She patted my arm. "Ruby, you don't have to drink it if you don't want to. But one glass of champagne isn't going to get you drunk."

"Well, I reckon I might as well try it." It was fizzier than Coke with a taste that was sweet and fruity and rotten at the same time, like preserves that were just about to turn. "Not bad," I said. "Kind of queer, but not bad."

Iris smiled. "Why don't you sit down, and I'll serve the stroganoff."

We sat across from each other at the candlelit table. "This is real good," I said after my first forkful.

"Our family cook showed me how to make it when I was a girl. That's probably why it's one of the few things I can cook properly."

She said "our family cook" so casually, like everybody had one. "You were talking about Europe a minute ago," I said. "Have you ever been there?"

She sipped her champagne. "After my second year of college, I took a wild hair and decided I was going to spend a year in Paris. My parents told me they'd pay for me to get there, but after that I was on my own. I got a student work permit, and because my French was pretty good, I got a job waiting tables in a seedy café. When I wasn't working, I just walked through the city, looking, looking, looking at everything that interested me. And everything did interest me, really. I lived in a filthy, one-room apartment with two other girls. It was on the fourth floor of a dilapidated building, and the stairs were rickety. But it didn't matter. We only went there to sleep, and none of us did much sleeping in those days." She refilled her glass. "In a lot of ways, that was the happiest year of my life. I was so completely and utterly free." She reached across the table and touched my arm. "I hope you'll have an opportunity like that, Ruby—to have a stretch of time when the only person you have to please is yourself."

"I can't imagine what that would be like," I said. "I don't think anybody in my family's ever been free like that. I guess we've always been too poor to be free."

"It's not fair, is it? I was just lucky to be born into a family with some money. But I do feel guilty about all the advantages I've had."

"Shoot, that's nothing to feel guilty about. You didn't get to pick what family you were born into. And even if you did, nobody would blame you for picking a rich one over a poor one."

"I guess you're right." Iris pushed her plate away. She seemed more interested in the champagne than the food. "After my year in Europe, once I started back to school, I felt like I was so much more sophisticated than all the college kids around me. And that's why I set my cap for Warren."

"You got him."

"And he got me," she said, but her tone wasn't all the way happy. "I bought a cake at a bakery in Knoxville. Would you like a slice?"

"Maybe you'd better wait to cut it till Warren gets home."

"He won't care. He has no sense of ceremony." She refilled her champagne glass before she got up from the table. "Why don't we have dessert in the living room? I like to eat cake with my feet up."

Once we were in the living room, Iris set her cake plate on the coffee table and walked over to the record player. "Let's have some music," she said. "Something soft that won't wake the baby."

The song was soft and swoony with lots of strings. We didn't say much for a while, just sat on the couch, enjoying the cake and the music.

After a while, she said, "Do you remember when I taught you how to dance?"

"Of course."

She drank the rest of the champagne in her glass in a few quick swallows. "Will you dance with me?"

I felt a little shiver. "Okay."

She stood up and opened her arms to me. I put one arm around her shoulder and took her hand. "Box step," she said.

I stepped with her, but somehow it felt different than when she was teaching me. This time, I wasn't thinking about the steps. I was feeling the music, and the movement came naturally. I was feeling her nearness, too. In her stocking feet, she wasn't much taller than me. Her hand was pressed against the small of my back, and she was so close that sometimes her breasts brushed against mine. She took a baby step closer, so we were in a sort of loose hug, and pressed her cheek against mine. Her skin was soft, her perfume sweet. Heaven.

"This reminds me of boarding school," she whispered, her cheek still against mine. "We'd have dances where we girls would dance together. Once a semester there'd be a mixer where the boys from another school would be invited, and most of the girls really looked forward to that. But I liked the all-girls dances best. Girls dance better than boys."

"You dance better than Aaron."

"This one girl, Miriam, was always my favorite dance partner. We were very close. She was a lot like you. Wise beyond her years. And of course, she was the age then that you are now."

"What happened to her?"

She sighed. I could feel her breath in my ear. "I don't know. We lose so many people in our lives. All we can do is hold on to who we have as best we can." She slipped out of my arms and looked right into my eyes. "I'm glad I have you, Ruby."

And then she was leaning toward me, her eyes closed, and just for a moment, her lips touched mine. My heart inflated like a balloon, and I felt other feelings, too—physical feelings I liked but wasn't used to.

Iris smiled, a little shyly. "I'm afraid I'm a little drunk. Maybe we'd better sit down."

We sat on the couch, and she rested her head on my shoulder. "I used to be able to drink and dance all night. But now give me two glasses of champagne, and I'm ready to pass out. I blame motherhood. It wears a girl out."

"I'm sure it does."

I stroked her hair, and she snuggled closer and said, "Mm."

We must've dozed off that way because the next thing I heard was the sound of a door opening. I opened my eyes to see Warren. Iris's head was still resting on my shoulder, and I jumped, startled.

"I didn't mean to frighten you, Ruby," Warren said. His eyes looked strained and tired. "I guess you ended up taking care of both my girls tonight."

Iris stirred. "Wha—?"

"Happy anniversary," Warren said. "I'm sorry I'm so late. Are you alert enough to drive Ruby home?"

"Yes, I can do it," Iris said, sitting up and stretching. "I think I've slept off my champagne. I know how much you hate to drive at night, and you've had to do it a lot lately with these hours Uncle Sam is making you keep."

After Iris got her purse and car keys, I said, "Good night, Mr. Stevens, and happy anniversary."

"Thank you, Ruby. And thank you for all you do to help out around here."

I don't think he could've said anything to make me feel more guilty. I don't suppose I had done anything wrong, exactly, and clearly Warren didn't think a thing about finding his wife asleep with her head on my shoulder. But how would he feel if he knew his wife had kissed me on their wedding anniversary?

Iris and I rode in silence all the way to my house. When she parked the car, I said, "Iris, I know you were kind of drunk, but do you remember everything from…earlier?"

I was relieved when she smiled. "I remember," she said, "and it's already a beautiful memory. You are lovely." She took my hand, and we sat there for a minute, hands clasped.

I think I'm starting to understand something about myself, and I'm scared of what it might mean. I feel about Iris the way I'm supposed to feel about Aaron. But I know better than to tell anybody. It's just one more thing about me that nobody would understand.

MAY 18, 1945

I haven't looked at this diary for nearly a week because all my time has been spent studying for tests and finishing my Jane Austen paper. But school is out now, and I ended the year with a straight-A average.

At first I was a little sad about getting out of school, but now I couldn't be happier.

After Iris and Warren's anniversary, I was nervous about seeing Iris again. I was afraid she'd be embarrassed about the kiss, about falling asleep with her head on my shoulder, about how close we were that night. But when I went to her house on Tuesday, she seemed to have no trouble looking me in the eye, and she talked to me like she always did, telling me that as soon as my schoolwork was done, I had to go to the library and check out this book by Dawn Powell called *My Home Is Far Away*.

And then on Thursday afternoon, Iris asked me to have a cup of tea and told me she had a proposition for me. "I was thinking," she said, sitting on the other end of the couch from me. Sharon sat between us, holding a cookie in each fist. "You're about to be out of school, which means you'll have some extra time on your hands. Might you like to help me out a few more hours a week during the summer? I talked to Warren about it, and he thought maybe you could come in for three hours a day on Monday through Friday."

"That's fifteen hours a week. Are you sure he's okay with paying me that much?" I didn't say I would be more than happy to spend fifteen hours a week with her for free.

"He's fine with it. He and I were talking about how you'll be going to college after this year and how nice it would be for you to be able to save a little money for living expenses."

"Thank you so much." I leaned over and hugged Iris, sandwiching Baby Sharon between us, who laughed and spat half-chewed cookie on my blouse. We hugged for a long time, tickling Sharon between us and joking about making a Sharon and jelly sandwich.

When we came out of the hug, Iris said, "It's me who should be thanking you. I'm always happy when you're here. On the days you don't come over, I spend too much time brooding. Sometimes I get downright obsessed with what Warren's doing all day, what this place is really about. I guess that's my nosy journalistic background. Oh, I'll try to amuse myself visiting with Eva and Hannah, but with them I always have to put on my best lady manners. With you, I'm just me." She smiled. "Of course, Warren thinks I want you around to help with Sharon and housekeeping. But mostly I want your company."

"Well, you can pay me for helping with Sharon and the housekeeping, but my company's free."

Neither of us said anything about the kiss. Probably I was the only one who thought about it after it happened. Sometimes in the movies I'd go see with Virgie, actors in tuxedoes and evening gowns would kiss each other as a greeting—a little peck to say hello or goodbye—no more serious than a handshake. Iris's kiss had probably been that kind of kiss—the kind that sophisticated people don't even think about—and the fact that I had thought about it a lot just went to show how unsophisticated and silly I was.

So I've decided to try not to think about the kiss. And what I'll think of instead is her saying, "I want your company." I want her company, too, and we're both going to get what we want. Plus, I get to earn some money to help out my family and some to save for myself. I do love school, and at first I was nervous at the thought of three months without it. But now I love the thought of these three months unfurling in front of me, as bright and colorful as a ribbon streaming from a Maypole.

MAY 30, 1945

I should be writing more. Samuel Pepys never laid down on the job. But the past week and a half I haven't even felt like myself because I've been so happy it feels like my life must surely belong to somebody else.

Mornings are nothing special. I help Mama with the washing or the dishes or the sweeping up and half-listen to my sisters giggle about one thing or another. But the whole time my body is in the house, my mind is elsewhere, anticipating the afternoon I'll spend with Iris.

Most afternoons we take Sharon to the playground. She likes to toddle around, examining the playground equipment and the bigger kids like she's a scientist doing research. And then she'll settle down in the sandbox, often with another little kid or two, and Iris and I will spread a blanket on the ground, stretch out, and read. There's something special about reading beside Iris. All my life I've been the only reader I know—the solitary girl whose parents and sister shake their heads in disbelief. To have somebody lying on a blanket beside me who's just as absorbed in her book as I am is a pleasure.

Some afternoons we stay home, and I help straighten the house while she fumbles around in the kitchen trying to fix something for supper and Sharon bangs on pots and pans. We listen to records and talk and laugh, and on these days I like to pretend that Iris's house is really her house and mine and that we live together and her and me and Sharon are a family, even though I know such things are not possible.

Yesterday Iris took a notion she wanted to play tennis and she wanted to teach me how. She loaned me this little white dress that made me look downright silly, and we put Baby Sharon in her stroller and walked down to the tennis courts, with me laughing and saying, "I ain't got an athletic bone in my body."

"Sure you do," Iris said. "You just haven't found it yet."

We parked Sharon's stroller by the fence on the edge of the tennis court, so she could see us and we could see her, but there was no danger of her getting hit by a flying ball.

"Okay," Iris said once we were on the court. "I want you to get on this side of the net. I'm going to hit some balls to you, and I want you to hit them back to me."

"Don't get your hopes up," I said.

Iris's little white tennis dress made her look pretty and graceful in a way mine did not. It was strange, too, to see her showing so much leg, but her legs, even in tennis shoes, were worth showing.

A ball whizzed by my head.

"Don't watch me. Watch the ball," Iris said, laughing.

"Okay. Sorry."

I watched the balls. I watched them sail past me as I swung my racket too soon or too late or too high or too low. Finally, when I was about to decide I was a lost cause, I hit one. Not hard enough to send it over the net, but I did hit it.

"Yay! You got one!" Iris jumped up and down like a cheerleader. "Look out, Bobby Riggs!"

Baby Sharon, I noticed, had fallen asleep in her stroller. Apparently, tennis, as played by me, wasn't a very exciting spectator sport.

Finally I got so I could hit about half the balls Iris served to me, but not with any aim or force. They went every which way but stayed on my side of the net.

I had just missed a ball that swiped my ear when I heard a voice say, "Iris?"

It was Eva Lynch. Hannah was standing beside her. Both of them were wearing white tennis dresses and had their hair tied up in scarves.

"Oh, hi," Iris said.

Mrs. Lynch looked over at me and then back at Iris. "Is playing tennis one of Ruby's responsibilities as a babysitter?"

Iris smiled, but it wasn't a real smile. I could tell. "I'm giving her lessons in exchange for her doing some extra work around the house. Before long she and I will be ready to play doubles with you and Hannah."

"Oh, I'm sure one of the wives in our neighborhood could play with us," Mrs. Lynch said. "Really, one should play with people one's own age."

"Hm," Iris said. "I never thought age was a particularly important factor in choosing the people I spend time with."

Mrs. Lynch smiled. "Well, I suppose it isn't for you. Or for your husband either, given the number of years between you." She flashed a syrupy sweet smile. "Have a lovely afternoon, Iris."

"You, too," Iris said, but she rolled her eyes at me once Mrs. Lynch's back was turned. "Well," she said, once they were out of earshot, "since I insist on playing with children such as yourself, can I buy you an ice cream?"

"You don't have to buy it for me. I can buy my own."

"No, I've got it. I feel like you should have something sweet after putting up with all the bile Eva just spewed. The funny thing is, despite your chronological age, you're much more of an adult than she is."

At the soda fountain Iris ordered a dish of vanilla for Sharon and a big chocolate soda with two straws for her and me to share. We watched Sharon paint herself with ice cream and took turns sipping through our straws. Once we both bent to drink at the same time, and our faces were almost touching, our lips puckered over our straws. We laughed and blushed and looked at Baby Sharon instead of each other.

I don't know how to explain things except to say I'm happier when I'm with her than I've ever been, and when I'm not with her, I think about being with her. And maybe it's just silliness or wishful thinking, but I'm starting to wonder if maybe she feels the same way about me.

JUNE 4, 1945

Today when Iris answered the door, she put her finger over her lips in a "shh" gesture. I followed her into the living room, where she pointed in the direction of the couch. Baby Sharon was lying on it in that special kind of deep sleep that belongs only to babies. "I'm afraid she'll wake up if I move her," Iris whispered, arranging cushions to protect Sharon from rolling off the couch. "Come keep me company while I smoke a cigarette."

I followed her into the bedroom, a room I hadn't been in before. She sat on the bed, propped up on a pillow, stretched out her legs, and lit a cigarette. I looked around for someplace to sit, but the only chair was at the desk which must be Warren's. "You can sit here," she said, patting the space beside her.

I sat, but I didn't stretch out like she did. Even though I was on a bed, I was sitting as straight and proper as if I was at my desk at school.

"I'm glad Sharon ended up napping early," Iris said, tapping her cigarette against the glass ashtray on the nightstand. "I've been wanting to talk to you about something, but now that I'm about to do it, I'm a nervous wreck."

"Don't be nervous. It's just me." But I was nervous, too.

Iris turned over so that she was facing me. "I know. And you're the one person in my life I can talk to." She took a puff from her cigarette and exhaled with a sigh. "Ruby, do you remember that night when we were dancing and I told you about how I used to dance with Miriam back in school?"

"Yes."

She hid her face in her hands for a moment. "God, this is hard. Ruby, when I said Miriam and I were really close, what I meant was that I loved her. Do you understand?"

I nodded. I understood perfectly.

"Miriam loved me, too. It's not unusual for girls in all-female environments to form passionate attachments to each other. And once these girls grow up and enter the real world, they date boys, get married, have babies. That's how it was with me. I went to college, had a couple of casual boyfriends, traveled a bit, then met Warren, and here I am." She blinked a couple of times and rubbed her index fingers under her eyes. "All these years I thought my feelings for Miriam were borne out of our teenage hormones and our close proximity to each other. But there had to be more to it than that, or else how do I explain my feelings for you?" Now she didn't try to stop her tears.

"Oh, Iris"—I reached out and touched her tear-streaked face.

"I love you, Ruby. I know I shouldn't. I know how many ways it's wrong, but knowing and feeling are two different things."

"I love you, too, Iris." My voice broke with the force of all the feelings I'd been hiding for so long.

Iris leaned toward me, then laughed and said, "Damn it, I've still got a cigarette in my hand. Just a second." She ground the cigarette out in the ashtray and said, "Now."

There was no mistaking the meaning of this kiss, and I fell into it like Alice falling into the rabbit hole, like Dorothy falling in her Kansas farmhouse into the wonderful Land of Oz. Our lips, our bodies, pressed together, wanting to be closer, closer. It was so different from Aaron's kiss, so much better than anything I'd ever imagined.

When Iris pulled away, her breath was ragged. "I have to remember you're just sixteen. I don't want to take advantage of you. Do you think you could be happy with just kissing?"

My hands were around her little waist. "Kissing you makes me very, very happy."

I was happy that way, lying on the bed with Iris, kissing and being kissed, until an hour passed and Sharon called out from the living room.

Iris pulled away from me and called back, "Mama'll be there in a minute, sweetie!"

We sat up and straightened our rumpled clothes. Iris put her hand on mine. "You know we can't tell anyone about this, right?"

"I know. It's just like that sign at the gate, 'What you see here, what you hear here, what you do here, keep it here.'"

"Yes, that's exactly what it's like."

"Don't worry. I'll keep it here." I gestured to indicate the bedroom. "And here." I took Iris's hand and put it on my heart.

"Oh, Ruby, I love you so much." She kissed my hand, and we got up to see to Sharon.

Iris's face was flushed, and her hair was fluffy and loose from where we'd been rolling on the bed. When Sharon saw her, she smiled and said, "Mama pretty."

Iris kissed the top of her head. "Thank you, sweetie."

Sharon looked at me. "Bee pretty."

"You're pretty, too," I said, gathering Baby Sharon up in my arms. "The whole world is pretty today."

JUNE 12, 1945

It's hard for me to focus on reading or writing these days. Love has made my brain as soft and sweet and mushy as banana pudding. Mama's worried about my appetite, and if she knew how little I'm sleeping, she'd worry about that, too. But I don't seem to need food and rest like I used to. I'm living on love.

I spend every afternoon with Iris, from right after lunchtime until right before Warren gets home. We do all our usual things—read together, take Sharon to the playground or the library, play tennis (I'm improving). Only now it's different because we know how we feel about each other, and sometimes we give each other this smile, and nobody else knows what it means.

The only time Iris and I kiss or touch is when Sharon is napping. We think it might confuse Sharon to see her mama and me loving on each other, and also Iris is afraid (though this seems far-fetched to me) that Sharon might find some way to tell her daddy if she saw us.

"She knows the words 'hug' and 'kiss,'" Iris said the other day as we lay on her bed, "and she's started to string simple sentences together, so she could conceivably say to her dad, 'Mama kiss Bee' or something to that effect."

"Well, we'll just make sure she doesn't see us, then."

"It's strange," Iris said, staring at the end of her cigarette. "I don't even know how Warren would feel if he knew. It might not even bother him. After all, it's not like you and I can do the same things he does with me."

I felt a wave of heat rising from my belly at the thought of what Iris and Warren did in the very bed I was lying on. At first I thought the feeling was embarrassment, but then I realized it was jealousy.

Iris must've felt my discomfort because she added, "Not that he and I have been doing much of anything since he took this job. He comes home exhausted every night."

Before I even thought about it, I asked, "Did you ever tell Warren about you and Miriam?"

She looked away from me. "No. Of course not."

* * *

My afternoons with Iris and Sharon are perfect. It feels like playing house when I was little, except with two mamas and a baby instead of a mama and daddy. And just like when I was little, I get so wrapped up in playing that I forget there's anything else in the world. So it's hard when 5:30 rolls around and I have to go back to my real house where nobody can figure me out—where mama is always asking if I'm feeling all right and my sisters go back and forth between thinking I'm pining away for Aaron or that I've got a new feller.

Sometimes, too, when I'm in my real house, I think of what Iris must be doing: eating supper with Warren, listening to music with Warren, lying down in the bed with Warren. And that hot surge of jealousy rushes up again, and no matter how hard I try to stop it, I can't.

But I shouldn't complain too much. You can't have pleasure without pain, right? And I'm willing to suffer the pains of jealousy, the loneliness I feel when I'm with my family, and if I believed in it, the fire of hell itself if it means that for five days a week, I can have a few perfect hours with Iris.

JUNE 19, 1945

Iris didn't let me in when I knocked today. Instead she came out, pushing Sharon in her stroller. "We're going to the library," she said. "But I can't tell you why yet."

"Okay." I fell into step with her. Her eyes were shining and staring straight ahead like they were already seeing the library in front of her. "You sure are being all cloak and dagger," I said. "I feel like I'm in one of those Nancy Drew mysteries."

Once we got to the library, Iris went straight for the big, dog-slapping dictionary they keep on its own little stand in the reference section. She flipped around in it, glanced down at a page, then looked at me with a big smile. "We can go now," she said. "I found out what I wanted to know."

When we were back outside, I said, "Can you give me a clue, Nancy Drew?"

"I'll tell you when we get home," she whispered.

In the house, she helped Baby Sharon out of her stroller and told her to play in her room. Iris sat on the couch and patted the place beside her.

When I sat, she leaned over and whispered in my ear, "Uranium."

"I beg your pardon?"

"Uranium," she said again. "Last night I had insomnia, so I was reading in bed. Warren started talking in his sleep. Most of it was mumbling I couldn't make out, but the one word I understood was 'uranium.'"

"So you went to the library to look up what uranium is?"

"I took my share of science courses in college. I know what uranium is." She leaned in close. "What I wanted to see was if anybody else has heard her husband say something about uranium. I figure Warren can't be the only man in this town who talks in his sleep. And do you know"—her hand rested on mine—"when I got to the page of the dictionary with *uranium* on it, that page had been flipped to and pored over so much it was thin to the point of transparency. And the entry for uranium had been fingered so much the print had faded to a smeary gray. Whatever they're doing here, Ruby, it's got something to do with uranium."

I remembered the worn-out state of that page when I'd looked up the word *urbane*. "I've heard of uranium," I said, "but I don't really know what it is."

Iris smiled. "What is the science department at that high school teaching you?"

"They're teaching me biology. I ain't got to chemistry yet."

"Well, in that case, uranium is a metallic element that has radioactivity. Do you know what radioactivity is?"

"Not really," I said, feeling dumber by the minute.

"When an element is radioactive," Iris said, lighting a cigarette, "it emits alpha rays, beta rays, sometimes gamma rays when the nucleus of the atom disintegrates."

She might as well have been speaking Swahili for all I was understanding. "You sure are smart," I said because I didn't know what else to say.

"No." She puffed on her cigarette. "If I were really smart, I'd be able to figure out what they're using the uranium for." She squeezed my hand. "Promise you won't tell anybody I talked to you about this, okay?"

"Okay." It was an easy promise to keep. After all, you can't talk about something if you don't at least halfway understand it.

JUNE 28, 1945

You know how in movies sometimes they'll show a sequence of a happy new couple doing fun things together and laughing and holding hands? That's how it's been with Iris and me the past week. If my life was a movie, you'd see images of us picnicking in the park, splashing with Sharon at the public pool, making fudge that turned out to be a hilarious disaster, and dancing close to soft music in the living room during Sharon's naptime.

But today when I went to Iris's she didn't come to the door. She hollered, "Come in!" in a choked voice, and when I did, she was curled in a ball on the couch, her face red and puffy, her hair uncombed, still just in her nightgown. Sharon was sitting on the floor in her pink pajamas, rolling a pull toy back and forth while giving her mother nervous glances.

"She…she needs changing, and she hasn't had lunch yet," Iris said. Her nose was so stuffy from crying she didn't even sound like herself.

"And what I can I do for you?"

"Just take care of Sharon. I—I can't right now." She curled up in a tighter ball, and her shoulders shook as she sobbed.

"All right," I said. "I'll take care of Sharon, but after that, I'm going to take care of you."

Her only response was to sob harder.

"Okay, Sharon," I said, scooping her up. "Let's get you out of your jammies and into some big-girl clothes." I carried her to her room and helped her out of her pajamas and soggy diaper. I powdered her down, diapered her up, and pulled her yellow sundress over her head. "Now why don't we get some big-girl lunch?"

Sharon took my hand, and we passed through the living room where Iris was still sobbing.

"Mama sad," Sharon said.

"Yeah, but she'll be all right," I said. "Don't you worry." Of course, I said this without knowing if it was true or not, and I was worried sick myself. But what was I supposed to tell a one-year-old about her mama? "Now how about I scramble a nice egg for your lunch?"

"No egg. Chee toe."

Being fluent in Sharonese, I said, "Cheese toast it is." I put a cheese-covered bread slice in the oven long enough for the cheese to get melty and poured Sharon a cup of milk. When she was settled in her high chair, I said, "Now remember you've got to blow on your cheese toast to cool it off."

She puffed out her cheeks and blew, looking like the way they always draw the North Wind in picture books.

It was strange. My heart felt like it was going to explode because I didn't know what was wrong with Iris, and yet here I was, talking nonsense to Sharon while she ate her cheese toast and drank her milk, acting like it was an ordinary afternoon. There's something about being around little kids that makes you able to act like everything's okay…maybe because you hope so hard it will be, for their sake even more than yours.

Once I got Sharon fed and settled down for her nap, I went to where Iris was still lying on the couch. She didn't say anything, but she reached out for me, and I sat down and held her while she cried.

"Shh," I said. "Shh. Whatever it is, you can tell me."

But she was crying too hard to tell me anything. She could only gasp and sob and hiccup with her arms around me, one hand flat against my back, the other hand clenched into a fist. When I pulled back from our hug, I saw the clenched fist was holding something. "What is that?" I said.

She held her fist out but did not unclench it. I gently peeled back her fingers to find a crumpled newspaper clipping. It was from the April 10, January 1936 issue of the Oakdale, Indiana *Banner*:

Auto Accident Proves Fatal

A one-car accident on Lakeside Road Friday night claimed the life of Mrs. Lucille Stevens, age 36. The driver of the car, Dr. Warren Stevens, an assistant professor in the chemistry department at Whitman College, was returning with his wife from a faculty party when, due to rainy conditions, he lost control of the vehicle, running off the road and crashing into a tree. Dr. Stevens suffered a broken arm and minor injuries and was treated at Oakdale Community Hospital. Mrs. Stevens was killed instantly. Her death was ruled an accident.

The reason I can write down what the article said is that I was in such shock I had to read it enough to memorize it before I could make sense of it. I must've read it a dozen times before I was able to ask Iris, "You didn't know about the accident?"

Iris looked at me with eyes that were swollen almost shut. "I didn't know he'd been married before." She fell into my arms again, sobbing.

"You're gonna have to talk to him," I said, which just made her cry harder, so hard I was afraid she was going to throw up or break a rib. Finally, I said, "Listen, you've got brandy, right? Let me get you some brandy."

I don't know why brandy came into my head except that I'd seen characters in movies give it to traumatized people, and

I knew it was what Saint Bernard rescue dogs carried in those little barrels that hung from their collars. Clearly brandy was some kind of help in an emergency, and I was willing to try anything that might help.

I poured a glass full of brandy and brought it to her along with her cigarettes and lighter. "Here. These will calm you down."

She took the glass in her shaking hand and knocked back several slugs. She set the glass on the table, put a cigarette between her lips, and let me light it for her. I sat beside her and let her smoke and drink in silence. I figured she'd talk when she was good and ready.

After a while she lit a second cigarette off the butt of the first one and said, "I feel like I'm in a story by Daphne du Maurier or one of those damn Bronte sisters—like I'm the young bride who has discovered a Terrible Secret about her husband's first marriage. It's a lot more entertaining in a book, believe me."

I glanced down at the crumpled newspaper clipping on the coffee table. "How did you find the article?"

"It was an accident." She shook her head. "Ironic, eh?" She dabbed at her eyes with a hanky. "You remember when I found out about the uranium?"

I nodded.

"Well, of course, it's just been gnawing at me—the curiosity about what they could be using the uranium for—so I thought I'd look up some more specific information on uranium in one of Warren's old chemistry textbooks. I grabbed a book, opened it, and the clipping fell out." A tear rolled down her cheek. "I wouldn't have minded if he'd told me, you know? And I would've been sympathetic about the accident, even if he felt like it was his fault..."

His fault. I thought of Iris telling me Warren didn't like to drive at night. I took her hand. "Well, there's no point in driving yourself crazy imagining things. The only person who can tell you anything is Warren."

"Well, clearly he doesn't want to tell me anything. Uncle Sam's secrets aren't the only ones he's keeping."

"Maybe he has an explanation. You've got to talk to him."

Iris shook her head, grabbed the brandy glass, and knocked the rest of it back. "You're the only person I can talk to, Ruby. You're the only person I trust."

Part of me wanted to say, *Go get Sharon, and run away with me.* But where would we run to? "Warren's still your husband, and you need to talk to him."

"He's a stranger. My mother always told me not to talk to strangers."

"He's Sharon's daddy." I stood up. "Tell you what I'm going to do. I'm going to run you a bath. You can get cleaned up, get your hair fixed, get dressed. Maybe getting fixed up on the outside will help you be fixed up on the inside a little, too... enough that you'll be able to talk to Warren when he gets home."

"You're so sweet to me, Ruby." Her voice was thick with brandy and sadness. "I love you."

"I love you, too." I kissed her forehead and then went to run her bath.

When I cut off the water, she was standing in the doorway.

"Stay with me, Ruby," she said. "I don't want to be alone."

"Not even in the bathroom?"

"Not even in the bathroom." She slipped off her thin nightgown. When Iris and I had gone swimming, I had blushed to see her in her bathing suit because it was easy when seeing her in it to imagine her out of it. And now I was seeing her, and she was soft and pale and delicate and beautiful. It was a shame, though, to be seeing her for the first time like this when she was so sad.

She stepped into the tub, then leaned back. "Life's too damned hard," she said, sighing. "It's too damned hard, and I'm not much good at it."

"Life's hard for everybody. You've just got to do the best you can."

"Thank you, Little Orphan Annie."

I knew there was nothing I could say to comfort her. "Iris, do you want me to wash your hair?"

"If you want. I don't care enough to do it myself."

I filled a cup with warm water, poured it over Iris's honey blonde curls, then filled and poured again. I let a dollop of Halo shampoo drop from the bottle into my hand.

There's something about washing a woman's hair—the weight and the silkiness of it in your hands, the feel of the foam, the way her head leans back with her eyes closed, trusting you, letting her touch you in a way she usually only touches herself. Iris's hair was spread out in the water behind her. She was beautiful, a mermaid, and I kissed her on each eyelid before I turned on the faucet for rinse water.

It's hard to hear much of anything while water's running, which is probably why, a couple of minutes later as I was pouring cupfuls of water on Iris's hair, in between lightly kissing her forehead and cheeks, I screamed to see Eva Lynch standing in the bathroom doorway.

Iris screamed twice—the first time because I screamed, I think—the second time because she saw Mrs. Lynch.

Mrs. Lynch clutched her purse in both white-gloved hands. Her lips were drawn into a thin line of outrage. "I knocked and knocked, but no one came to the door," she said. "I shouldn't have come in. I don't know what's going on here, but this house is clearly no place for decent people!" She spun around, and the next sound we heard was the front door slamming.

Iris looked at me, her eyes streaming with fresh tears. "Ruby, sweetheart, I think it would be best for you to leave now."

JULY 2, 1945

Friday and today I went to Iris's, and nobody answered the door. I'm worried and scared, but there's nobody I can talk to about how worried and scared I am. You know how in movies they show those sequences of happy couples doing fun things together? Usually those scenes come before something terrible happens.

JULY 4, 1945

Today is all red, white, and blue and marching bands. Everybody's celebrating but me. When I went to Iris's and nobody was home again, I left a note on the door that said,

Dear Iris,
I keep coming here in the afternoons like always, but you're never home. I need to know that you and Baby Sharon are all right. If you get this note, can you send a message to me so I won't worry so much? You know where to find me.
Ruby

My hand itched to write "Love, Ruby," but I didn't. I knew it wasn't safe.

JULY 6, 1945

Daddy came home from work today around eleven o'clock. Mama set down her iron and turned off the radio and said, "What's the matter? Did you get hurt? Are you sick?"

"No," Daddy said, but his color wasn't good, and his jaw was tight. "But I need to talk to Ruby by herself for a few minutes. Why don't you take the other girls to the show or something?"

Mother looked at Daddy, then at me, then at Daddy again. I could tell she was nervous. "It's kindly early to go the show, ain't it?"

"Well, then, take 'em to Woolworth's and buy 'em some candy," Daddy said. "But get 'em out of here."

"All right, girls, let's go," Mama said with a quaver in her voice, then she rushed over and whispered in Daddy's ear.

"Naw, it ain't nothing like that," he said. "You'uns just make yourselves scarce for half an hour, all right? Go visit a neighbor or something."

I sat at the kitchen table and watched my mother and sisters file out of the house. My jaw was clenched, and my lips were pressed together tight. If I opened my mouth, I was sure I'd scream or throw up or both.

Daddy sat down at the table across from me. "Is there any coffee left?"

"I think so."

"Get me a cup, would you?"

With shaking hands, I poured him a cup of coffee, set it on the table in front of him, then sat back down.

He didn't drink his coffee. He just looked at it, maybe because looking at it was easier than looking at me. "This morning a soldier come over to the job site and took me over to one of the offices for questioning," he said. "I told 'em if I liked answering questions I would've stayed in school, but people like that don't have no sense of humor."

"What did they ask you about?" I said, but the sick feeling I had made me think I already knew.

"Well, they set me in this big white room with all these old army fellers who looked like they'd shoot me soon as look at me. I didn't have no idea what they might ask me about, but I have to say I was mighty surprised when they commenced to asking about you."

"Me?" I swallowed hard to push back a wave of nausea.

"Mainly they was asking about you working for Iris Stevens. What did you say about her, what did I know about her, that kind of thing, so I reckon they was trying to find out about her more than they was trying to find out about you."

"What did you tell them?"

"I didn't tell them much cause there wasn't much to tell. I said you said Mrs. Stevens was a real nice lady and that she paid you regular."

I was crying hard by this time. I wiped my eyes with my fists like a little kid.

Daddy handed me the red bandana he always carried in his pocket. "What you crying for?"

"I'm scared."

He covered my hand with his big, rough one. "There ain't no need to be scared. You ain't in trouble. You ain't never been in trouble in your life, and you ain't in trouble now. I think your buddy Mrs. Stevens might be in a speck of trouble, though." He took his hand off mine. "This is what the army fellers told me to tell you: They don't want you going over to the Stevenses' house no more, and they don't want you working for Mrs. Stevens no more. They want you to stay away from her. You understand?"

"Yes, sir," I managed to say, though I was crying even harder now. How could I not cry when a force as powerful as the United States government, which was supposed to promote freedom and the pursuit of happiness, was telling me to stay away from the person I loved most in the world?

"She's been paying you by the week, this summer, right?" Daddy finally took a sip of his coffee. "She owe you any money?"

"A little bit."

"I'll go over and collect it on Monday," Daddy said. "But you're never to set foot over there again. Them old boys made it real clear that if you did, then you, me, your ma, and your sisters would be put on the next bus to Kentucky."

I wiped my eyes. "I've been going over there the past few days to work," I said. "But nobody's answered the door."

"Something they said made it sound like Mrs. Stevens took sick and has been in the hospital, but that she's coming back home. It's all right peculiar." He set down his coffee cup. "It got me to wondering...did anything queer ever happen when you was over there? Or did you ever see anything that made you think Mrs. Stevens might be a Jap spy? Did she eat a lot of rice or anything like that?"

"No. She just seemed...nice."

Daddy stood up. "Well, you never can tell about people, I reckon. I'd better be getting back to work."

"Daddy," I said, my voice choked. "I'm sorry I caused you so much trouble."

"Shoot," Daddy said as he was halfway out the door, "you ain't caused me a minute of trouble in your life. You're the best girl I got."

His words just made me cry harder, for him, for Iris, for me, for all the things about ourselves and other people that we can never understand.

JULY 9, 1945

"Did you see her?" I asked Daddy when he handed me the five-dollar bill. It was a dollar more than the Stevenses owed me, but under the circumstances, I figured it was best not to argue.

"No," Daddy said, pouring himself some coffee from the pot on the stove. I never can understand why people drink coffee when the weather's so hot. "I talked to him. Mr. Stevens."

"What did he say?"

"Not much, to tell the truth. He said you was a good girl and that you'd been a big help around the place and that he didn't want me to get the wrong idea on account of you not being allowed to come back. He said none of it was your fault." Daddy sat down at the kitchen table. "What do you reckon he meant by that?"

I blinked hard and looked away. "I don't know."

"Oh, and I plumb forgot. I put it in my dinner bucket so I wouldn't lose it." He got his dinner bucket from where he'd set it near the sink, opened it, and took out a book. "Mr. Stevens said his wife wanted to make sure this here book got returned to you." He looked at it. "I ain't never seen it in this house before. Is it yours?"

I took it from him. It was *My Home Is Far Away*, the Dawn Powell book Iris had recommended to me. "Yessir," I said, because the book was mine now. "A teacher at school gave it to me. I'd loaned it to Iris." It was the only time I've ever told a lie right to my daddy's face.

Once I could get a minute alone, I flipped through the book. I opened it and held it upside down and shook it to see if Iris had left anything—a note or message of some kind—tucked between its pages. But she hadn't, probably for the same reason I hadn't written "love" on the note I'd left for her. It wasn't safe.

If Iris had wanted me to have this book, maybe it was because there was something in it she wanted me to understand. Desperate to understand something, anything, I started to read.

JULY 15, 1945

If I wasn't so sick with sadness, I'd be taking great pleasure in reading *My Home Is Far Away*. It's every bit as good a book about being an imaginative, difficult child as *A Tree Grows in Brooklyn*. But all the sadness in the book deepens the sadness in my heart. When the little girls in the book lost their mother, I cried for them at first, but then I cried more for everybody I've lost. Miss Connor and Virgie, gone and far away, never to be seen again. And Iris, gone but nearby, which is even harder, and if I was to try to see her again, it would be a betrayal of my family and my country, too, because the U.S. government has forbidden me to see her. So I cry for my losses, but I know how little they are compared to so many people's in this terrible war. But these losses are mine, so I have to cry.

I can see a lot of myself in Marcia, the little girl in *My Home Is Far Away*, and I'm sure Iris saw a lot of herself and a lot of me in her, too. When I got to chapter 23, I saw a passage Iris had underlined: "The biggest jolt in growing up was to discover that you didn't like what others liked and they thought you were crazy to like what you liked."

Had she underlined it for herself because it struck her as particularly true? Or had she underlined it for me?

JULY 19, 1945

I won't go to her house because I promised Daddy I wouldn't, and I don't want to cost him—well, cost all of us, really—his job. But I figure it wouldn't be disobedient if I just happened to run into Iris, at the park playing with Sharon or at the A and P waiting in line for rations or at the library returning a book. And so I walk up and down the wooden sidewalks, guessing where she might be, all the while trying to look like I'm just out running an errand in case I'm being watched.

When we first moved to Oak Ridge I always read the signs: the three monkeys, the housewife who killed somebody just by talking, the loose lips that sank ships. But after a while I stopped seeing them just like you don't notice the furniture that's in your own house. Now, though, I see them again, and this time they scare me. As I walked the streets today, I froze in front of one sign: an index finger positioned over a pair of lips with the caption *Keep Our Secrets*.

I knew the sign was about the war, but it made me think about the secret life Warren hid from Iris—another wife, a terrible accident in a car he was driving, and his years of saying nothing, of a silence that was the same thing as a lie. But Iris had her secrets, too. She never told Warren about Miriam, never told him how she kissed me and held me, about the secret life we led while he was working on his secret project. Her secrets seem smaller than his somehow, but maybe they aren't.

And now that Iris and I are separated, I feel like my whole life, my whole self, is a secret that's been locked up where I can't find it. And maybe I should do the opposite of what Pandora did in that old story and not go snooping around where I'm told not to. But I don't think secrets always keep us safe. Secrets stop us from understanding. And I want to understand. Like Pandora, I won't rest till I rip the lid of that box open even though I know that when I do, I probably won't like what I see.

JULY 24, 1945

I won't write again till I see her because I'm so empty there is nothing left inside me and so nothing to say.

AUGUST 3, 1945

I knew she wouldn't be able to stay away from the library, so after a while I stopped wandering the streets and started going to the library right after breakfast and staying till it was time to go home for supper. The librarian said she wished she could give me a special award for summer reading.

Iris came in today around two o'clock. She looked a little thinner than when I last saw her, and she was pale, but that might have been because she was missing her usual red lipstick. She was still beautiful, though. I can't imagine her not being beautiful. Our eyes met, and then we both looked away, making sure nobody was watching. She looked at me again, nodded ever so slightly, and then disappeared into the fiction stacks.

I counted to twenty in my head, then got up and followed her.

She was in the third row of fiction, crying silently.

"I want to hug you so bad," I whispered.

"You can't."

"I know. But I still want to." My eyes were full of tears. "Could we talk for a minute?"

"We're not supposed to."

"I know. But we already are." I could almost see the shadow of a smile.

"I'll tell you what," she whispered. "Meet me in the woods behind the park where we used to take Sharon. But if you see anybody who might see us, keep walking. Go home, and forget about me."

"I can go home, but I can't forget about you."

"Oh, Ruby." A tear spilled down her cheek, and she wiped it away like it was evidence of a crime. "Wait fifteen minutes, then come find me."

She walked away, and I watched the clock.

I found her in the woods, leaned against a tree, smoking a cigarette. I opened my arms to hug her, and she said, "No. Someone might see."

"Who? The birds or the squirrels?"

"Or a spy. You never know in this place."

It was strange to see her without Sharon, and Sharon's absence worried me suddenly. "I wish I could see Sharon, too. Where is she?"

"She's with my mother in Evanston. Warren sent her there when everything happened. Mom's coming down here to bring her back tomorrow, though, and she's going to stay a couple of weeks to help me and keep an eye on things." She laughed, but it wasn't really a laugh. "Which means keep an eye on me."

"You said *when everything happened*, but I don't really know what 'everything' is."

"Maybe you shouldn't know. Ruby, you're so young. Part of me really wants to keep you innocent of all this sordidness."

"Being innocent is the same thing as being ignorant." My firmness surprised me. "And I don't want to be ignorant. I want to *know*."

"All right." She sighed. "Maybe we should sit."

We sat on the soft, mossy ground. "The day you last saw me—when Eva barged in on us—God, Ruby, I didn't know days could be that bad. When Warren got home from work, I handed him the newspaper clipping, and he turned white as a sheet, but he didn't say anything, so I asked him why…why he hadn't told me." Iris lit a cigarette and didn't bother to wipe the tear that slid down her cheek. "He told me that Lucille's death still haunted him, that he still had nightmares, that he had been drinking at the party and had always thought he could've prevented the accident if he'd been sober. I told him I understood why he might not want to talk about her death, but why hadn't he told me he'd had a life with someone else before me?" She paused and sucked in a big gasp of air. "It's the only time I've ever seen him really angry. He didn't raise a hand to me, but he did raise his voice. He said that some people were determined to live in the past, but he wasn't one of them. He lived in the present, and I was welcome to join him there, but in the meantime, he was going to be staying at his friend Bill's apartment. And he stomped out and slammed the door behind him."

"Oh, Iris, I'm so sorry." Without thinking, I reached out to touch her hand. She pulled it away.

"You have nothing to be sorry for. Why is it that some people say they're sorry even when they haven't done anything, and other people won't apologize no matter what they do?"

I shrugged. "Human nature, I guess."

"Different humans have different natures." She hugged her knees to her chest. "Would you believe that what I've told you isn't even the bad part?"

"No," I said, not because I didn't believe her, but because I didn't want to.

"Two days later a pair of soldiers came to the door and told me I had been called in for questioning. I had to leave Sharon with Hannah, and they escorted me to this…this chamber where I expected Torquemada to show up any minute. It was a panel of soldiers—not privates, but colonels and generals—not exactly the kind of people you want to pour your heart out to…"

"They questioned my daddy, too."

"About me?"

"Yes."

She nodded grimly. "I'm not surprised. They asked me if I'd ever been a homosexual or had ever been involved in homosexual activity."

"Why do they even care? What business is it of theirs?"

"They care because they think homosexuals are a security risk. They're easy to blackmail, so they might be willing to divulge government secrets to protect themselves."

I swallowed hard. "What did you tell them?"

"I told them that when I was a teenager in boarding school, there had been a flirtation with another girl, but that it was just silly, schoolgirl stuff, something I left behind once I grew up." She looked at me, her eyes misty. "And then they asked me if I was having a homosexual relationship with you. I denied it, of course."

It wasn't the knowledge that my privacy had been invaded that scared me. It was the knowledge that here, there is no such thing as privacy. "How...how could they know?"

"Oh, I think you know as well as I do how they know. There are spies planted all over this town—people who may seem like nice neighbors or harmless coworkers, but they're on the lookout for information all the time. And when they see someone who behaves in any way out of the ordinary, they write a letter and send it to this post office box, and before you can turn around, that person gets called in for questioning. And if the answers aren't satisfactory, he's on the next bus out of Oak Ridge."

"Do you think Mrs. Lynch is..."

"I'd be willing to bet a significant sum of money on it. The way she was always coming in unannounced, always snooping, always judging. But of course, I didn't think a thing about it because I've known ladies like her all my life." She sighed. "And probably every one of them would've done the same thing Eva did. Warren got called in for questioning, too, of course. Ironically, that's what got the two of us talking again, so we could 'circle our wagons.'" She stared down at the glowing coal of her cigarette. "What 'circling our wagons' meant was following the orders the government had placed in regard to me which would allow Warren to keep his job and stay in town." She recited the next items coldly, as if they applied to somebody other than herself: "Sharon was to be temporarily removed from my care. I was to be hospitalized and observed for a week by a psychiatrist and various doctors and nurses. My official diagnosis, by the way, was a 'nervous breakdown.' After being released from the hospital, I was to begin psychoanalysis once a week."

"Psychoanalysis for what?"

She laughed, but somehow it was without humor. "My history of lesbian tendencies. It's not the first time I've had my head shrunk for the same reason. One time, the dorm mother caught me kissing Miriam. My parents pulled me out of school and put me in psychoanalysis with this gruff old German woman. She asked me about my mother and my father and my dreams, and I talked and talked until I ran out of things to say, at which time I was declared cured. My last session, though, the shrink took me to visit the state mental hospital so I could see where I might end up if I regressed to my old ways." She shook her head. "They took me to this ward filled with young women, and Ruby, it was awful. Awful. Their hair had been clipped as short as soldier boys', but messier, choppier-looking, like whoever was cutting it hadn't been paying any attention to the way it looked, and they were all wearing those awful hospital gowns. One girl who was at least your age was carrying around a rag doll and talking to it like it was a person. Another girl sat in the corner, rocking back and forth and yanking out her eyelashes. Then there was the girl who screamed and screamed the way you'd scream if somebody was stabbing you over and over." Iris ran a finger under her eyes. "The worst part, though, Ruby, was the way the nurses talked about the girls—like they were funny or like they somehow deserved to be in that condition. It was as if the girls were prisoners instead of patients. If the shrink showed me that scene to scare me into sanity, it worked. At least for a while."

"But you were sane to start with."

"By my definition, yes. But not by society's."

"I was just thinking about that passage you marked in *My Home Is Far Away*."

"Yes. It's true, isn't it? And then there's that Emily Dickinson poem, 'Much madness is divinest sense/To the discerning eye/

Much sense, the starkest madness/'Tis the majority in this, as in all things, prevail.'"

It was one of my favorite poems, too. "Assent and you are sane/Demur, you're straightaway dangerous/And handled with a chain," I finished.

"I love you, Ruby," Iris said, looking so deep into my eyes it felt like she was touching me. "I'm sorry we can't see each other anymore."

"I love, you, too," I said, my voice so clogged with tears it didn't even sound like my own. "I wish it could be some other way."

"It can't." Her tone was matter-of-fact. "I need to live my life in such a way that I can be a good mother to Sharon. And you"—she smiled through her tears—"you have to finish school and go off to college and travel and write and have adventures and be very, very happy. Will you do that for me, Ruby?"

"I'll try," I said, but as I left her in the shadowy woods and walked into the sunlight, I knew I'd never fall in love again, and I couldn't imagine ever being happy.

AUGUST 6, 1945

Mama had come in to turn up the radio so she and my sisters could hear it while they were outside washing clothes. I was sitting at the kitchen table where I'd been sitting since breakfast even though I couldn't bring myself to eat anything. I'd been claiming to be sick ever since Friday, but since I didn't have a fever or any symptoms except profound misery, Mama seemed to be getting suspicious.

"Them dishes has been sitting in the sink for over an hour," Mama said. "When you was planning on washing them?"

"I'm sorry, Mama," I said. "I don't mean to be lazy. I just don't feel good, and I don't feel like doing anything."

"Well, if there's one thing I can teach you about being a woman, it's that the work don't go away just cause you don't feel like doing it."

Mama turned up the radio, but the music that was playing was cut off by the announcer's deep voice: "We interrupt this broadcast to bring you a special announcement issued by President Truman." Opal and Garnet and Baby Pearl tripped over each other getting through the door to hear what the announcement was. As we listened, the world changed.

The message was from President Truman, but it wasn't his voice on the radio that said, "Sixteen hours ago an American airplane dropped one bomb on Hiroshima, an important Japanese army base. That bomb had more power than 20,000 tons of TNT." He went on, "It is an atomic bomb. It is a harnessing of the basic power of the universe. The force from which the sun draws its power has been loosed against those who brought war to the Far East."

"Did Japan just get blowed up?" Baby Pearl asked, but Mama hissed, "Shh."

The announcer went on to talk about all the scientific knowledge that was needed to work on the project and how everything had to be top secret. I had guessed where the bomb was made before I heard him say "Oak Ridge," but apparently my mother and sisters hadn't figured it out yet because they said, "Did you hear what he said? He said Oak Ridge!"

Opal started jumping up and down. "Daddy helped make the bomb that ended the war!"

"The war's not over yet, honey," Mama said, but her face was lit up, too.

"It will be soon, though, won't it, Mama?" Garnet said. She was holding Opal's hand and jumping up and down with her. "The Japs can't fight back if we just keep bombing 'em and bombing 'em."

At first I wanted to tell Opal that Daddy hadn't helped make the bomb. He had just built houses for workers here. But then I thought better of it. Everybody who worked here was helping make the bomb because without the bomb none of us would be here in the first place. It put me in mind of that nursery rhyme "This is the House that Jack Built"—*This is the man who built the houses to lodge the workers that made the bomb that crossed the ocean to end the war by killing the people who started the war*...Oak Ridge. This is the town the bomb built.

Everybody was laughing and talking at the same time except me. Mama asked, "What's the matter, Ruby? Ain't you glad?"

"I don't know. I'm glad the war might be over soon. I'd like to know more about this Hiroshima place. Do you reckon it was just military men there, or do you think there might have been some regular people, too, like families?"

Mama looked at me like I was the most peculiar person she had ever seen. "Well, shoot, honey, I don't know. Whatever was there, it ain't there no more. And I'm glad. Serves them right for what they did at Pearl Harbor."

I held back from saying what I was thinking, that if there had been any little babies in Hiroshima, then surely they hadn't been responsible for the bombing of Pearl Harbor. There was no point in saying anything. Mama and my sisters were happy and proud, and it feels better to be happy and proud than it does to think.

At first neighbors just talked to neighbors, but by the middle of the afternoon everybody had poured into the Townsite—housewives, soldiers, plant workers, scientists—to celebrate and to finally break the silence by talking about the project. Loudly.

"So that's what we were doing," I heard one young woman plant worker say, laughing. "I had no idea."

A middle-aged bespectacled man in a suit shouted, "Atoms! I've been dying to yell that word for two years now! Atoms! Atoms!" His face was joyous, and I couldn't tell if he was drunk on liquor or just drunk on his accomplishments.

Newsboys wound through the crowds with issues of area newspapers calling, "Extra! Extra! Power of Oak Ridge Atomic Bomb Hits Japs: Truman Reveals Use of World's Greatest Bomb!"

Daddy found us in the crowd and hugged Mama and then all of us girls together. His eyes were shining as he said, "Girls, I want you to remember this day as the proudest day of your daddy's life. I always wanted to be a part of something big, and there ain't nothing bigger than this."

"Congratulations, Daddy," I said, like he had thought up the bomb and built it all by himself.

* * *

Scanning through the crowd, I saw Iris's face. She was on the wooden sidewalk on the other side of the street in a cluster of cheering housewives. Sharon was in her mother's arms, wearing a pink and white checked sun suit, and I was shocked to see how much she'd grown in the few weeks since I'd seen her. I watched Warren, wearing more of a smile than I would have thought him capable of, as he pushed through the crowd toward his wife and child. He kissed Baby Sharon on the forehead, then kissed Iris on the cheek. Iris said something to him and smiled, but it was a small smile, one that flickered and faded.

I know Iris's heart enough to know that she, like me, couldn't take pure joy in what her husband and others like him had created, not when the purpose of their creation was destruction. Like me, Iris is a thinker, somebody who will turn things around in her mind and examine them from every possible angle and worry and brood while everybody else is having a party in the street.

I was staring at her, and I knew I should stop because if I didn't, after a while she would see me, too. And I knew we couldn't look at each other again without falling to pieces. We had already seen too much.

AUGUST 5, 2006

Dear Reverend Stevens,

I'm sure you don't remember me, but I've danced with you and held you and kissed you. Before you get too nervous, let me also say that I've changed your diapers. Back in Oak Ridge, during what we used to call "the war" (like there wasn't ever going to be another one), when you were a baby and I was just a girl, I was your babysitter.

I'm writing because of an article I saw about you on the Internet. Yes, I did "Google you," as my great-nephews would say, but don't worry. I'm old, but I'm not crazy, and I'm not a stalker. I figured I probably wouldn't find you because your name might be different, but you popped right up on the first page. You can imagine my surprise when I saw the picture of you in the Champaign, Illinois newspaper. For some reason, I imagined you'd be younger, but then I did the math and realized that of course you wouldn't. But the real kicker was seeing you in your black shirt and white collar. An Episcopal priest! When

I was taking care of you, I never would've even imagined there could be such a thing as a woman priest, let alone that I was bouncing a future one on my knee!

In the interview I read, you had just come to the church in Champaign and were talking about your ministry. You said you felt a special calling to help the mentally ill because your mother spent most of your childhood and adolescence in a mental hospital while your father left you in care of your grandparents. The only time you saw your mother was for short, supervised visits, and she died of breast cancer when you were just twenty-two.

Reverend Stevens, I don't know what your daddy or your grandparents told you, but your mama wasn't crazy. Not when I knew her, anyway. And if she was crazy later, it was because she was driven to it.

Your mama was special. She was special and different in a time and place when people—especially women—were expected to be the same. The old, musty notebook enclosed with this letter is a journal I kept during my time in Oak Ridge. It's as much about your mother as it is about me. I hope it lets you see her as she really was, as someone who thought and read and laughed and loved and was loved.

I stopped writing in my journal right after the bomb dropped. I was too sad and too scared to keep spilling my secrets onto its pages. I meant to burn it, but something always stopped me, and so I kept it hidden instead. I kept it hidden when my family moved back to Kentucky, and I kept it hidden in my dorm room at the teachers' college. Your old babysitter didn't do so badly for herself, you know. I loved college so much that I went on to The University of Tennessee, where I got a master's degree. I worked for many years as a high school English teacher and later, a principal. I also met a wonderful woman with whom I've spent the past thirty-seven years. At one point in the journal, I wrote that I would never be happy again. I was wrong.

Throughout the decades, I always kept my girlhood journal secreted away. Whether out of habit or out of fear, I don't know. But when I read the interview with you, I knew it was time to let it go. I knew the words I'd written all those years ago had finally found their audience. And so this yellowed journal, as old and wrinkly as I am, is for you. I hope you come to know and love the woman in its pages. The time for secrets and hiding is over.

Acknowledgments

While this book is a work of fiction, it owes a great deal of authenticity to the work of historians, librarians, and other experts who have made the story of America's "secret city" available to the public. Charles W. Johnson and Charles O. Jackson's *City Behind a Fence: Oak Ridge, Tennessee, 1942-1946*; Russell Olwell's *At Work in the Atomic City: A Labor and Social History of Oak Ridge, Tennessee*; James Overholt's *These Are Our Voices*; and the wonderful Thelma Present's *Dear Margaret: Letters from Oak Ridge to Margaret Mead* were particularly indispensible titles in my research. Also very helpful was time spent in the Oak Ridge Children's Museum, The American Museum of Science and Energy, and the City Room of the Oak Ridge Library. My thanks also go to Mariella Akers, who gave me a guided tour of Oak Ridge's Manhattan Project-era dwellings.

After writing the first draft of this novel, I learned (with some trepidation, at first) about the existence of another novel for young people set in Oak Ridge during World War II, Connie Jordan Green's *The War at Home*. I promptly read Ms. Jordan Green's book and found it to be both excellent and (to my relief) very different from my own; I recommend it highly to readers looking for another fictional perspective on daily life in the Atomic City.

As always, my thanks go to Linda, Jessica, Becky, and the impressive team of women at Bella Books, and to editor extraordinaire and literary goddess Katherine V. Forrest.

Bella Books, Inc.

Women. Books. Even Better Together.

P.O. Box 10543
Tallahassee, FL 32302

Phone: 800-729-4992
www.bellabooks.com